Open and Closed

Other Five Star titles
by Mat Coward:

Over and Under
In and Out
Up and Down
Do the World a Favour and Other Stories

Open and Closed

A Don Packham and Frank Mitchell Mystery

Mat Coward

Five Star • ?Waterville, Maine

This novel is a work of fiction. Names, characters, places and incidents are either the product of the author's imagination, or, if real, used fictitiously.

First Edition, Second Printing.

Published in 2005 in conjunction with Tekno Books and Ed Gorman.

Set in 11 pt. Plantin by Liana M. Walker.

Printed in the United States on permanent paper.

Library of Congress Cataloging-in-Publication Data

Coward, Mat.
Open and closed / by Mat Coward.—1st ed.
p. cm.
ISBN 1-59414-274-2 (hc : alk. paper)
1. Packham, Don (Fictitious character)—Fiction.
2. Mitchell, Frank (Fictitious character)—Fiction.
3. Political activists—Crimes against—Fiction. 4. Police—England—London—Fiction. 5. London (England)—Fiction.
6. Public libraries—Fiction. I. Title.
PR6053.O955O64 2005
823′.914—dc22 2005019071

Dedication

Dedicated to the library workers of the world—
on liberty's front line, now more than ever.

Chapter One

"That's quite a storm outside," said Frank Mitchell, as he stood in the entrance lobby of Bath Street Library, trying to reassemble his windblown umbrella sufficiently for it to be collapsed.

"Best place for it," said the uniformed officer who'd admitted him.

Frank gave up on the umbrella—it seemed to have grown several extra spokes during the short journey from car to building. "I'll just stick this in a corner," he said. "Can you make sure someone marks it, so Scenes of Crime don't end up logging it in as the murder weapon?"

"I'll do my best," the PC promised, in a voice devoid of either enthusiasm or optimism. A tubby, greying man well into the final trimester of middle age, he was known around Cowden nick as Cheerful Charlie—though Frank had never been quite sure why, given that the name on his warrant card was Police Constable Nigel Chester.

"Thanks, Nige. Whereabouts are we, then?"

PC Chester nodded skywards. "Top floor."

"There are only two floors, aren't there?"

"That's right. Ground floor and top floor."

"Right." Frank flattened his reddish hair, wiped the rain

off his boyish face with a clean handkerchief, and looked around him. Something had been bothering his peripheral vision, and now he realised what it was. Here and there, dotted about the library's main room, its open staircase, and its gallery, were little huddles of shock-faced men and women. "Awful lot of people around, for a public library at two in the morning?"

PC Chester signalled for the detective constable to follow him towards the staircase. "That's because it's being occupied," he explained.

"Occupied?"

"That's right." Cheerful Charlie nodded. "By an occupation."

"Wait a minute." Frank laid a detaining hand lightly on his colleague's forearm. "There's an occupation *and* there's a body in the library?"

"Both." He set off upwards again, leaving Frank no choice but to follow.

"So which were you called to?"

"The body—the occupation's not subject to an official complaint yet. I don't suppose anybody at the council would know about it until opening time."

As they reached the top of the stairs, Frank managed—by dint of younger legs and longer strides—to slip ahead of Cheerful Charlie, forcing the latter to stand still for a moment. "And the three nines call came from . . . ?"

"The branch librarian, Ms. Dolores Estevez. She couldn't sleep, apparently."

"Couldn't *sleep?*" Frank was losing track of all this. "What, she couldn't sleep so she came back to the library in the middle of the night to catch up on some shelving?"

"No, no, she was already here. She's part of the occupation."

"Oh, right," said Frank, relieved, at least, that he wasn't dealing with some sort of hostage situation.

"And they were all downstairs—the occupiers—sleeping, or whatever. But Ms. Estevez couldn't sleep. I got the impression she rarely does, which believe me, Frank, I know all about. I might as well sell my half of the bed, the amount of use I get out of it these days."

"The branch librarian couldn't sleep," Frank prompted him, "so . . . ?"

"No, fair enough, you don't want to hear my problems. Got plenty of your own, I'm sure. She couldn't sleep, so she came up here to do some paperwork." Without Frank noticing, they had shuffled their way along a corridor and arrived outside a door marked "Staff Only," which PC Chester now opened. "And she found, sitting at her desk . . . this."

It was a small office, made considerably smaller by the four white-jumpsuited figures working intently within it—not to mention the fifth occupant of the room, an elderly man who sat awkwardly on a swivel chair in front of a desk. Frank wasn't entirely sure what the technical term was; he'd have to check before he wrote his report. Was it garrotting, when the victim was choked from behind with some kind of cord? Whatever you called it, it wasn't an especially pretty way to die.

One of the white jumpsuits looked up. "Ah, Frank. Shall we step into the corridor? Not enough room to hear yourself think in here."

Frank was not reluctant to leave the room. "Morning, Dr. Walker. I suppose even you're happy enough to say this one wasn't an accident?"

Sam Walker went to scratch his beard then evidently remembered he had his gloves on, and settled for stretching his shoulders instead. "I'm not going to call it murder, DC Mitchell. That's your job."

"From what I saw, Doctor, I can't imagine what else it could be."

The doctor shrugged, obviously unwilling to concede on so important a point of procedural principle. "A sex game gone wrong?" he offered, but only half-heartedly.

Frank had been hoping to get Dr. Walker to commit himself to the magic word before the DI arrived—it would have been one less thing for the detective inspector to get in a mood about—but clearly he had hoped in vain. "Always supposing, by some unlikely chance, that the old fellow in there was unlawfully killed by another's hand . . . well, you know the questions I'm going to ask, Doctor. Better than I do, probably."

Dr. Walker smiled. "I'm not sure about better than you, but I've certainly known them a few decades *longer* than you. All right then: it would have taken reasonable strength to kill in this manner, but not to such a degree as to rule out a female assassin. The deed may well have been accomplished without significant noise, provided it was done with confidence and determination, and without warning; it wouldn't be a long job, given the age and comparative frailty of the victim." He waited a few moments for Frank's note-taking to catch up. "He's been dead, I should say, an hour or two at the most. Does that complete your little list?"

"Admirably, Doctor, and concisely. Many thanks. You didn't happen to spot a weapon in there, while you were wielding your thermometer?"

"There is a thin, strong leather belt—found under the desk and currently encased in a SOCO's plastic bag—which, if I were ever to have need of one, would serve me quite nicely as a ligature."

"Lovely," said Frank, his pen moving again. "Many thanks for that, too."

"Not that it's very likely, is it?"

"I'm sorry?"

"That I would have recourse to a ligature. Not what you'd call a doctor's weapon, at all. My parents scrimped and saved for many years to ensure I avoided a life of manual labour, after all."

Frank smiled as required. "Will there be much forensic on the killer? If there is a killer, I mean, and given that I am seeking merely your hypothetical opinion."

"On that basis, I would say you could get lucky—but don't bank on it. If he knew what he was doing, he should be able to avoid anything too exciting. There's no blood, of course. There'll be contact traces, obviously, but nothing that couldn't be explained in a dozen non-incriminating ways. A hug on greeting, a helpful shoulder up the stairs, that sort of thing."

Frank conferred next with the uniformed sergeant who'd taken charge at the scene pending CID's arrival. "Do we have an identification, Sarge?"

The sergeant—who was trying to do seven things at once even though, as he would have been the first to tell you, he was really only up to doing six—dragged his notebook out of his tunic pocket one-handed, dropped it, picked it up with both hands, and found his place in it using one wrist and half a chin. "Deceased is a white male, aged eighty-four, Mr. Bert Rosen, and we've got a local address for him."

"Do we know what Mr. Rosen was doing here?"

"Taking part in a protest, apparently." The sergeant snorted. "You'd think the old git would know better at his age, wouldn't you?"

Frank had no immediate plans to involve himself in philosophical discussions, no matter how erudite. "And could you point me at the person who reported the body, please? I believe it's a Ms. Dolores Estevez."

It was *Dot,* in fact, as the librarian in charge of the Bath Street branch told him twice within the first three minutes of their acquaintanceship. Dot was a lively, perhaps even frenetic woman of about fifty, her spectacles encased in enormous, multi-coloured frames, and her greying hair giving the impression that it had urgent business to attend to elsewhere and in several different directions. Her long fingers twined and danced in time to her curls, but on the offbeat, and Frank considered it quite an achievement when he finally persuaded her to sit down in the staffroom and take an occasional sip from a mug of tea.

"I just can't believe," she told him, adding: "I mean, Bert was completely—I mean, *entirely*—what this will do to, I just . . ."

It was clear that she was dreadfully upset; at Bert Rosen's death, and, from what Frank could make out in the gaps of her fractured and gasped sentences, at that death's implications for her library. He felt that for now, he would be best sticking to practical questions which had simple answers.

"How many ways out of this building are there?"

"Just two," Dot replied without hesitation, thus confirming Frank's guess that her managerial instincts would, given the right prompting, gain temporary mastery over her human feelings. "The main entrance, and a fire exit—right at the back there, beyond the disabled toilet."

"And were either or both of them open during the night? This night, I mean, not a normal night."

She shook her head. "The door was locked from closing time last night, until I opened it to admit the ambulance people just before half past one this morning. I had the only key, and if anyone wanted to go in or out they had to ask me."

Frank had learned early on in his police career that the one question you must never fail to ask is the obvious one. "And did anyone enter or exit through that door?"

"No one after about nine thirty last night."

"Absolutely no one?"

"Absolutely no one." She met his gaze firmly, if sadly, and he knew that she understood what that meant; if no one had left the building since closing time the previous evening, then Bert Rosen's killer was still amongst them.

"What about the fire door? Was that locked, too?"

Dot looked quite shocked at the suggestion. "Certainly not! You don't lock fire doors, not under any circumstances. But if it's opened, it sets off an alarm—and that alarm cannot be disabled from this site. It's mainly an anti-theft measure, to be honest."

"Right. And I'm right in thinking—"

"The alarm didn't ring at any time during the night."

"Thank you." Frank's pen rushed to keep up with his ears. "How about the windows—could someone have decamped that way?"

"Definitely not. They don't open."

"None of them?"

"None of them at all, to the daily regret of everyone who works here and most of the readers. We have air-conditioning, instead, so that we're boiling hot in summer and—"

"—and freezing in the winter," said Frank. "Yes, we have the same system where I work. Right, now . . ."

He continued asking bread-and-butter questions, about ingress, egress, and numbers, until he overheard a nearby PC muttering to a colleague *Oh Christ, look who the gale's blown in!*

Frank was confident that only one man in the borough of

Cowden could elicit such a heartfelt moan merely by arriving at a crime scene. He made his excuses to Dot, and went to greet his boss.

"An eighty-four-year-old white male," said Frank, as he showed Detective Inspector Don Packham into the librarian's office, "identified as—"

"Bert Rosen," Don cried, at his first glimpse of the deceased's face. "Bloody hell, that's old Bert Rosen!"

Frank blinked. "What, you know him?"

"No, Frank—I was *guessing.*" Don shook his head, though whether at the dead or the living, Frank wasn't certain. "Of course I know him; don't you? I thought everyone in Cowden knew Bert the Bolshie."

"Bert the Bolshie?"

"The only Communist ever elected to Cowden Borough Council. You don't suppose the CIA's finally caught up with him, do you? Poison-tipped Havana cigar? I can't think why anyone else would want to kill him."

"I'd never heard of him," Frank admitted. "Was he still on the council?"

"God no, this is years ago—before my time in Cowden, let alone yours. But the council was just part of his CV. What he really was, was an activist. I had the great honour of arresting him once; he'd chained himself to the army recruitment place in the high street, to protest against the British presence in Northern Ireland."

"Well—" Frank began, but Don hadn't finished reminiscing.

"Well, well, old Bolshie Bert Rosen, his sword sleeps in his hand at last."

"Sword?" Frank's stomach turned over. He *couldn't* have missed a sword, surely?

"He'll be missed—and not just around here, either. You'll see a funeral now, Frank, believe me. They'll come from all over, the young and the old especially: a great convocation of nose-rings and Zimmer frames. I pity the disc jockey at the wake—he won't know whether to have them doing the pogo or the Charleston."

"I don't think you have disc jockeys at wakes," said Frank.

"Are you sure?"

"Yeah. I think you must be thinking of wedding receptions."

Don's frown cleared. "Oh, well, there you are, then."

"What sword?" Frank really wanted to get this cleared up before they went any further. "You said his sword was sleeping in his hand."

"Jerusalem." Frank looked blank, so Don began to sing the old socialist hymn: *"Bring me my bow of burning gold . . ."*

He could hold a tune, could the DI, and he wasn't singing all that loudly by his standards, but even so it was the kind of behaviour liable to cause surprise amongst onlookers, when indulged in at half past two on a Saturday morning in a suburban public library in the presence of a murdered Bolshevik, so Frank took an executive decision to move the conversation along. "It's a windy night, but," he noted, "you can't step outside without losing your hat, your hair, and your teeth."

Don stopped midway through his chariot of fire. "What?"

"I was just saying, that's quite a gale blowing outside."

"Well, where else would you expect it to blow? Be reasonable." Don took a deep breath, closed his eyes and opened his mouth.

"Did you know Mr. Rosen well?" Frank asked. "Apart from arresting him the once, I mean."

Don opened his eyes, and chuckled. "He was a charming bloke; really, a bona fide birds-from-the-trees merchant.

Very nice manners, always a friendly word and a joke, even with coppers. In the car on the way back to the nick, after I'd lifted him at the troops out demo, he said he hoped he'd be processed and released without too much delay, because he'd forgotten to feed the tortoise. I said something like, you know, 'Oh, you've got a tortoise, have you?' and Bert said, no, not my tortoise—Mark's tortoise."

Don grinned, and a silence ensued. Don said nothing because he was waiting for Frank to laugh. Frank said nothing because he didn't realise the anecdote was at an end. Eventually the silence became uncomfortable for both men, and one of them broke it.

"Mark's tortoise," said Don. "Marx taught us. Yeah? *Mark's tortoise.*"

"Right," said Frank. "It was Mark's tortoise, not Bert's. Right."

Don groaned. "No, Frank, listen—"

"But apart from that hilarious occasion," Frank interrupted, "you had other dealings with him, presumably?"

"Our paths crossed now and then over the years. I never had to nick him again, I'm glad to say. So, Frank, have you nicked his killer yet?"

Frank outlined the good news on that front—that it appeared that the killer was still in the building. However, he couldn't, in all conscience, omit the flaw in the argument which was nagging at the back of his mind. "Of course, as far as we know, Dot Estevez could have let someone else in or out through the main door. We've only her word that she didn't."

"Fair point, Frank. But assuming we can establish that she's telling the truth about that, then how many suspects are we looking at?"

"In the library as a whole, there were about a couple of

dozen. But I understand that a large group of them were gathered in the children's library, playing Scrabble." He leaned over the gallery, and pointed down into the main body of the library to illustrate his reasoning. "You can see, coming out of there, it's one direction to the lavatories, but if anyone from that group came in *this* direction instead it'd be noticeable to the rest of them."

"Yeah," said Don, "that works. Okay, so assuming the Scrabblers all account for each other, how many are we left with?"

"I make it seven people."

"Ah," said Don, "sounds like a quorum. Hold on . . ." He had returned his attention to the corpse, and this time was peering at it rather more intently than before. "Has the body been searched for personal effects?"

"No need," replied a woman dressed in a disposable spacesuit. "We already had identification."

"Then do you mind if I have a quick rummage in his pocket?"

The SOCOs conferred by means of glance, and then nodded in unison. "Go ahead, Inspector."

Don put on a pair of crime scene gloves, crouched down beside Bert Rosen's remains, and carefully inserted his right hand into the rear, right-side pocket of the old man's voluminously baggy trousers.

"Well I never . . ."

"Sir?"

"His murder might come as a terrible shock to the people of Cowden, but it looks as if Bert himself was expecting it." Slowly, Don withdrew his gloved hand, and its prize—which came out upside-down, awkwardly and reluctantly, but was instantly recognisable, even so. "Why else would an eighty-four-year-old man take a handgun into a public library?"

Chapter Two

On an island stand near the issue desk, there stood a generous display of books, leaflets, and DVDs under the general heading of "Health." They ranged from dietary advice to spiritual growth, dropping in along the way at massage and aromatherapy, holistic parenting, and allergy prevention.

Don, who'd never felt fitter in his life, dismissed the whole lot with a single grunt. Health, he reflected, was just astrology for graduates.

It was a fine library, though, he couldn't deny it: it seemed spacious without being barn-like, modern but soulful. He had seen something in the local paper about proposals to close it down—even though it had only opened a couple of years earlier—and he'd tutted, but he'd had other things on his mind. Still had, really.

Not a bad way for Bolshie Bert to go, Don thought as he wandered from Science Fiction A–Z to the Web Access Area: defending a public library against those morons in the town hall.

It was getting on towards breakfast time, Saturday morning, and beyond the library's picture windows the birds were busy amid the breezy remnants of last night's storm. Bert's body had been removed, the gun had gone to where guns go, and divers uniformed and plainclothes officers and technicians were doing their bits of busyness here and there about the building. Preliminary interviews and searches were being concluded before the witnesses—including those who fell into the awkward category of witness/suspect—were released back into the wild. The library was gradually quieting, just in time for it to get noisy again. It had missed a whole night's sleep.

Never mind; it would be able to catch up today. Only today, he hoped; Don was determined to let Bath Street branch reopen to the public as soon as possible. As a policeman, he was required by oath to be scrupulously neutral in all matters of political controversy, which he had always interpreted as meaning that it was his job to screw the authorities at every possible opportunity.

"Inspector?"

He turned from Local History to find a human hurricane bearing down on him from the direction of World War I. It was, he thought, quite an attractive sort of hurricane, with its peripatetic hair and its psychedelic glasses.

"Yes, I'm Don Packham. Are you the branch librarian?"

"I'm Dot," she confirmed, stretching forward to shake his hand, as if she didn't have time to take the extra step towards him that would have made the stretching unnecessary. She looked like the sort of woman, Don thought, who had so much energy she even made *herself* nervous. "Your friend Frank said you'd probably want a word."

"Just an informal chat, if you've a moment. I won't keep you—I realise this has been a dreadful night for you. I'm sure you're keen to get home."

"Home?" said Dot. "Well, yes, I suppose—"

"Hello, Dot." A young woman wearing a paramedic's overalls gave the librarian an encouraging smile as she passed them on her way to the exit. "How's John?"

"Oh, hello, love." Dot returned the sad smile. "Much the same, thanks."

"John?" Don asked.

"My husband. I should be getting back to him, he'll be worried. I've given my statement to the constable . . ."

"Of course. I was just wondering if you could give me an idea of what you were all doing here last night. Some sort of protest?"

Her hair vibrated as she tried to shake some clarity of thought into her head. "Yes, it was—we were planning to occupy the library. You know it's been scheduled for closure?"

"I did hear something. But I thought it had only just opened?"

Dot sighed. "Eighteen months ago. Madness, isn't it? But the council changed hands, you see, in a by-election last month."

"Ah, right," said Don, remembering. "From Labour to LibDem, wasn't it?"

"That's it. And our new lords have new plans. Though, to be fair, I should stress that we've had support from across the political spectrum. There was at least one senior LibDem here last night, who opposes the closure. James was chatting him up for us."

"But the new council's first priority is cutting the library service?" Don knew the world was full of crazy people with insane plans, but even so—closing libraries!

"It's not a cut," she explained, wearily. "The council's very firm on that point."

"Closing a library isn't a cut?"

"Oh dear me, no. It's a horizontally integrated customer-centric re-branding project."

"Of course it is," said Don. "I should have known that.

Has Bath Street not been a success, then?"

"It's been a huge success! Issues are much higher than predicted, footfall is up, the customer satisfaction index is the second best in the borough."

"Then . . . ?"

"It's been a huge success by every possible measure, except one. They don't use the actual word—they've got some lovely jargon for it, which I can't quite remember at the moment, it's been a long night—but what it comes down to is, Bath Street isn't profitable."

"But it's not supposed to make a profit! It's a public service."

"Oh, Inspector!" She squeezed his arm for a second. "Welcome to the dinosaurs' club. Everything has to make a profit these days, even if only a notional profit. Didn't you know? That's the only way you can possibly judge whether anything is working. Every department and section and every bloody *desk* has to make a profit in competition with every other department and section and—"

"Bloody desk? Yes, I see. And you're fighting this?"

She nodded her head, firmly, and for once her hair stood still, as if in solidarity. "As hard as we can. It's my last battle—I'll go down with this ship, if need be."

Don took her hand, and shook it solemnly. "Then I'll tell you what—if you are guilty of murder, I promise not to tell anyone."

That set her hair off again. "I can't imagine *anyone* killing Bert. He was such a lovely . . . unless, you don't think? Oh God, I hope not, that really would be—you don't suppose it's because he's Jewish?"

Bloody hell! Don hadn't thought of that—and now that it had been thought of for him, he quickly exiled the idea from his mind. If the killing was a hate crime, he'd have to hand it over to a task force.

So distracted was he by this disagreeable idea, that he'd put a small cigar between his lips, and was on the point of lighting it, before he remembered where he was. "Sorry, Dot, I suppose this whole building is non-smoking?"

She laughed. "You're not even allowed to smoke in the staffroom these days."

"The council's a caring employer."

"You're allowed to be attacked by drunks, druggies, mad people, and thugs, because it would cost too much to have enough staff on duty to prevent it, but you're not allowed a fag with your coffee break, because it's bad for you."

"I think I'll just nip outside, then," he said, waving his cigarette-sized cigar towards the door. "Will you join me?"

"Oh no," said Dot, "I don't indulge. I just wish our masters would learn what's important and what isn't, and spend more time trying to do something about the things that are and less time buggering about with the things that aren't."

What a wonderful woman, thought Don. He hoped her husband was a smoker; it'd be a bloody waste, otherwise. "Did anyone go outside for a smoke during the night?"

"No," said Dot, lowering her voice and giving the library a quick security sweep from the corners of her eyes. "I declared the staffroom smoke-friendly for the duration. But please don't tell anyone—*seriously,* they might not sack me for taking part in the occupation, but they would definitely sack me for that."

The phrase *funny old world,* Don thought, as he took his leave of the battling book-stamper, had been rendered pathetically inadequate by the sheer strangeness of life in the twenty-first century.

Outside the library, but still within the shelter of its glass and steel, Don was amused to discover that he was not alone.

Two men stood hard against the wall, fighting the wind for control of their smoke.

"Good morning, PC Standfield."

"Morning, sir." The uniformed constable dropped his cigarette, without ceremony, and covered it with a size ten boot. "Ah, this gentleman wished to have a smoke—you know, for the shock, like—so I said I'd escort him."

"Very kind of you, Les," said Don. "But you can get back in the warm, now. I'll take over from here."

PC Standfield hurried to obey. Don lit his cigar, using the moment to study the civilian; one of the witnesses, obviously—and one of the suspects, too? He was in his forties, though probably not for much longer, of noticeably erect bearing, and from what Don could glimpse in the gaps of his hurriedly buttoned overcoat, he wore clothes so glaringly inappropriate that they'd probably be rejected by a Texan golfer at a fancy-dress party.

"Detective Inspector Don Packham."

"Cyril Mowbray. How d'you do."

They shook hands, and Don felt the tremor from Mowbray's pass into his own. "If you'll take a word of advice, Cyril? When they let you go, I wouldn't drive home if I were you."

"Not home?"

The man looked quite lost for a moment, so Don hurried to reassure him. "Home, by all means—but you're probably not in the best state for driving."

Mowbray looked at his hands. "No, you're right. Not driving, as it happens—came by bike. But the same thing applies."

"I'm sure they'll let you leave it in the library until you can collect it."

"Don't know why I'm in such a state." He finished his cigarette and lit another. “I was in the army until a few months ago—I’ve seen worse than this.”

“But you don’t expect it, in a setting like this. That makes it different, I imagine.”

“Very different.” Mowbray nodded. “Completely different.”

“Are you married?”

Busy drawing on his cigarette, Mowbray gave an affirmative *Mm.*

“Perhaps your wife could collect you?”

“Oh no, I don’t think . . . best not to disturb her, this time of night. Morning, whatever. Don’t want to worry her. There’s a minicab place just round the corner, that’ll do me.”

Don was taking his time with his cigar. If he carried on asking questions once he’d finished smoking, he was sure, Cyril Mowbray would subliminally register the change from chat to interrogation. “Did you know Bert Rosen well?”

“Just through this business, really.” Mowbray gestured towards the library. “But during that time, I suppose I got to know him reasonably well.”

Don waited for the cliché customary to such statements—*seemed a nice bloke,* or something of that ilk—but it didn’t come, leaving the sentence seeming oddly unfinished. “Hard to think why anyone would want to kill him,” Don prompted.

“Well, chap like that, must have had his enemies, I suppose.”

“Chap like that?”

Mowbray shrugged. “Politico, you know. The people’s flag is deepest red, and so on.”

“I suppose you’re right. Did he have any enemies, as far as you noticed?”

“Well . . .” He seemed to give the question due consideration, but then shook his head. “No, can’t say I did.”

Fair enough, thought Don; we'll come back to that another time. "You're one of the library occupiers?"

"Yes, indeed, certainly. Glad to help out. Use the library all the time, you see. Splendid place. Bloody politicians, buggering about, changing their minds; had enough of that when I was in uniform. Had to put up with it then—don't have to now. Don't intend to." As the conversation continued, Don noted, the ex-soldier's shakes were diminishing. Colour was returning to what had been a chalky face, and his voice was by now almost as loud as his shirt; it boomed and bounced around the flagstones.

"And what do you do for a living, now that the Queen no longer has need of your services?" *Businessman,* Don predicted, silently. They always call themselves businessmen, when they stumble out of the Forces. Or consultants.

Sure enough, the reply was: "Company director. Keeps me out of trouble, you know."

"I imagine it does," said Don, wondering whether murder counted as "trouble," or merely as an inconvenience, amongst ex-soldiers. Or amongst company directors, come to that.

Quite what Don thought he had to complain about, Frank really couldn't imagine. If he didn't like sitting in the car to eat his breakfast—bacon baps dripping brown sauce, and tea which was mysteriously colder than the polystyrene in which it dwelt—then he had only himself to blame. Frank would have been perfectly happy inside the only place nearby which was open for breakfast *and* offered seating. Don, however, dismissed the idea on grounds of principle. For one thing, it would be collaborating with the forces of global imperialism, and for another, he'd rather go hungry than eat in a place where the staff wore paper sailors' hats with their names on.

So why was he moaning, now? Well, yes—because he was Don Packham, that's why.

"Interesting watching the market set up, isn't it?" Frank said, hoping—though without much optimism—to deflect the DI from his obsession with the staffing policies of transnational burger corporations.

"Market!" sneered Don. "Markets take place in market towns—pigs and potatoes, that's what you get at markets. Not plastic cigarette lighters, three for a pound, and kids' toys with all the instructions in Latvian."

"Right," said Frank. "Still—"

"People think everything for sale in car-park markets is nicked, and that's why it's so cheap—but it's not: the reason it's so cheap is because it's crap."

Frank had been thinking of nipping round to one of the stalls over by the public lavs and stocking up on cut-price batteries—shop early for Christmas, sort of thing—but perhaps, on reflection, that could wait until next week. "They've only just started cross-referencing the initial witness statements," he said, consulting his notebook, "but it seems pretty clear that there are only seven people who can't fully account for their own movements, or each others', during the significant hours."

"All members of the occupying forces?" Don asked, his voice muffled as he was concentrating on wiping bacon grease off his tie with a rapidly disintegrating paper serviette.

"More than that: all members of the committee of LOFE."

Mopping-up operations ceased, mid-dab. "Loaf?"

"No, not LOAF." Frank grinned. He was quite enjoying this; he'd quite enjoyed his breakfast, and now he was quite enjoying this. "That point was made to me by Dot Estevez quite firmly."

"Get on with it, Frank." Don resumed his scrubbing.

"Did you not enjoy your breakfast, sir?"

"Get *on* with it!"

"LOFE is Libraries Open For Everyone. The group that's campaigning against Bath Street Library being closed. They couldn't call it LOAF, as they had originally intended, because—"

"Libraries . . ." Don forgot all about his saucy neckwear, as he screwed up his eyes and concentrated on the puzzle. "Libraries . . . Open . . . Libraries Open And Free! How's that?"

"Double top, first dart, Don. You win the goldfish."

"But they couldn't use that because . . . ?"

"Because some other organisation was already using the acronym. Nothing to do with libraries, something else. Don't know *what* else, though, Dot couldn't remember."

Don's lips worked silently for a moment or two. "League Of Anal Fetishists? It's a Kylie Minogue fan club; very hardcore."

"Possibly." Frank'd had a little longer to think the matter over, and hadn't wasted his head start. "Or perhaps, Leominster Ornithologists And Friends."

The sideways look Don gave him was appraising, as much as it was approving. "And friends?" he asked.

"Aye, well—it's a social club, you know. They organise outings and that. It's not just non-stop ornithology, day after day. There's theatre visits and all sorts. So the ornithologists—"

"Bring their friends along," Don said. "Yes, fair enough, that makes perfect sense. I'll bet it's a thriving club. And it probably does them good to get out of Leominster occasionally."

"There was another group before LOFE, apparently, but

I'm not sure what that one was called," said Frank, who *always* enjoyed breakfast, now he came to think of it, even when it consisted of nothing more than a gulp of tea and a rumour of toast. "Anyway, LOFE: the leading members of which took advantage of the occupation of Bath Street to hold a committee meeting."

"At one in the morning?"

Frank shook his head. "No, the meeting was much earlier—but because of it, our seven didn't get involved in the rank-and-file's board games and what-have-you in the children's library."

"Hence neither they, nor the games players, can account for any of the seven's movements through the rest of the night."

"That's it."

"Do we have any security footage?"

"Nothing inside," said Frank. "There are CCTV cameras around the outside, so we will know if anyone has entered or left the library, but there's nothing inside the building. The way Dot explained it to me, the union wants internal cameras because of assaults on staff, and the management wants them so they can do secret time-and-motion studies . . ."

"And since both of them want it, neither side will let the other have it?"

"It's 'a matter subject to ongoing discussion,' is how Dot put it. But the way she smiled when she said it, I suspect that your version is spot on."

"So, Dot Estevez herself is one of the seven, I suppose?"

"Her, and one other member of staff: Kimberley Riggs, she's the union rep at the branch, and as such, chair of the LOFE committee. Then there's a member of Cowden Council—by the name of James Pomeroy."

"Pomeroy? You're joking."

"You know him?"

"By reputation. He was almost kicked out of the Tory Party a few years back, for being too right-wing."

"Funny guy to find on an anti-cuts committee." Frank made a note. "Other than that, the other four are just library users. Keen ones, I suppose."

"All right. Now, any word from anyone about the gun?"

"Nobody volunteered anything." The officers conducting the interviews had been instructed not to mention the weapon unless any of the witnesses raised it first. "The gun itself has gone to the Yard. They reckon they'll have an initial report later today, or Monday morning at the latest. They did say that since it hasn't actually been used in any crime—as far as we know—it might not get top priority."

"I should have shot that PC I caught smoking," Don suggested. "Might have bumped it up the list a bit. From everything I know about Bert Rosen, carrying a shooter is totally out of character."

"It'd be fairly out of character for any eighty-four-year-old, I should have thought."

"True enough."

"Nothing interesting in his pockets: a few quid, a plastic bag, his keys—and his wallet, so he wasn't robbed."

"And a gun. Presumably, he was carrying it to protect himself."

"From the person who did, in fact, kill him?"

"Well, let's hope so, Frank. Otherwise he had *two* mortal enemies."

"But he didn't have a chance to use it, when he was attacked. Despite the fact that he was expecting to be attacked—by that very person."

"Doesn't make a lot of sense, does it? Though, come to

think of it, the awkward position of the gun in his pocket suggests that he wasn't exactly ready for a quick draw. Anyway, someone must know who he was afraid of. He was a widower, I think—didn't he have kids?"

"Next of kin is a daughter."

"Okay. Let's start with her."

Frank phoned the daughter's mobile. "You'll never guess where she is," he said, when his call was done.

"So?"

Frank pointed out of the window. "She's over there. Manning a market stall."

Chapter Three

"I can always tell a copper," said the young man with green hair and eyebrow-rings, as soon as Frank and Don came within his radar-range. He pointed at Frank. "And you, citizen, are a copper."

"Detective Constable Frank Mitchell, Cowden CID," admitted Detective Constable Frank Mitchell of Cowden CID. "We're looking for—"

"What about this one?" The green man nodded towards Don. "Is he an informer, or have you just arrested him?"

There was a pause—*He's not starting another bloody cough, is he?* thought Don—before Frank said: "DI Don Packham. He's my boss."

The boy was visibly shocked. "Bloody hell! I must be losing my powers."

Don was delighted. Not looking like a police officer was one of his chief aims in life.

Frank tried again. "We're looking for Mrs. Ledbury."

"Rosa? Yeah, she's just fetching some coffees. Here she comes now."

A solidly built woman in her early sixties, with a helmet of grey hair—and no visible body piercings, Don was slightly disappointed to note—marched across the car park towards them. She was scarcely in earshot when she called out to them. "I trust you've signed the anti-Star Wars petition while you were waiting."

"Anti-*Star Wars*?" said Frank.

"Quite right," Don said. "Formulaic crap. Give me *Doctor Who* every time."

"There you go, Ryan." Bert's daughter handed one of the polystyrene cups to the green-haired lad, and cleared a space for the other on a trestle table full of leaflets, pamphlets, badges, and petition forms. Behind the display was a board bearing the famous Campaign for Nuclear Disarmament peace sign, above the words "Cowden CND," and a phone number and Web site address. "We're collecting signatures against Britain being used as an aircraft carrier for the U.S. Missile Defence system, also known as Star Wars. I've got a pen, if you've lost yours."

She smiled at Don, who smiled back and was reaching for her biro when Frank coughed and said: "Police officers aren't actually allowed to sign petitions on duty, Mrs. Ledbury."

As you are perfectly well aware, thought Don, catching the laugh in the woman's lively eyes. It wasn't there long, but it had to be a healthy sign, he thought, in one so recently and so shockingly bereaved. "I'll come back and sign when I've retired," he promised her. "Meanwhile, please accept my condolences on your loss—Bert was a remarkable man, and Cowden will miss him."

"Well cool," agreed Rosa's young colleague, before breaking off to deal with an enquirer. The stall seemed to be doing good business, Don noticed. Pity people only thought about disarmament when they were scared, though; inevitable, perhaps, but a pity all the same.

"I must say," he continued, "we weren't really expecting to find you on a stall in the market this morning." He gave the sentence an upward inflection at the end, the way young people did, in the hope of removing any hint of disapproval.

"Better than sitting at home. I'm all alone there—my daughters are on their way home, obviously, but one of them's in New Zealand on holiday, and the other's just moved to Cardiff. I couldn't sleep anyway, after the police had woken me to tell me about Pops."

Don nodded. "I'm sure you're better off keeping active."

"The only mistake I made was in forgetting to forget my mobile. I switched it off after speaking to you two."

"Too many sympathy calls?"

"People mean well, but—well, you can imagine. Bert Rosen? The phone will be ringing twenty hours a day for the next few weeks. I'd rather be out here."

"Don't mourn, organise," suggested Don. "I'm sure it's what your father would have wanted."

"Oh, I don't know," she said, the twinkle in her eye again. "I think Pops would be very glad to know people were mourning as well as organising! He wasn't a saint, he was a man—and a man who was very proud of his achievements."

"With good reason," said Don.

She looked away over the car park, and past the car park. "People in the Labour Party were always trying to get him to defect. There's more than one Member of Parliament over the years who's told Pops that if only he'd given up the CP for Labour, he'd have ended up as a cabinet minister." She must have seen—or imagined—some passing damselfly of scepticism flit across Frank's face, because she addressed her next remarks directly at him. "You may be too young to remember it, but for the best part of a century in this country we used to routinely elect working-class men to parliament."

"Now it's only middle-class women," said Don.

"It used to be commonplace for a man to be working down

the pit on Wednesday, elected on Thursday, and sitting in the House of Commons on Monday."

"Wearing a suit and calling for wage restraint," added Don.

Rosa was still educating Frank. "We had our first working-class prime minister in 1924."

"And our last, I fear, in 1976," Don said, rather enjoying Frank's buffeted look.

"But can you imagine a postman or a train driver, or even a schoolteacher ever being elected to national office in the United States, or France? Unthinkable!"

"Blasphemous," Don agreed.

"But instead of the rest of the world catching up with us . . ." The realisation that there was no elegant way of finishing that sentence gradually disported itself across her face. She abandoned the clause mercilessly and changed tack. "But then that's the fatal flaw in reformist politics—a generation of the working class rises up in solidarity, and makes life better for its children or grandchildren . . . who promptly become middle class, buy bungalows, and vote Conservative."

"But that rule didn't apply in your case?" Don asked.

She smiled. "Well, I was a primary schoolteacher all my working life, which didn't offer many opportunities for embourgeoisement. But one of my daughters is a dentist and the other's a lawyer. Still, in their defence, they are both active in the peace movement."

"And their father . . . ?"

"We're divorced," she said. After a moment, she added: "He was a teacher, too."

In Don's experience, cradle Communists didn't get divorced very often; he wondered if that had been an embarrassment to Bert.

Frank—who Don had noticed before had a regrettably

short tolerance for chit-chat with suspects—spoke up. "We have to ask, Mrs. Ledbury; can you think of any reason why anyone might have wished your father harm?"

"No. No, I really can't. I suppose it's possible that it could be to do with his politics, but it's hard to believe. He didn't have a real enemy in the world, as far as I knew."

"In recent weeks, you didn't notice that he was particularly worried about anything, preoccupied?"

"I don't think so." She shrugged. "He just seemed normal, really."

Don wondered whether to mention the gun at this stage. Perhaps not, he decided; he'd still rather keep that up his sleeve. "The campaign at Bath Street Library—was your father particularly close to any of the people involved in that?"

"Not that he said. I'm sure he knew most of them, to some extent—he seemed to know everyone in Cowden. Growing up with him as a father was like living in a village."

"Was he one of the founders of LOFE?" asked Frank.

"I think he was, yes, but he wasn't as heavily involved in it as he would have been a few years ago. He was getting on, after all. Since his second wife died, he was content to be a rank-and-filer, really. He saw himself more as a facilitator, I think, these days. Encouraging the youngsters, that was a big thing with him."

"But his contacts would still have been essential, I imagine," said Don. "To any campaign he was active in."

She nodded. "Oh, I'm sure. And he had contacts across the board, too—he was very proud, for instance, of getting our former Tory MP to write a letter in the local paper opposing the library closure." She was lost in thought again, for a moment. "With him gone, it might well be that the campaign has less chance of success."

"It might lose some of its broad support, you mean?"

"That, and also just that, well I'm sure you know yourself, in any committee or group there's ten times as much blather as there is—oh, mind out: witches' knickers."

Which, even Don had to admit—and making allowances for bereavement—was a fairly eccentric thing to say. But before he—or, more likely, Frank—could ask her what it meant, Rosa had darted between them, bent over at the waist with her right hand close to the ground. She looked, Don thought, not entirely unlike a curling champion on the verge of releasing a stone.

"Gotcha!" said the retired teacher, straightening up and displaying her quarry to the detectives: a plastic carrier bag, bearing a supermarket's logo. She started to stuff it into a pocket of her windcheater, but it was only halfway in when her shoulders sagged and her chin crumbled and for a horrible second Don Packham honestly wondered if she'd been shot.

But it wasn't an assassin who'd taken her; it was only grief. The tears lasted for seconds, not minutes; she finished stowing the prize she'd won from the wind, and blew her nose on a robust linen handkerchief.

"Witches' knickers?" Don asked.

"It's what the Irish call them. Plastic snow, that's another name I've heard." She patted her pocket. "This is a habit I seem to have inherited from my father. As far back as I can remember—as far back as there have been plastic carriers—he's always gone around collecting them up, putting them in the bin. Hated the things; wouldn't accept them at the checkout. Pops always took his own canvas bag with him when he did the shopping."

"He had a point," said Don. "They do get everywhere, blowing around the place, never rotting away."

"One of the happiest days of his life, when they put a carrier bag recycling bin outside the old library. Enough shopping bags are thrown away in the UK every year," she said, with a self-conscious smile, to let them know that she knew she sounded like a teacher, "to cover London over three times."

"Not a bad idea," said Don. "Don't you reckon, Frank?"

"Mrs. Ledbury is a native, sir," Frank replied. "We should maybe keep our prejudices to ourselves."

"Quite right, DC Mitchell. Now you come to mention it, Rosa, didn't I read somewhere that the Greens want people to post all their old carriers to 10 Downing Street . . . ?"

"That's right. It's part of a campaign to bring in a plastic bag tax. They've done it in Ireland, and it's worked wonders."

"Was your father from round here, originally?" Frank asked, and Don made a mental note to have a word with the boy about his impatience. In detective work, you never knew which bit of inconsequential trivia might turn out to be significant. Besides, the days would be so boring if all they ever did was ask sensible questions.

"No, he was born in the East End, in 1920. My grandparents were Jewish refugees from Tsarist Russia."

"Political exiles?" Don asked. "Bolsheviks or anarchists?"

"I don't think they were especially political, except in as much as all Jews had to be back then, just for survival. Pops found his politics on the street, not in his mother's milk. He joined the CP after the Battle of Cable Street, as so many did."

"He'd have served in the war, presumably?"

"Yes, he was on convoys. The Battle of the Atlantic, the longest battle of World War Two. Before the war, he'd been apprenticed to a tailor, but I think that was his mother's idea, not his, and after he was demobbed he worked at various jobs here and there, doing a few stints as a full-timer with the Party."

"He was married twice, I think you said?"

"That's right." She drank the last of her coffee, and made the obligatory grimace. "Twice married, twice widowed. He married my mother on leave, in 1940. She was killed during the second blitz, when I was a baby. I don't really remember her. I was grown up by the time he married again, in 1965, and my brother was born the next year."

"Does your brother live locally?" Frank asked.

She shook her head. "No, Tom's up in Edinburgh. He's a researcher for one of the Trotskyite members of the Scottish parliament. Pops doesn't really approve, as you can imagine. There's a little estrangement there, you could say."

There's an opportunity for a trip up to Scotland, there, thought Don, making a mental note to put in a formal request.

"And after the war," Frank persisted, "your father moved to Cowden?"

"Oh, I am sorry! That was where we began, wasn't it? Yes, after he'd got married again, they decided to move out to the suburbs, and I followed when I got married, which was not long after. Pops by then had a steady job selling insurance for the Co-op, which he did until his retirement."

"I'll bet he was good at that."

"He was, yes. Yes, he was! He was humorous, friendly, generous . . . everybody liked him, he was happy company. And you could see he was honest just by looking at him."

"Which is probably how he managed to get elected to the local council, in a basically Conservative borough," Don said. "What was that, early seventies?"

She giggled, and momentarily looked, Don thought, forty years younger. "That's right, 1971. There were special circumstances, but even so it was quite an achievement. Pops used to say it was one time when he had succeeded against overwhelming sods. The only Communist councillor in the borough's entire history; that's quite something." She found a pen and paper in her pockets, and wrote herself a note. "I must make sure the *Gazette* has a photo of election night, for its obituary."

"There'd be plenty of photos to choose from, I imagine," said Don. "From all through the decades."

"Oh yes. All the time, non-stop, from Cable Street until yesterday, he was involved in causes, involved in the community. He always used to say, 'A revolutionary is just a reformist who never gives up.' "

"Your father's address," said Frank, rather too urgently for Don's taste, "is the same as your own, is that right?"

"Yes, he sold his place when he was widowed. We were both on our own by then, so it made sense to double up."

"We'll leave you to your peacemongering, Rosa," said Don. "Looks like your comrade there is getting busy. Just one thing—do you mind telling me, what's your strongest memory of your father? If people say his name to you, what's the image—or sound, or smell, or whatever—that immediately comes to your mind?"

Bert Rosen's daughter closed her eyes for a moment and was smiling when she opened them. "This," she said, and drummed her fingers on the edge of the CND table, in a rhythm that was unfamiliar to Don.

"He was a Morse operator during the war. Tap-tap-tap . . . anyone who's ever used Morse code will tell you, once learned it's never forgotten. All his life, he'd tap out messages with his fingers or a pencil, or his fork at dinner. Most of the time it was just an unconscious habit, but when I was little it was our secret—like, our version of pig Latin. He taught me a few simple phrases. You know: 'Are you bored?' and 'Soon go home,' that sort of thing. That's how I picture him: forever tapping out messages with his left hand."

"There you are, Frank," Don said, as they made their way back to the car. "Bet you he tapped out the name of his killer even as he lay dying. Now all we've got to do is find someone who heard it."

He saw the look Frank gave him. He didn't care. If he ever said something like that, and Frank *didn't* give him a look—that's when he'd start worrying.

Some detectives hold their meetings in offices, thought Frank, as they sat in his car, getting their thoughts in order.

A political motive for the killing of Bert Rosen would have to be considered, given his controversial career. Neither Frank nor Don particularly fancied it. True, the killing of communist workers was still an everyday occurrence in various parts of the world, generally at the behest of household-name corporations, but it seemed an unlikely occurrence in the north London suburb of Cowden. As far as Don could recall, no one had ever been killed for his politics in Cowden. Snubbed at the golf club, possibly; ignored at Christmas by his mother-in-law, quite likely; but not actually killed.

Neither did the hate crime angle seem one especially worth pursuing, though even so all the suspects would be checked for prior involvement with anti-Semitic organisations. ("Hate crimes," said Don. "Ridiculous expression. Murder is very rarely a crime of indifference, in my experience.") There had been racist assaults in the borough, with the victims almost invariably Asian, but the cold-blooded killing of an elderly Jewish man in a public library, presumably by a friend or acquaintance, hardly seemed to fit the profile.

"I suppose strangling someone with a ligature is a pretty hateful thing to do," Frank mused. "It suggests passion, of some sort."

"Possibly." Don wasn't convinced. "Or it could just be efficiency. You need him dead, and you need him silent, and cutting off his air supply meets both criteria quite nicely. Plus, you don't get covered with blood, as you would with a stabbing or a bludgeoning. In fact, you could say the method of killing is indicative of good planning."

"Tell you what, though," said Frank, remembering his first sight of the late Bert, "you'd need something about you to go through with it, wouldn't you?"

"When he started struggling," said Don, "and clawing, and you had to pull tighter to make sure? My God, yes. I couldn't do it. Unless the victim worked in telesales, obviously."

"Obviously," Frank agreed. "I saw this programme a while back, on BBC4—"

"Did you?" said Don.

Frank ignored him. He knew the truth was Don enjoyed nothing better than chewing on ideas sparked by his colleague's suggestions. "They've done studies on infantrymen, over the years, and they reckon that in the First World War, only two percent of soldiers actually aimed their guns at the enemy during battles with the intention of killing. The taboo against killing your own species that's built into all animals by evolution is so strong, you see. The only people who can overcome it easily are psychopaths."

"Or heroes, as they're sometimes known."

"They reckon the people who are able to kill the enemy right from the start are people who are used to killing animals. As farmers, or for sport, or whatever. It's a kind of practice—it breaks down the inhibition. There's never been a serial killer known to science who didn't start on pets."

"So all we need to do," said Don, "is arrest any suspect who grew up in foxhunting country." But Frank could tell from Don's narrowed eyes that what he'd said had grabbed the DI's imagination. "So what are you saying, Frank—that all murders, as opposed to acts of manslaughter, are by definition psychopathic? In which case, why do we put most killers in prison, instead of in hospital?"

"I don't know," said Frank. "Because prison's cheaper?" That was enough hypothetical, tangential speculation, as far as he was concerned. He could see the DI's point—or, more accurately he had *come* to see the DI's point—but he still reckoned there were limits. You could spend all day on the general, if you weren't careful, and end up forgetting all about the specific.

His phone rang at that moment, bringing news from the incident room. "Looks like Bert's will is a wash-out," he told Don. "There's a fair amount of money involved, all in mutually owned banks and building societies—"

"Is there, indeed?"

"Presumably from the sale of his house, when he moved in with Rosa."

"Oh, yeah. I suppose anyone who sold a paid-for home in Greater London these days would be cash rich. Until they had to buy another one, at least."

"But in any case, the bulk of his estate favours his daughter, with large bequests to his son, to the People's Press Printing Society, whatever that is, and to the Marx Memorial Library in Clerkenwell Green. So, I don't think it helps us, unless one of Bert's children is in league with one of the people occupying Bath Street."

There had been something else Frank had meant to ask Don about; he quickly ran through his mental checklist . . .

Oh yeah, that was it. The Battle of the Atlantic he'd just about heard of, but Cable Street? He had a feeling there was a Cable Street in the East End somewhere. Don's reaction, when Rosa had mentioned it, suggested that he knew what she was talking about. Should he ask Don about it now, or look it up on the Internet when he got home?

A better idea came to him: *I'll save it for a day when I need to cheer Don up by giving him an opportunity to educate me.*

Chapter Four

They decided to see a certain Stanley Baird next, since he was, according to Frank's notes, the secretary/treasurer of LOFE.

"Which unless I'm very much mistaken," said Don, "is short for Lawyers Oppress Angry Fish."

"You're getting confused, surely," said Frank, and Don realised immediately that he was right, damn him. "Surely you meant to say Lentils Oscillate Fertile Elephants."

"I did, Frank, good point."

Stanley Baird's flat, a mile from Bath Street Library, was of a decent enough size, in a nice enough street, though there was something cheerless about it; apart from anything, the place was under-heated and under-furnished. It was obvious from every inch of it that he lived alone, and for no specific reason he could have pointed to, Don got the strong impression that Stanley was a bachelor, rather than being divorced or widowed.

The man himself was tall, thin, and mostly bald. His clothes looked of good quality—or expensive, at least, which in Don's mind was rarely the same thing. His almost constant lip-licking and brow-wiping were evidence of the nervousness he felt in the presence of the two detectives, but that was only natural after all. Don often felt the same way, himself.

The tea which Stanley Baird served them turned out to be so weak as to be almost hallucinogenic, and Don was fairly certain he was in the presence of a re-user of teabags. Sadly, there was no statute forbidding that odious practice, and Don knew, because he'd looked. If you wanted to get full value out of every pinch of tea, then by all means feel free to dry the stuff out and smoke it in a pipe—but double-dunking was simply beyond decency. What was the betting this bloke worked in banking? "What exactly is it you do for a living?"

"I took early retirement, in fact, five years ago."

The slightly defensive way in which he said this made Don wonder if early retirement was a euphemism for redundancy. "From what?"

"I was a payroll manager."

Close enough. "Were you one of the founding members of LOFE?"

"No, before I became aware of it, the group had been running for a little while, in its own manner."

Odd way of putting it, thought Don. He saw Frank look up from his notebook; so it had clanged against his ear, too. "How did you become aware of the campaign?"

"There was a sign on the library notice-board, advertising a meeting. I decided to go along and see if I could be of assistance."

"Obviously," said Don, who was beginning to realise what sort they were dealing with here, "the library must be of great personal importance to you? For you to give up your time in retirement to fighting to save it. You spend a lot of time there, I suppose?"

"Not especially. I'm not a big reader." He said this with the simple pride of a busy man.

Yes, indeed; Don recognised his type now. Stanley Baird

was a pressure group hobbyist. He might just as easily have become involved in societies concerned with steam engines, choral singing, or dominoes, but Don suspected he'd chosen campaigning groups, consciously or otherwise, because they found it harder to fill their top-table vacancies.

"I wonder," said Don, "if you could just give us an outline of the case against the closure of Bath Street. I'm sure we can get the arguments in favour from the council, but it would be a great help to us, in understanding the background to this case, if you could—"

"You're asking the wrong person, I'm afraid." Baird showed not a hint of embarrassment, Don had to give him that much. "I'm by no means an expert on the whys and wherefores."

"But if I had a question about LOFE's rules and constitution . . . ?"

"Oh, yes." He nodded enthusiastically. "Then, I'm your man."

He was quite shameless about it—and, it occurred to Don, why shouldn't he be? A man needed a pastime in retirement, and not everyone had the knees for tai chi. Subtle probing proved entirely unnecessary, as Stanley was perfectly happy to talk about his activities. It quickly became apparent that he sat on more committees than he had pairs of trousers and that he did so, invariably, as secretary or treasurer. Or both. There were committees to save this, and steering groups to get rid of that, along with the occasional society for the suppression of the other. It was equally apparent that anyone looking for ideological commitment to any of these undertakings, or even a reasonably detailed awareness of their objectives, should look elsewhere. Stanley Baird's delight lay not in campaigning, but in keeping the books and typing the minutes.

Even after the detectives had understood and accepted

this concept, Baird proved still capable of causing their jaws to drop. Frank had asked him that most standard of standard questions—How well did he know the deceased?—and he had replied, predictably, "Not very well," adding, less predictably perhaps, "but his death is a great loss. A very great loss, indeed."

"It is?"

"Certainly. Mr. Rosen knew his Citrine." Clearly, there could be no higher praise.

"Ah, yes," Don smiled. "I noticed that your copy of old Walter was well-thumbed." A crack-spined hardback of the legendary book of procedure for meetings, Walter Citrine's *ABC of Chairmanship*, straddled the arm of the chair in which Baird sat.

A frown spread across Baird's face. "Yes . . . I was seeking the solution to a problem arising from last night's events."

"A problem?"

"You see, last night's gathering—"

"The occupation of the library?"

"Technically, you understand, that entire event was a committee meeting."

"Was it? I see."

"But as such, it was never formally ended or suspended. Instead it was—well, broken up, I can only say, by the discovery of Mr. Rosen's body, and subsequent matters arising."

It took the detectives a few moments to process this statement, let alone formulate a response. Eventually, Don managed: "Right . . ."

"So you can see my problem, Inspector. How does one minute such an eventuality? It's very tricky."

"It must be, yes." Don tried to signal to Frank that his

mouth was still hanging open. "Still, I'm sure you'll be able to sort it out."

"Well, I hope so . . ."

"You were saying, you formed a positive impression of Bert Rosen?"

"Yes, certainly. A sound committeeman. He invariably conducted himself properly in meetings, always addressed his remarks through the chair, which I have to say—" But whatever it was he had to say, he clearly decided at that moment not to say it. His mouth closed, and then opened again just enough to allow his tongue to dart out and dab at his neat moustache.

"Some of the others, perhaps," Don prompted, "were not quite so well-schooled in procedural etiquette?"

Baird said nothing.

"You get on all right with the others, do you?"

"Yes, yes." Baird wiped his brow with a small, off-white handkerchief. "Yes, of course."

Never mind, Don told himself; we'll come back to it. "Can you think of anyone on the committee who was not on good terms with Bert? Or perhaps, someone who had a row with him lately, even a minor disagreement?"

To this, at least, Stanley Baird was able to offer an assured response. "No, definitely not. I anticipated your question, and I can confirm I have double-checked and that there is nothing in the minutes suggesting anything of the sort."

Oh, enough! thought Don. Time for an early lunch.

A phone call from the firearms forensics officer assigned to Bert Rosen's gun decided Don and Frank's lunchtime arrangements for them. If they fancied getting a quick verbal report now, rather than waiting for the full details on Monday, they were welcome to meet him in half an hour or so at a certain pub near his workplace. They would know him by the plate of Scotch eggs, chips, and cheese and onion sandwiches behind which the top of his head would just be visible.

Frank duly forwarded this message to Don, who expressed approval. "Sounds like a sound man," he said. "People who have small lunches are generally untrustworthy."

Eamon Soper, they soon discovered, had been exaggerating about the size of his platter of pub grub—but not to the point where anyone would call him a liar. Frank felt a little faint at the sight. Then again, Eamon did have a lot of space to fill. A big, solid man—if he wasn't actually a regular rugby player, then he could probably be arrested on a charge of attempted deception simply for walking down a street—he wore a black T-shirt and jeans (the autumnal weather didn't seem to interest him) and his head was shaven. What Frank fancied was a Maori tattoo snaked up one shoulder towards his tree trunk of a neck.

While Don queued at the bar to buy pints for himself and Eamon, and a tonic water for the DC, Frank watched the big man finish his meal. It was not a drawn-out business; great hands tirelessly shovelled skillfully loaded forkfuls of food into a surprisingly small mouth, where mighty teeth masticated with ruthless efficiency.

Once all three were sitting with their drinks in front of them, and Don had received permission from his table-mates to enjoy a small cigar, Eamon wiped his hands fastidiously on a series of paper serviettes, before shaking hands with the two CID men.

"You're a Kiwi?" said Don.

"Damn—now that you've found me out, will I be deported?"

"What on earth made you leave New Zealand for London?"

"Oh, I don't live here," Eamon explained. "No offence, but I couldn't stomach that." He enjoyed Don and Frank's puzzled looks for a second or two, before continuing. "My home is still back in New Zealand; I work two months on, two months off. I bunk with a mate in London. Work all the hours while I'm here, mind. Your lot pay better."

"Sounds idyllic," said Don. Frank smiled, but thought that commuting was commuting, whatever you called it. "So: our gun."

"Right. Well, the reason I can give you a preliminary, informal report on the gun you sent in is because there's nothing to report, basically. And that's pretty much what the report will say, when you officially receive it."

"Typical," said Don. "What do I always say about physical evidence, Frank?"

Nothing, as far as Frank could recall. "That it's not worth the effort of planting?" he guessed.

"That it's like a third party vote in a general election—promises everything, delivers nothing."

"The DI prefers the dialectical approach," Frank explained.

"Ah, well," said Eamon, "it may be that what the gun doesn't tell us in fact tells us a good deal."

"Yeah," sneered Don. "That's what you physical evidence junkies always say. Go on then, impress us with what you haven't got. But leave the technical stuff for the written report; I prefer to ignore it on paper rather than verbally."

The Kiwi opened his notebook, and perched a pair of delicate, gold-rimmed half-moon spectacles on his nose. Frank was careful not to catch Don's eye. Policemen were trained to avoid unnecessary risks, and he felt that laughing at four-eyed giants probably came under that general heading. "Okay," said Eamon. "First of all, it's a conversion—a modified replica."

"Not a real gun?" said Don.

"It's real enough now, in that it could shoot you well enough. But it started out life as an expensive toy. Most of the guns on the street these days are activated replicas. Easily the majority of gun incidents in Britain involve converted replicas or air pistols. And there's plenty of them; I don't know how many of them you see in suburbia, but you take a walk around the right parts of London, and the bulges you notice in the pockets of the kids' baggy jeans aren't aerosol canisters any more. Graffiti is passé, compared to posing with your piece."

"We get our share," said Frank. "Unless you believe what you read about the gun epidemic in the newspapers—in which case, we should be knee-deep in the things."

Eamon made a dismissive gesture. "Media shit," he said. "Don't get me started. I used to believe in freedom of the press before I came to London, jeez. But one thing they have got right is that if you want a handgun in this city today, all it's going to take is a couple of phone calls and about a hundred and fifty pounds. Cheaper than that if you're buying for function more than looks. Blank shooters, or the guns used in paintballing-style sports: they can be converted for fifty quid. Takes a couple of hours. There's guns so cheap, crims treat them like disposable razors: use 'em once and dump 'em. The only reason there aren't more guns in circulation, you ask me, is because the cops don't carry them."

"You mean, so the criminals don't need to?" said Frank.

Eamon smiled. "Well, that too, I guess. What I meant was, so the CID can't flog them in pubs."

That earned him a laugh from Don. "Didn't I read that the number of deaths from firearms is actually falling?"

"Though knowing the lovely British press, I'm sure you

read it in *very* small print. The exact number goes up a bit, down a bit, year on year. Last year was high: eighty-one deaths in the whole UK. To put that in context, the murder capital of Britain is Glasgow—murder capital of western Europe, as it goes—and Glasgow has a homicide rate of 58.7 people per million. Britain's rate as a whole is nineteen per million. Compare that to Washington DC, which is 428.7, and New York City, home of Zero Tolerance, which is 86.5. Now—"

"Did I mention that I'm not keen on technical details?" Don interrupted.

"Sorry." The New Zealander made a face which could only be described as sheepish, though Frank hoped he would never meet a sheep that big except in his nightmares. "Anyway, my point is that gun crime is still comparatively rare in this country."

"You're safer in the cities than you are in the countryside," Don announced, "where some farm worker goes mental and shoots a pub up with his shotgun. In the cities, most gun crime is drug related, and therefore restricted in its effects. Or are you going to tell me that's an urban myth?"

"No, you're dead right. It's all about drugs. But you see, it's in everyone's interest to hype up gun crime—criminals get more respect and fear, cops get more resources, politicians can abolish centuries-old freedoms without anyone minding, and above all the media get frightening stories."

"Which are the only kind that sell," Don agreed.

"Too right. Truth is, the number of people in the UK who've ever *seen* a gun except on TV is infinitesimal. Knife culture is the real problem—there's a whole generation of youngsters carrying knives routinely now, but that's not as sexy as guns, so nobody talks about it. Plus, obviously, there's a race element. The press drools at the idea of 'black on black violence,' and 'gun culture,' because it allows them to be racist while still keeping a big, innocent look on their faces."

"So if it's not guns," Frank asked, "how do people get murdered in this country?"

Eamon grinned. He was obviously enjoying himself. "Okay, stabbing is number one—that's about two hundred and seventy killings a year. Poison or drugs is also pretty high, then a big drop to punching and kicking, halve that to get shooting, followed by strangulation, then the legendary blunt instrument—not nearly as common as folk suppose—and twenty-odd people a year are murdered by means of a motor vehicle."

"How do you keep all that in your head?" Don asked, genuinely impressed.

"I play a lot of chess. Point being, if you're an ordinary citizen, your chances of getting shot dead in this country are so low as to be invisible. But there you are: it's human nature to worry about the wrong things. Everyone's terrified of phantom terrorist conspiracies, when what's really going to do us all in is global warming. Optional illusions, I call them. Still, it all makes work for the working cop to do, right? My overtime's looking lovely! Building myself a new house back home."

"I'm very glad for you," said Don. "So, which category does our gun fit into—the fifty pounds or the hundred and fifty?"

"It's at the cheaper end—a disposable. This particular model is currently popular with would-be gangsters. I don't mean *gangster* gangsters—I'm talking about kids, dealing drugs or whatever."

"More for show than for use?"

Eamon took a sip of his beer; the glass emptied, instantly, like a conjuror's trick. "Good for both, but probably leaning towards the former. Your gun has been fired at various times in its life, but of course I can't tell you whether the targets were tin cans or crack house guards." He smiled. "You'll have to rely on the old dialectics for that. And, before you ask, the gun will almost certainly be impossible to trace."

"Any prints?" Frank asked.

"Only the deceased's. It had been wiped pretty thoroughly in the recent past. One thing you haven't asked me though, guys: the ammo."

"What about the ammo?"

"Funny you should ask. There wasn't any. The gun wasn't loaded. Did your man have any ammunition on him?"

"No . . ." said Don. "Though come to think of it, that makes more sense, not less. From what we know about the man who had the gun, an unloaded weapon could be more in character."

Frank saw his point. "You mean Bert might have been willing to threaten his attacker with an empty gun, but he wouldn't have taken the risk of pointing it at anyone if it could actually have gone off. Still makes you wonder where he got it from, but. I can't see a respectable octogenarian buying a shooter under the table in some dodgy pub."

"Don't let Bert Rosen's ghost hear you calling him respectable," Don warned. "But you're right; it is a mystery."

"There's another possibility," Eamon offered. "The gun wasn't his. The killer planted it on him."

"It's got his prints on, you said."

"Okay, so he tricked the victim into handling it before he killed him."

It wasn't impossible, Frank had to admit. Except—"Why

would you want to leave a gun in someone's pocket, after you've strangled him?"

"To confuse the cops, maybe?" Eamon shrugged. "After all, no offence guys, but—it's done that all right, you got to admit."

Chapter Five

"We need someone willing to speak ill of the dead," said Don, as they sat in Frank's car, checking the list of suspects. "Didn't someone say that there was an earlier group, before LOFE? The Legion Of Ferret Exterminators, that is."

"You're right," said Frank, flipping back through his notebook. "One of the library users on our list is a widow, Mrs. Marjorie McDonald. Before LOFE, the Leicester Office of Further Education, came into being, she chaired the Friends of the Library. She lives near that halfway-house for alkies," he noted, thinking of what that must have done to the price of her property.

"Good. We'll do her next, Frank: with any luck, she'll be seething with jealousy and resentment at being usurped. That might even be why she killed Bert."

As they turned into Marjorie McDonald's quiet road, ten minutes walk from Bath Street Library, they found themselves behind a sleek German sports car. Frank had no particular interest in cars—any more than he had a particular interest in electric kettles or vacuum cleaners, just as long as they performed the function for which they'd been bought—but even he recognised this particular motor as rather special.

"Well, well," said Don, as the sports car parked, next to a

cheap estate car, in front of the very same pleasant, semi-detached house that was the detectives' destination. "Male driver: maybe the boyfriend or son?"

A black man in his twenties, wearing a smart suit and holding a leather briefcase, got out of the car. They approached him with smiles, and with warrant cards in hand, intending to introduce themselves before asking if Mrs. McDonald was at home. The opportunity to do so, as it happened, did not arise.

"Oh, *Jesus!*" The young man slammed his briefcase onto the car's ticking bonnet, making Frank fear for the paintwork. Or for the leatherwork; perhaps; actually, it'd be interesting to see which came off worst. "God, I don't believe it—outside my own sister's house! Actually in her fucking drive! I do not believe it, you people are incredible."

"Hold on, sir—"

"No I will not hold on!" He pointed at Don. "Can you tell me which piece of legislation you wrongly imagine gives you the right to stop me? Because I would be very—"

"We didn't stop you, mate. You were already stopped. We just—"

"You just follow me to my sister's house and start harassing me on the doorstep!" He shook his head in apparent astonishment. "Do you have any idea how many unsolved burglaries there have been in this area in the last month alone? Does it never occur to you that you might be better occupied—"

"Irwin!" All three men jerked their heads towards the front door of the semi, which now framed a slim woman in her thirties, wearing jeans, a tracksuit top, and an expression halfway between amusement and what-will-the-neighbours-think. "Irwin, calm down—I think the officers are here about the body in the library. Isn't that right, gentlemen?" The remaining traces of her musical Jamaican accent contrasted with her younger brother's dull, classless London tones.

"That is right, Mrs. McDonald," said Don, stepping forward to shake her hand. "If you can spare us a few moments?"

Marjorie McDonald's brother Irwin, a City solicitor, could not have been more apologetic. In fact, after several minutes of his apologies and explanations, Frank decided that he'd found him less annoying when he was angry.

Don, however, was magnanimous. "Don't you worry, pal—anyone whose first instinct on seeing a copper is to shout abuse, is okay by me."

"Ah, now . . . I don't think I was actually abusive, as such," said Irwin, clearly a lawyer first, last, and always. "Not within the meaning of the Act." Nonetheless, his apology stretched to him insisting that his sister sit down in the living room with her guests, while he made tea for them all.

Frank was mildly embarrassed to find himself a little surprised by Mrs. McDonald's house. For one thing, it was untidy; nothing extreme, just lived-in, but added to that there were no visible religious symbols, no sounds of scrubbed children practicing the violin. And Marjorie McDonald herself—well, she didn't wear a hat, and looked as if she didn't even own one. She was slim, somewhat sloppily dressed, and only a few years older than Frank himself.

The truth was—and Frank always liked to know the truth, because you never knew when it might come in handy—that she did not fit his preconceptions of West Indian women, especially widow women: churchgoing, obsessed with education, and fiercely house-proud, that was the template he had unconsciously expected Mrs. McDonald to fit.

Still, he was pretty sure that he personally, in his uniformed days, had never stopped a black man purely for driving a nice car, so perhaps things evened out. And he had to smile, when he realised where his stereotype had originated: in an anti-stereotyping course he'd done during his training. Ah, well; he made a mental note not to mention cricket, should a need for small talk arise. For all he knew, she might be a golf fan.

Once the tea and cakes had been distributed to everyone's satisfaction, Irwin presented the court with further evidence in mitigation concerning his earlier misunderstanding. "It becomes second nature, I'm afraid, for any black man who drives a decent motor. I myself have been stopped by the police, for no reason whatsoever, at least thirty times. I know a black judge—in his sixties, lives in Hampstead, drives a Roller—he's been stopped four times in the last year in his own *street!* The last time he was handcuffed in the back of a police car, and his wife had to come out and identify him."

"It's an unqualified disgrace," said Don. "There is no excuse."

"Luckily, his wife is white, so they believed her. Still, I should have given you a chance to state your business, and I'm sorry."

"No problem." Don gave the young lawyer his business card; Frank was astonished—he thought the DI had thrown them all away the day they were issued. "Next time it happens, phone me."

"Thanks, Inspector, but complaints are a complete waste—"

"To hell with complaints," said Don. "I'll pay someone to beat them up."

They shook hands, and parted on superficially good terms as Irwin told his sister he'd take her kids off for a burger while she was busy.

"He's been brilliant," she told them, once two delighted children had been squeezed into the small but perfectly formed car. "Since my husband died, my two couldn't have hoped for a better uncle."

"He seems like a good sort," said Don. "I imagine family help has been invaluable. Do you go out to work?"

"Well, sort of. I worked in a bank when I left school, and I would have gone back to it when the kids were old enough—I loved it, it was great. People think it sounds dull, banking, but if you're working with the right people . . ."

"I wouldn't know," said Don. "All my colleagues are coppers."

She smiled. "Trouble is, being on my own, I needed something with extremely flexible hours to fit in with the kids. Hence . . ." She stood up, and signalled that they should follow through the kitchen to the garage. It was packed, almost floor to ceiling, with packages in plastic courier bags. "I do small deliveries for mail order firms. They deliver them here by lorry or van, and I take them to the customers' houses in my car, and get them signed for. Or, at least I get them signed for on the rare occasions when people are actually at home."

Not much of a living, Frank thought. Couldn't be; how much would she get paid per parcel? She'd have to be doing a hell of a lot of them every week to make anything worthwhile. With various state benefits it'd maybe just do—well, obviously it did, in fact, as they seemed to live decently. Perhaps the mortgage had died with the husband; that'd help.

Back in the living room, conversation moved on to the Friends of Bath Street Library; a long-standing group, of which Marjorie had been a leading light. "I was a school governor at my daughter's primary, years ago, and you know how these things go—once they've seen you're willing to volunteer for one job, they scent blood, like wolves, and before you know it they're all over you, tearing a piece of you off to sit on this committee, and another piece to chair that meeting, and so on."

It wasn't clear whether she took her complaints seriously herself, but Frank was confident that he and Don shouldn't do so; the liveliness in her eyes, and the pride in her voice, made it clear that she was perfectly content to be dismembered by the wolves of civic duty. Some people were like that, Frank knew from his own family; whenever something needed doing, they were the ones who ended up doing it, even though they were already using up more hours in each day than actually existed.

"You said the Friends had been around for a while, but Bath Street only opened a couple of years ago?" said Don.

"Yes, I don't know if you remember, but there was a long, hard campaign to get a new library built in this ward. All we had for years was a hut, basically, a prefab left over from reconstruction after the war. We were *decades* overdue a new facility, no exaggeration. The council always reckoned we were too well-served by other branch libraries nearby, but nearby is a relative term if you're a busy mum with a couple of kids and no car."

"So the Friends was originally a pressure group lobbying for a library, rather than a support group for a library that already existed?"

"That's how it started, yes."

Aye, aye, thought Frank; there was a little hint of bitterness there, just as Don hoped there might be. "So, once the new library came under threat from the council, a new organisation took over?"

"So it seems." She put her mug down on the table, having cleared a kid's homework book out of the way first, and directed a look of puzzlement at the two policemen. "I know it sounds silly, but I sometimes wonder if the Friends would have come out of it all a bit better if we'd had a snappy acronym."

"Like LOFE, you mean?" Don said.

"Quite. But I suppose when we originally named the Friends of Bath Street Library Group we just weren't thinking."

"Fobslug," said Frank.

"Foobyslog," Don corrected him.

Marjorie McDonald laughed, but when Don raised his eyebrows at her invitingly, she just shook her head. "It's a fool's errand, Inspector. It's unpronounceable. Mind you, before the library was built, we called ourselves Bath Street Library Campaign Group."

"I won't even attempt that one." Don smiled at her. "Still, once LOFE had taken over the leadership of the anti-closure campaigning, you joined their committee?"

"No, no I did not."

"Oh, I beg your pardon. I understood—"

She shook her head. "No, I'm not a member of the committee as a member of LOFE. I act purely as a liaison between LOFE and the Friends."

"I see. So, the Friends still exists?"

"There has never been any suggestion of dissolving the Friends."

"Right," said Don. "And what sort of membership does the Friends enjoy these days?"

She folded her hands in her lap. "I don't think headcounts are a relevant way of looking at the issue."

So just you, then, thought Frank.

"Anyway," Don said, "you're all on the same side now."

She made no verbal response to that; a nod of the head was all she deemed it worthy of.

"In any case, you were part of the occupation of—"

She held up a hand, palm out. "No, Inspector, I must make that clear. I was present at the occupation—I was not *part* of it. The Friends does not support non-legal campaigning methods."

Don gave Frank the nod, and the DC asked the two questions which everyone involved would hear over the next couple of days, or had already heard in the last few hours.

Yes, she knew Bert Rosen fairly well; until his wife died, he'd lived only a few doors away. Then he sold up, quite suddenly. Her tone was properly regretful, Frank felt, but not especially warm; and she did seem, generally, like a warm woman.

"And were you aware of any tensions within the LOFE committee?" he asked her. "Was there anyone who didn't seem to get on with anyone else? Not necessarily Bert, but anyone?"

She appeared to give the question due consideration. "Not really. I mean, Cyril and Stanley can't stand each other," she said, "but quite frankly, it would be a very strange committee if the people on it actually liked each other."

"Genocide USA" was what it said on Kimberley Riggs's T-shirt. Don wasn't entirely sure whether the slogan was an accusation, an exhortation, or the name of a rock band. Could be all three at once, he supposed, these days.

In any case, he was careful not to stare at the rune for too long, because Kimberley was nineteen years old and had very nice breasts, and men in their mid-forties did well to observe certain proprieties. Don prided himself on his proprieties. Besides, for all his po-facedness, a certain DC Mitchell was not above dealing out the odd sarky smirk.

Luckily, she was busy covering up her ideological affiliations at this very moment, in accordance with the regulations of her municipal employers, and with them into the depths of a baggy green jumper went certain of the more prominent aspects of her loveliness.

Don, Frank, and Kimberley Riggs were in the small, slightly mildewed staffroom of another branch library, where she'd been posted to cover a sickness absence, her own workplace being temporarily unavailable.

"You've only just got in to work?" Frank asked; a little sternly, Don thought.

"Yeah, your lot had all their questions, and then I went home, had a quick kip, a shower, by then it was lunchtime—you know."

"Surely they'd have given you compassionate leave for a few days?" said Don. "After the ordeal you've been through."

"I'm sure they would, to be fair. But . . ." She shrugged. Don looked at the ceiling. "I don't know what I'd be doing at home. Just moping about. Might just as well come in." She looked about her and sniffed. "Wish I was back at Bath Street, though. This place mings."

"I'm surprised to find you still standing," Don said. "You must be exhausted."

She smiled up at him from underneath her fringe of orange-blonde hair. He looked at the ceiling again. "To be honest, two hours sleep on a Friday night is about average for me."

"Ah, of course. Much the same is true of my colleague, here."

She looked at Frank with a puzzled smile, as if she thought she'd placed him and now wasn't so sure. "You go clubbing?"

"No," Don explained, "he's got a four-year-old."

"Oh, that's nice."

"Who sleeps through the night, thank you, and has done for some time," said Frank.

"You've got time to talk to us before you get back to collecting the overdue fines?" Don asked her.

"Oh, sure. I've arrived just in time for my tea break, anyway." She wrinkled her nose. Don looked at the ceiling. "I would offer you a cup of something, but quite frankly . . ."

Don smiled. "We'll manage without. Just hope we don't have to use the loo while we're here."

"Well if you do, remember to whistle. There's no lock. This place was supposed to be closing down in the new year, for complete refurbishment. Gutting it and starting again, basically. God knows what'll happen now, with the new council."

"Of course," said Don, "you'd be very involved in that sort of thing, I suppose, being a union rep."

She nodded, and blushed. He couldn't look at the bloody ceiling again, Don told himself; she'd think he was seeking divine guidance. He glanced over at Frank, instead. That was no bloody help—Frank was blushing, as well. Not from the same cause, of course; Frank was blushing because Kimberley was blushing. Nature's blushers, of whom Frank was one, found blushing as contagious as yawning. The young shop steward, he suspected, was blushing because her union activities were something she felt passionate about.

Damn. He looked at the ceiling.

"Yeah," she said, "I'm the steward for three branch libraries. Not including this one, thank God." She lowered her voice and leant forward; she found herself glancing at the ceiling for a second, but wasn't sure why. "The steward for this branch is *useless.* Mind you, it's mostly old women work here, part-timers. You wouldn't get my members putting up with a staffroom that stinks like the town tip, and no lock on the bog door."

Her unremarkably pretty face had worn a quite fierce expression during this short speech, Don noticed. This pendulum swing between stammering and scowling, blushing and blustering, was something he'd seen before in the committed young, who enjoyed complete confidence in the rightness of their causes but still endured the remnants of an adolescent reluctance to speak out loud.

It did Don's heart good to see a youngster so involved, but he couldn't think of a way of expressing that which wouldn't insult her and humiliate him. And make Frank blush. So instead, he said: "You've certainly got your hands full at Bath Street, fighting the closure."

"I know!" The anger and the passion were both radiant on her face. She pushed her fringe off her forehead as if it had personally offended her. "It's crazy—they spend a fortune on a really good, state-of-the-art library, and then a couple of years later they want to close it. And you know why?"

Don knew his chances of getting out of that room alive didn't really depend on his answer to this question, but looking at her burning eyes, he could almost believe it. "Because they're a bunch of tossers?" he suggested.

Kimberley giggled. Don blinked. "That, too. But mainly I think it's simply because the other party opened Bath Street—so this party has to close it."

"You're right," said Don, "that is crazy."

"Right!" Her fringe had misbehaved again, evidently. She gave it a really good shove this time; that'll teach it, Don reckoned. "God, even my dad put a 'Save Bath Street' sticker in his car. And believe me, that's like a *really* big deal."

"Your father a bit conservative, is he?"

"No, just apathetic. Mum and Dad were really into the anti-racist movement in the seventies. I mean, really into it—that's where they met, picketing a police station. Love at first cavalry charge, according to Dad."

"But not any more?"

"No!" Her baffled disbelief made her eyes as big as discuses. "They've been totally inactive for years."

Inactive apart from the trivial business of being parents, Don supposed; but he could see where some of Kimberley's passion came from, anyway—a need to pick up the baton dropped by her disappointing elders. "Well, people get older, I suppose."

"That's no excuse," she said, and blushed harder than ever. Her fringe was taking a real beating now. "Look at Bert—he was over eighty, and he never stopped. One of the readers who'd known him for ages said to me, 'Bolshie Bert's been an Angry Young Man for seventy years.' Isn't that great?"

"You were obviously a fan."

"Bert was wonderful," she said, managing to keep talking through her tears—a trick which evolution had gifted only to women, in Don's experience. When men started crying during an interview, it was all over. You'd be lucky to restart within the week. To women, tears seemed to be an inconvenience to rank with sneezing. Kimberley took from her Greenpeace shoulder bag a packet of tissues, and a big, hardback book: *The Battle of the Atlantic*. "He fought in the Battle of the Atlantic, did you know?"

"Yes," said Don, "I did. Longest battle of World War Two, wasn't it?"

She nodded. "That's right. It lasted from the first day of the war in 1939 until the German surrender in 1945. There were eighty thousand Allied dead by the end. And a lot of those were just kids, like Bert. You know what Churchill said about it?"

"Not off hand," Don admitted. "Frank?"

"Can't quite put my finger on the exact quote," said

Frank, who was sitting with his notebook open but ignored on his lap. He was making a heroic effort, Don knew, not to look bored or sound impatient.

Kimberley was flicking through the pages of the plastic-wrapped library book. "He said that only one thing truly frightened him during the whole war—not the Blitz, but the U-boats. You see, the convoys that Bert served on, they had to escort the merchant navy on the trade routes to North America. Protect them from submarines. If the battle had been lost, Britain would have starved, and that would have been it—the war would have been over, before it even became a world war."

"So it was a pretty simple equation?" Frank, Don could see, was getting interested despite himself.

"Perfectly simple: if Germany could sink merchant ships faster than the shipyards could replace them, then Hitler had won. If it was the other way around, he'd lost. And do you know . . ." She was off, dashing through the pages again. "Did you know that the German navy finally got enough U-boats to finish the job in 1945? If they'd had them a couple of years earlier, we'd probably be speaking German today. D-Day was nothing compared to the Atlantic. This bloke," she said, lifting the book to indicate her source, "reckons four battles decided the outcome of the whole war: the Battle of Britain, the Battle of the Atlantic, Stalingrad, and Kursk."

"Not what the war films tell us," said Don, grinning.

"Yeah, and who made them? Bert told me, the only thing you need to know about the Hollywood version of history is that it's one hundred percent wrong one hundred percent of the time!"

"It sounds like you and Bert became good friends."

"Yeah, we did. He was great, I'm really going to miss him. I just can't believe anyone could do that to him."

"You're on the LOFE committee, I presume, as union rep?" Don asked. "So, tell us about that—is it a good committee? Is it really united, or are there the usual personality clashes and differences of opinion?"

She thought about it, but it seemed to Don that she hadn't yet realised quite why the question was so significant. "Marjorie McDonald can be a bit of pain, to be honest. She's always going on about how we have to do everything through the proper channels and not be too militant. But how many rights would people have today if no one had ever broken the law?"

"And more importantly," said Don, "Frank and I wouldn't have jobs. We'd have to work for a living."

"To be fair," she continued, "Marjorie generally abides by the decision of the majority. She was very upset about the occupation, for instance, but once the vote had been held, she went along with it. I think mainly she's just pissed off because she used to run a Friends of the Library group that LOFE pretty much took over from. But it was obvious we needed a militant, union-led campaign, less of a do-goodery thing."

"The rest are mostly of a similar mind, are they? Concerning tactics and so on."

Along with the mixture as before of fierce and shy, her face now showed another archetypal ingredient of youth: scorn. "Actually, some of them just seem to turn up for the cup of tea at the end of the meeting! I don't know how Bert kept his patience with them—he had more fire in him than most of them put together. Can you imagine what he must have been like when he was younger?"

"Still, you're lucky that your immediate boss is so supportive."

"Dot?" She opened her mouth to say more, then closed it again. She took a swig from a bottle of mineral water, before adding: “Yeah, she’s lovely. Everyone loves Dot.” Not the most ringing endorsement of union militancy he’d ever heard, Don thought; perhaps poor Dot’s crime was that she wasn’t an eighty-four-year-old veteran of one of World War II’s forgotten battles.

Chapter Six

"It must be sex," Don announced, once they were back in the fresh air.

"Sex?" Frank echoed, but at a slightly lower volume. "What, you mean the motive?"

"Has anyone offered anything better?"

"Well, aye, no, but . . . sex? The guy was eighty-four."

Don waggled his hand, scattering the smoke of his small cigar into the autumnal afternoon. "Doesn't matter, Frank. This murder took place in a library, and libraries are full of sex."

"Are they?" Frank had always thought of libraries as being full of books, mostly, and that rather unpleasant plasticky smell you got from the protective book jackets.

"Of course they are. It's all those stacks and shelves and nooks and crannies. Sex between the staff, sex between the readers. Sex between the readers and the staff."

"Well, if—"

"Lot of young people work in libraries, Frank, don't forget that. Public libraries have a disproportionate number of young, highly intelligent staff."

"True enough," said Frank, who didn't know whether it was true or not, but hoped it was a diversion.

No such luck. "I used to go out with a library assistant. Years ago, before they invented steam trains. When she was on late turn, I'd come in and keep her company."

"Right," said Frank, who always tried to avoid his Uncle Harold at family gatherings for precisely this reason. "That's us, behind that Hyundai."

"I'll tell you, Frank, in the springtime, in some libraries—there'll be a queue outside the Disabled Toilet stretching right round Crafts and Hobbies, past Eastern Cuisine, as far back as Do It Yourself Plumbing. A queue of people in wheelchairs keeping their legs crossed."

They got into the car. "Well," said Frank, who had learned that it was always wiser to offer at least token resistance to one of Don Packham's blitzkriegs of fancy, "all I could smell in that library was stale milk."

Don sighed, shook his head, and looked at the ceiling.

Doug Ticehurst, lay member of the LOFE committee ("That's the Lesser Orifice Festivities Executive," Don reminded Frank), answered his mobile phone in a breathless and hurried manner. He was at work, he explained. Even so, he was told, the officers did need to speak to him. They were, after all, investigating a—

"Yes, okay. But we'll have to talk while I work."

"No problem," Frank assured him, meaning that when they got there they would take him to a different part of his workplace from the one that he actually worked in, so as to avoid distractions, and that therefore there would, indeed, be no problem. "Whereabouts are you?"

"At the moment we're in . . ." His already thin, vicarish voice faded, until Frank thought he'd lost him altogether.

"You still there, Mr. Ticehurst?"

"Sorry, just checking—if you're more than about ten minutes, you'll find us in Tudor Gardens. I've got to go now, sorry."

What? Was the guy moving office today? And what bloody number, Tudor Gardens?

"Ah, I see," said Frank, quarter of an hour later, pulling into a broad, residential street on the other side of the borough from Bath Street Library. "That'll be him, over there," he said, pointing towards a small lorry which was kerb-crawling fifty yards from where the detectives were parked. Frank phoned Doug Ticehurst's mobile again, and sure enough one of the two figures moving around the lorry reached into his pocket.

"Hello, Mr. Ticehurst—it's DC Mitchell. We'll be with you in ten seconds."

"I quite fancy that job," said Don, as they got out of the car. "Wonder if they've got any vacancies."

"On the recycling lorries?" Hard work, in all weathers, for unimpressive wages. Frank was pretty sure they'd have vacancies—permanently.

They stood and watched the recyclers labouring for a moment. The two workers would collect the plastic crates of household waste from outside each front gate, and sort their contents into wire cages on the open-sided vehicle: cans, newspapers, old clothes, white glass, brown glass, green glass . . .

"It's a nice methodical job, that," said Don. "Sorting everything out like that. And I love that lorry, don't you? I always wanted to be tractor driver when I was little, but I reckon this'd be even better."

"Where I live, the recycle van comes early in the morning," Frank said, after they'd made themselves known to Doug Ticehurst. "I didn't realise you worked this late."

"We're running behind," said Ticehurst, "because of the

storm. Yesterday's rounds got backed-up, so it's all a bit hectic."

"But you can't have had much sleep," said Don. "Wouldn't the council give you just one afternoon off, under the circs?"

Ticehurst was in his early thirties and good-looking, Frank supposed, in a sort of wet, Hollywood-Englishman way. He even had the requisite floppy hair, which his bright orange cap couldn't entirely tame. His chewed lips and habitual-looking frown suggested a man who was not often at ease with himself, and he certainly seemed on edge just now. His feet and hands were engaged in constant, jerky movements, reminiscent of a dance from the golden age of rock'n'roll, while his eyes kept flashing longingly towards the lorry and the crates of rubbish.

"It's not council," he replied. "It's contracted out. There's no union." He lowered his voice; superfluously, Frank thought, what with the lorry idling and his colleague tossing wine bottles into its belly. "One girl, they wouldn't give her a morning off for her great-aunt's funeral. They said if it had been an aunt, okay, but not a *great*-aunt."

"That's a bit harsh," said Don.

"I suppose it's true, though, what they always tell us—if all this lot isn't recycled, it's just choking the planet, and that'd be down to us." Like a fawn who'd lost sight of its mother, he jerked his head towards the lorry as it moved forward a few yards. Its crew consisted of only two people, Frank saw; there was no dedicated driver. Now he came to think of it, he recognised the stop-start rhythm of the job, usually heard rather than seen as he ate his breakfast on a working day: a few minutes of clanging and smashing and thudding, followed by a few seconds of vehicle noise, and then the clanging began again, as the driver leaped down from the cab to return to his duties as a collector, sorter, and flinger. Frank's four-year-old son could no doubt have described all this to him, if he'd ever asked; Joseph never missed the weekly appearance of the recycle van, his face right up against the window for all the time the lorry was in sight, like a granny watching a soap opera.

"Look, I'm sorry," said Ticehurst, "but could you please ask your questions as you trot alongside me?"

Frank knew instantly that this would count as one of the most treasurable moments of his year.

"Trot alongside you?" said Don.

"I'm sorry, it's just, we're not supposed to stop for any reason at all. All the task timings are carefully calibrated according to Best Practice Parameters."

"Trot?"

Oh, yes, thought Frank: that face. Wonderful. What he wouldn't give to have a photograph of that face! For a moment—only a moment, admittedly, but a moment which did, nonetheless, exist—he thought of whipping out his mobile phone and actually taking a souvenir snap of the DI's horrified, outraged, disbelieving, never-been-so-insulted-in-its-life phizog. Instead, he remembered who he was and what he was doing and told the twitching recycler: "I'm not sure that would really be practical, I'm afraid."

"Oh but please, you see—"

Rescue came in the form of Doug's partner, a young black woman with blue hair who, even in this weather, was proudly (or nonchalantly, Frank couldn't really tell which) displaying, by means of a cropped top and an open jacket, the ring which pierced her bellybutton. "For heaven's sake, Doug!" Her tone was a mixture of exasperation and sympathetic patience. And maybe just a hint of flirtation, too. "Talk to them, will you? Your mate's been murdered—that is quite an important business, yeah? I'll carry on while you're speaking to the officers, it'll be fine."

Ticehurst looked at her, and then back at the van. "But the rules . . ."

She put a hand on his shoulder, and he looked grateful for it. "I've told you before, Doug, it's morally wrong to obey rules."

"Will you marry me?" Don asked her.

She laughed over her shoulder, as she returned to her crates. "Let me finish this lot, first, eh?"

And so, at last, they managed to separate Doug Ticehurst from his duties, and took him to Frank's car to talk, partly to get out of the cold but mostly to make it harder for him to escape back to the old shoes and bags of used tinfoil.

They established that he was divorced, though how long he'd been in that state seemed to be something he had to think about. "Um . . . about six months," he told them, a large part of his attention still fixed beyond the car's window. They further established that he lived alone, in—judging from the address, which was familiar to both CID men—an area of bedsits in which the most popular letting agency was the probation service. From Ticehurst's clear embarrassment, it was obvious that he, too, was perfectly aware of his home street's reputation.

Frank received Don's eyebrow semaphore from over the suspect's head, and interpreted it as meaning "Make a note of that; he's short of money." Frank duly made a note; as far as they were aware, there was no monetary motive in this case, but Don had taught him well that when it came to murder, money was rarely irrelevant.

Had Doug always done this job, Frank asked, knowing perfectly well that he hadn't, since the job hadn't existed ten years ago; the UK's conversion to the recycling faith had been almost farcically slow.

Under the pressure of interrogation, Ticehurst admitted that he was an English graduate, and that he'd done various jobs— "Nothing in particular" —over the years. "I've just been on the vans for a few months, but I like it. Out in the fresh air, you know, doing something worthwhile. You've got to start by feeling good about yourself, that's what all the books say."

"And, indeed," Don told him, "it's really quite a responsible position. For an English graduate." Ticehurst seemed to find this a little less amusing than Don did.

Questioned about his background in politics or protest, he revealed that before joining LOFE he had never so much as signed a petition in his life. Neither detective found this hard to believe; Ticehurst did seem an innocent sort of bloke, with his wide eyes and his uncertain smile. Frank thought he knew what Don would say about the man later: that he'd wandered into LOFE out of loneliness, following his divorce. Even an evening spent at a committee meeting would be preferable to one spent alone and broke in his one-room home.

"How did you get involved with LOFE?" Frank asked.

"I use that library quite a lot, it's a very nice place, and I just think it's very sad if they close it."

"That's why, Doug," Don pointed out, not unkindly. "We were asking about how?"

"Sorry, yes. I don't know, I just sort of wandered into it, I think. Someone asked me if I wanted one of the 'Save Bath Street' badges, and I said yes, and they said why didn't I come along to a protest meeting, and I said, well, okay, I suppose so, and . . . It's terribly sad about poor Bert, isn't it? I mean, it's just terrible."

For the first time, Frank noticed, all of Ticehurst's attention was focussed on the matter at hand; he was momentarily deaf to the lure of the lorry. "You liked him, did you? You got on with him?"

"Oh, good heavens, yes—he was such a kind man, he'd do anything for you. He'd help anyone." There was, now Frank came to look for it, a redness around Ticehurst's eyes; Bert Rosen was, it seemed, being mourned by many, just as Don had predicted.

"So what do you make of the political world, Doug," Don asked, "now that you've experienced its joys?"

"Joys, well!" He was back to staring out of the window, Frank saw. "I'm not sure it's somewhere I'd like to spend too much of my time."

"No?"

"No. It's all a bit—well, factional, you know?"

Frank could almost see Don's ears pricking up. "Is that right?"

"Oh God, where is she?" Ticehurst slid out of the open car door so fast he almost bounced on the tarmac. "I can't see the lorry!"

"Don't worry," Frank told him, "it's just turned the corner."

"I've got to go," Ticehurst said, and went. They watched him run off in pursuit of the steadily diminishing sound of breaking glass.

It was getting dark. "I don't care who we talk to next," said Don, "as long as he works indoors."

Frank knew just the man. "How about Councillor James Pomeroy?"

"Ha! Yes, I think we can safely assume he's never had an outside job in his life. Or, indeed, a job that involved working on Saturdays."

Councillor Pomeroy was recovering at home, the detectives were informed over the telephone. "Who was that you spoke to, do you reckon?" Don asked Frank as they set off towards an address in the very south of the borough. "His butler or his boyfriend?"

Frank pondered, aware that when Don said something which sounded like a cheap dig, it usually turned out to be a serious inquiry. "Don't know," he eventually replied. "Couldn't really tell. Does he have a butler, then?" He'd be damned if he was going to ask "Does he have a boyfriend?" He'd give Don his due, sure enough, but he didn't see why he should give him his sport.

It wasn't a butler, but a partner. "I'm James's partner," said the polite young man who opened the door to them. "If you'd like to go through, James will be with you in a second."

"Not 'boyfriend,' Frank," said Don, in a reproving undertone. "He prefers 'partner.' "

"Bloody hell," said Frank, referring not to semantics but to interior design. "I've seen football pitches smaller than this living room."

The London Borough of Cowden was very mixed—by income, by race, by type and age of property—and most of its neighbourhoods and even individual streets were diverse microcosms of the blended whole. The road in which James Pomeroy lived, however, was Cowden's one true claim to an authentic, North London–style, leafy avenue. Admittedly, there were blocks of council flats at each end—stubborn remnants of a more egalitarian era—but the bulk of the tree-lined street, the gazelle in the boa so to speak, consisted of flats in old conversions like this one. Deceptively narrow from the outside, and seeming squashed together in terraced rows, they were breathtakingly gigantic within.

Elegantly and minimally furnished, the room seemed warm and full of light, and—what was this? *Can't be!* thought Frank.

"Mind where you're treading, Don."

"You're joking!" said Don, looking at his feet. "Oh, I see what you mean. That is flash, isn't it?"

"You like that, do you?" said Councillor Pomeroy, approaching them across the bare floorboards on appropriately bare feet. It took him a while to arrive.

"I'm not sure whether I like it or not," said Don, as they shook hands. "It's certainly impressive. I've never seen a room with a stream running through it before."

Pomeroy laughed. His soft, southern Irish accent and rather doughy face made him, in the flesh, considerably less intimidating than his reputation. "Not a stream, as such, Inspector. It's a loop running from, and back to, an ornamental pond outside, there." He pointed towards what was, in effect, a glass wall, rather than merely a very big set of sliding patio doors. "We used to have koi in the pond. But we have cats, and we got fed up with tripping over fish—these floors can be quite slippery. Please, sit down."

The partner continued his impersonation of a butler, bringing in coffee on a tray, and then gliding out again. Pomeroy served his guests and himself, Frank being the only one to decline cream; a revolting and strange habit, to his tastes. Still, he couldn't bring himself to ask for milk, so he pretended that he always took his coffee black.

"Helps you stay awake, I expect," said Pomeroy, "through all those tedious interviews, asking the same bloody questions over and over."

"It helps," Frank agreed. Councillor Pomeroy was charming, no doubt about it. Even Don, who Frank knew had little time for politicians, let alone rich Conservative politicians, seemed relaxed and smiling in this particular politician's company.

In the car on the way over, the DI had told Frank what he knew about James Pomeroy, which amounted, as he admitted, to little more than that he was a bona fide colourful Cowden character—a right-wing version of Bert Rosen, in a way—with some small but growing fame beyond the borough as one of a new generation of openly gay young Tories, with extreme libertarian views. "The sort of professional noisemaker," Don had concluded, "that newspapers and discussion shows love best."

Now, sitting on the noisemaker's leather sofa, Don went straight in. "What on earth is a Tory borough councillor doing supporting the workers and peasants in occupying a public library?"

"Let me just say, Inspector, that I'm not overly keen on the word *Tory*."

"Of course, how insensitive of me." Don leant forward; Frank hadn't seen him enjoy an interview this much in months. "For an Irishman, the word has particular resonance, I realise. How about Conservative?"

Pomeroy put his cup down on a marble-topped table. "I'm not mad on that one, either, to be honest."

"Really? You're beginning to realise there's no career future in Conservatism, are you?"

"I simply think these terms are outdated. Tory is utterly meaningless, and as for Conservative—why would I wish to saddle myself with a label implying a philosophy based on opposition to change?"

"No danger of you answering the question, I suppose?"

"Ah! Well, let me admit that I'm still enough of a tribal politician to be happy to support anyone who opposes any policy of the LibDems. If the LibDems want to close Bath

Street Library, then I want to keep it open."

"Fair enough. But you opposed the opening of the library in the first place, didn't you?"

Pomeroy spread his hands. "And in doing so, I was opposing Labour Party policy. I reserve the right to be consistent in my own way. You know, I wasn't the only Tory there last night; there was a smattering of local politicians, from all three parties. We all chatted together, politely enough."

"You are, as a libertarian, opposed to public libraries, aren't you? In principle."

"No, no." Pomeroy held up a long finger to show that this bit was important. "I'm not opposed to public libraries; I'm opposed to publicly funded libraries; there is a difference."

"Of course," Don began.

"What is the difference, exactly?" Frank interrupted, ignoring Don's irritated glance at him. "If they're not publicly funded, are you suggesting that the private sector might run them? Hard to imagine a library making a profit."

"You must remember, Constable, that the original public libraries were charitable institutions, not organs of the state."

"I see," said Don. "So that's what libertarian Conservatism comes down to—abolish the state, and go back to the mill owners dipping into their pockets for loose change every time the number of child prostitutes gets too high?"

"Now you're being silly, Inspector." Pomeroy smiled broadly. "I like that in a copper."

"But despite your ideological distrust of state-run public services, you took an active part in the campaign to save Bath Street. Crude politicking apart, I still find that a little difficult to understand."

Pomeroy stroked his chin with steepled fingers. "Did you know Bert Rosen, at all?"

"I'd met him," Don replied. "An interesting man."

"Well, he was the reason I supported the LOFE. It pleased him to have me there, and it pleased me to please him. As you say, an interesting man—an admirable man, too."

"Admirable?" said Frank, struggling to grasp why someone on the rightmost fringe of mainstream politics should admire an elderly Communist.

"He lived his beliefs; that's unusual enough these days to be admirable, in my opinion."

"So," said Don, "we can put your membership of LOFE down to Bert's legendary ability to build unlikely alliances?"

"I admired the old Tankie," Pomeroy repeated. "And I liked him, too. I was there as an act of friendship, simple as that."

"What exactly do you do for a living, Councillor?" Don gestured at the football pitch and the stream. "A local politician's attendance allowances don't pay for this lot."

"I'm a businessman."

"What does that mean, precisely?"

"It means that I'm in business." Pomeroy sipped at his coffee.

"Could you be a bit more specific, perhaps?"

"Inspector, if you have a specific question, please ask it. Fishing trips are so vulgar."

Don bowed his head, and smiled. "Do your business interests include any PFI contracts?"

"I have some such interests, yes."

"So you make money out of private sector involvement in public services, and yet you campaign to preserve a public library. That's very noble."

"Thank you." Pomeroy mimicked Don's bow and smile.

Don looked about him for a while, apparently in no hurry to be anywhere else. He took his time enjoying his coffee. When he was quite ready, he said: "So, tell me again—why you were at the protest?"

Pomeroy laughed out loud. "You think I was there to kill dear old Bert, Inspector!"

Don shrugged. "But you weren't, of course, so why were you there?"

Again, Pomeroy made the spread hands gesture which Frank recognised from watching public figures interviewed on television; the gesture which meant, *Joking aside, here comes the truth now.* "Well, apart from anything, no matter my own views, I have a duty to represent my constituents."

"Bath Street isn't in your ward."

"It's in an adjoining ward. Many of my constituents use it, and they overwhelmingly oppose its closure."

"I didn't think libertarians believed in mob rule," said Don. "Or 'democracy,' as the old-fashioned statists call it."

"When one accepts election one must accept certain obligations."

Don's face said he was far from convinced. Frank wondered whether he was, in actual fact, far from convinced, or whether that was merely what he wished to convey. And whether Councillor Pomeroy would be able to tell the difference.

"You could oppose the closure at a distance, surely; you don't need to be quite so hands-on."

"I'm a hands-on sort of fellow." Pomeroy showed no signs of discomfort, as far as Frank could see. But then, that was the advantage of his kind of good manners—they could cover, or convey, any amount of rudeness, as their owner chose.

"But to take part in an illegal occupation of a council-owned building?" Don persisted. "All a bit Che Guevara for you, I'd have thought."

"Ah, well there you have me, Inspector. I wasn't intending to be part of the lock-in, at all. But I got talking to old Bert, and one thing led to another, and I didn't notice the time passing . . . and you know, the fact is, I never was an early-to-bed type."

"And you'd had no falling out with Bert? Or with anyone else in LOFE?"

"Certainly not." For the first time, Frank thought, the councillor looked just a little riled. Perhaps the idea that he might engage in anything so common as a falling-out had got under his skin.

"Were you aware of any other tensions or enmities?"

"More so than is normal on a committee?" Pomeroy smiled again, and stood up. "Nothing. But thank you for coming round, gentlemen, and please do keep in touch."

Chapter Seven

"Not convinced," said Don, as Frank drove him back to the library to collect his own car.

"No?"

"No way. Okay, Bert may indeed have been a persuasive old bugger, and Pomeroy an unusual Tory, but even so—whoever heard of an ambitious Conservative councillor taking part in a sit-in?"

It did sound odd, Frank couldn't disagree. "I suppose a businessman and a politician is a decent candidate for a murder suspect."

"Blackmail, you mean?"

Frank was a little surprised—and, truth be told, a tiny bit put out—to hear unmistakable doubt in Don's voice. "You don't reckon? Pomeroy's got money and a career: plenty to lose."

"Yeah, I know Frank, but ask yourself—even if we try to picture Bert as a blackmailer, what could he possibly have with which to embarrass an openly homosexual libertarian Tory? It'd have to be something pretty strong, don't you think?"

"And there's no hint of any such thing," Frank admitted.

They drove in silence for a while, until Don spoke again.

"Nobody bats an eyelid at gay politicians these days. Even ten years ago, the idea of a cabinet minister's lesbian girlfriend being formally introduced to the Queen at a Buck House reception would have been incredible—but it happens all the time now, and nobody even notices. All the parties now accept that having a gay candidate doesn't create even the tiniest blip in either the opinion polls or the real polls, in any constituency on mainland Britain. That gay marriage act went through parliament with only a handful of geriatric nutters opposing it, and the general public not even vaguely interested. Nowadays, the quickest way to ruin your political career is to make an anti-gay remark."

Frank couldn't help chuckling at that. "You sound almost regretful, Don."

"No, don't get me wrong. That's one part of our brave new world that's undeniably made the country more civilised, not less. Politicians should be judged on what they do in office, not in the bedroom. I just can't quite get used to living in a world where Tory sexual hypocrisy is history, that's all."

Now Frank was really laughing. "You mean you miss all the sex scandals."

"I do, I admit it! There's no sense in buying the Sunday papers any more."

"All right, so gayness isn't even notable any longer, but you're always saying politics is bland and colourless now—so surely Pomeroy's libertarian stuff still has the power to shock?" Frank recalled some of the councillor's political positions, as outlined to him earlier that day by Don himself. "Didn't you say he thinks the old age pension should be scrapped, for instance, and heroin legalised?"

Don shrugged. "Legalising drugs—most of the doctors and half the police chiefs advocate that, nowadays. And as for privatising the old age pension, that's official European

Union policy, isn't it?" He gave a heartfelt sigh as they pulled up outside the library. "The Americans have got the right idea, Frank—all their right-wingers are nutcases, and all their left-wingers are weirdoes. That's how it should be. *That's* democracy."

In theory, Saturday night at Frank and Debbie's meant a Chinese takeaway and the telly—though in practice, Frank just as often spent the evening on stake-outs, interviews, and filling in forms. With an active murder investigation less than twenty-four hours old, the best Frank could promise his wife was that "I'm off for the night, unless they ring with anything."

Luckily for him, and no one should ever imagine that he didn't appreciate the fact, his wife had never been one of those copper's spouses to whom the working practices of the police service came as a shocking affront, anew and afresh, every time they intruded into her plans. It helped, no doubt, that she'd worked as a nurse until becoming a mother. She knew as much as he did about unsocial hours.

The Chinese was therefore fetched (Frank reckoned it took longer to arrive when it was sent out for, and he liked his bean sprouts warm—or, more precisely, he disliked them cold) and dished onto oven-warmed plates, which were in turn placed on mats, showing scenes from the Lake District, which protected a low table in front of the sofa. Frank had one glass of red wine, and Debbie one and a bit. Neither of them were big drinkers really, but it was what you did, wasn't it? If you were a young, middle-class couple, sitting on a sofa on a Saturday night, you drank some wine. Frank would have preferred a beer, really—it was thirsty work, he always found, was Chinese food—and Debbie was gasping for a cup of tea, but it was what you did, wasn't it? On a Saturday night, you drank a glass of wine.

"Very nice this, isn't it?" said Frank.

"Very fruity, isn't it?" Debbie replied.

"Think I'll stick the kettle on, but," said Frank.

"I wouldn't say no," Debbie replied.

Before eating, they'd watched a quiz show on television with their son, Joseph, sitting between them on the sofa. For some reason, Joseph thought the answer to every question on the quiz was "Pants." He was wrong, but each time he said it, after the first few times, his parents squeezed against him from either side, as if planning to crush the life out of him, which made him shout with laughter loud enough to disembowel a guinea pig—should there have been one present, which luckily there was not.

With Joseph in bed, and the Chinese ingested, they sat together on the sofa, watching nothing.

"Don didn't fancy carrying on late into the night, then?" Debbie asked. "Does that mean he's on a down?"

"No, I wouldn't say so. In fact, these last few days he's been remarkably cheerful. Not *up* exactly, not anything as unnerving as that. More . . . I don't know, as if he's happy about something."

This was a strange concept, indeed—DI Packham happy, rather than ecstatic or depressed—and they pondered it in silence for a while. Then they stopped pondering it, also in silence.

Frank watched some rugby highlights—Scotland getting thrashed by a country the size of Margate—while Debbie read, with apparent fascination, a magazine about metal detecting. Neither of them had ever been metal detecting in their lives, but that didn't bother Debbie; she judged magazines on their own merits, not those of their subjects.

The phone rang once, around eight fifteen, but it was a

wrong number, and after that Frank knew his luck was in for the night.

Over time, Frank had learned that there was little point in questioning Don on matters about which he did not wish to be questioned; it wasted the questioner's time, and annoyed the DI.

On Sunday morning, Don had invited his younger colleague to join him, at his home address, for "a late breakfast or an early lunch."

"Brunch?" Frank had suggested.

"Stupid word," said Don. "Made-up word."

It occurred to Frank that all words were made-up, because otherwise how would they come into existence, but he didn't waste time on that. Instead, he pinned Don down on a precise time for this between-meals meeting, and the address at which it was to be held.

A comfortable, somewhat rambling garden flat, just over the borough border into Harrow, at ten thirty in the morning, was the answer. It was a pleasant day, and the kitchen in which Frank found Don excitedly occupied was warm and swimming in sunshine. Frank had never seen, or even heard of, this flat before. But he didn't ask.

Early lunch or late breakfast, whichever it was, it turned out to consist mostly of popcorn. "You ever seen one of these, Frank? They're brilliant."

Not only had Frank seen a popcorn maker before, he had two of the bloody things in a cupboard at home. Both Christmas presents. Both from the same aunt. Different years, though, to be fair. They'd used the first one once, out of respect, but they hadn't felt the same sense of obligation about the second one. They kept meaning to take it down to the charity shop. Or give it to someone for Christmas.

"Looks great, Don. Can't beat homemade popcorn. Very healthy."

"Look!" said Don. "Watch this, it's starting!"

Frank watched. After a while, he said: "I don't know if it's mentioned in the instructions at all, but it might be an idea to place some kind of receptacle underneath the spout of the popping machine."

"Receptacle?"

"To catch the popped corn as it flies out."

Don surveyed the kitchen counter; and then the kitchen floor. "Actually, Frank, that's not the worst idea you've ever had. Let's do another lot. You're in charge of receptacles."

Over popcorn and tea—tea, mostly, on Frank's part—they talked about where they were in the case so far. Not very far, was the gist of it.

"We've met all the suspects," said Don, "but I don't really feel we've come up with much in the way of motive. Do you?"

"Not a lot." Frank made a list on a blank page of his notebook. "I suppose the best we've got, using the word best in its broadest sense—"

"You can say that again."

"There's Marjorie McDonald, and the possibility that she bears a grudge because of LOFE eclipsing her group. But she'd have to have gone completely mad, surely, to kill an old man over that."

"A mid-LOFE crisis, sort of thing?"

"Aye, that sort of thing," said Frank, "only funnier."

"And you raised the possibility of James Pomeroy as a blackmail victim."

"But only because of who he is—well off and high profile, I mean. Not for any better reason than that."

"Not to worry." Don scooped up the rest of his popcorn.

"Something better will turn up eventually."

"I hope so," said Frank.

"Well it must, mustn't it? Because poor old Bert did get killed, and therefore someone did have a reason for killing him."

"Aye, I suppose so."

"And then, of course," said Don, "there's the rhinoceros in the launderette."

"The what in the where?"

"The gun. That is totally baffling. Made more so by the fact that Bert was toting this shooter around with him, like a sheriff in a Western, and yet no one we've spoken to seems to have been aware of him being scared or preoccupied or nervous, or bloody anything."

"I suppose it's possible," said Frank, "that even the killer never knew he had a gun. Took him by surprise, had him half dead before the old guy could ever get his hand to his pocket."

"And, come to that, perhaps the person who was a threat to him didn't know he was a threat." Don shook his head. "But we're tying ourselves in knots, here. Forget the gun for the moment. I'd like to know where it came from, but it's essentially a distraction."

"I suppose so. Back to motive, then? Or the lack of one. How much difference would Bert's death make to the campaign?"

"Not a fatal difference, I wouldn't have thought. There's still Dot, and young Kimberley. And from what Councillor Pomeroy said, public opinion is firmly on LOFE's side."

"It is." Frank nodded. "I was reading up on it in last week's local paper, this morning. They seem to think the new council has bitten off more than it can chew."

"So it's not practical, even if it was imaginable, to kill Bert to stop the library campaign. In any case, if we're right about our seven suspects, they were all there to *support* the campaign."

"So we're back to looking for something within LOFE which somehow led directly or indirectly to the killing?"

"Yeah. Doesn't have to be Bert versus someone, it could be someone versus someone else with Bert somehow ending up as collateral damage."

"Apart from Marjorie," said Frank, after a few moments' thought, "the only obvious unpleasantness seems to be between Cyril and Stanley."

"Right then." Don stood up, and reached for his leather jacket. "Never let it be said that Cowden CID despised the obvious. Let's go and see Cyril."

So this was Cyril Mowbray's *company directorship,* Don thought. Not much of a company: he didn't even have a lad to hold his bucket, so far as Don could see.

"Surprised to find you up there on a Sunday," he said, as the former soldier clambered down his ladder. "I didn't know window-cleaners worked weekends." Cyril's trousers reminded Don of something, and he just couldn't put his finger on what it was. Apart from the pavement outside a kebab house at chucking-out time.

Cyril shook hands with them both, and Don could see the bluster, which he was sure was the man's customary style returning, as if by an act of will; replacing the obvious annoyance at the detectives' arrival which he had briefly displayed from the top of his ladder.

"Best day," he said, his voice echoing around the courtyard of the small block of flats. "Only day they're home, most people. If they're home when you do the windows, you get paid. If not—you've got to come back. Inefficient, you see."

"Good point," Don admitted. "Does your company employ a large staff?"

"If you want a job done, do it yourself." Cyril's face suddenly closed in on itself, as he realised even a copper would understand that this answer meant that he worked alone. "Expanding all the time," he added. "Always expanding. Essential to have a business plan, you see."

Rupert the Bear! That's who he'd got the trousers from—or from the same tailor, at least. "Must seem a bit quiet, I suppose," said Don, "window cleaning. After the army, I mean."

"Well, people say that." Cyril reached into an inside pocket and withdrew a much-creased newspaper cutting. "Very interesting: window cleaning is the most dangerous occupation in Britain, according to a list drawn up by life insurance underwriters."

"Is it?" Don looked across at Frank, but Frank was apparently studying his notebook. "I never knew."

"People don't," Cyril boomed. "Most people don't realise. Window cleaners, you see, are ahead even of other people who work aloft, because we have to juggle various implements at the top of a ladder. You see? Our sense of balance has to be perfect, otherwise . . ." His free hand mimed a fatal plummet.

"What about police officers?"

Cyril frowned. "Well, I suppose a sense of balance is also—"

"No, I meant, where do we come in the list?"

"Ah. Right. Yes." He looked at the press clipping for a while, reluctant, Don suspected, to reveal what it had to say on the subject. "Yes, indeed, police officers are in the top group.

As are firemen." He refolded the piece of paper and put it away again. "But window cleaners are *way* out in front."

"Congratulations," said Don.

"Circus performers," Cyril Mowbray scoffed, "are Second Division." He gave a superior smile and looked about him, as if searching for clowns to taunt.

"So what's the safest job?" Frank asked.

"Health and safety officers, and insurance brokers."

Both detectives laughed aloud at that. Cyril waited for them to stop, with a puzzled but patient expression on his face. This league table of doom was obviously important to him, Don understood; presumably because he had to convince himself that what he was doing now was a suitable occupation for one who had once worn his country's uniform. Well, why not go along with him.

"It must worry your wife more now you're a window cleaner," Don said, with a chummy smile, "than it did when you were a soldier."

Cyril, who had been squeezing his chamois into his bucket, froze. "What do you mean by that?"

"Well, you know, what with window cleaning being so dangerous." What Don wanted to say was *What the hell did you think I meant?* Whatever it was, you weren't happy about it, were you?

"Ah, right!" Cyril relaxed. "Yes, absolutely!"

"Does your wife work herself?" Don saw himself, sometimes, as being a bit like a dentist; where he sensed pain, he dug all the deeper.

"Not just now. She's in Chelmsford, looking after her sick mother."

"Oh, I'm sorry. Has she been there long?"

Cyril shrugged. "Little while. Not to worry, be home soon, got to be done."

They'd get nothing more there for the moment, Don was sure. Onwards and upwards. "So, with poor old Bert dead, how do you think LOFE will manage?"

"We'll press on. You're tasked with a mission, you just get on with it, don't you? Same in your business, I imagine."

"Oh, absolutely." He was going to have to have a word with Frank about that troublesome cough. Perhaps the boy needed an x-ray. "Of course, it must help to be under such good leadership."

Cyril looked blank.

"Stanley Baird, I'm talking about."

"Ha!" Cyril barked what Don took to be the officers' mess equivalent of a laugh. "Leadership isn't the first word that comes to mind."

"You don't get on with Stanley?" Don asked, innocently.

"Not a question of not getting on, Inspector. That doesn't arise. It just so happens that I consider Stanley Baird to be a hapless prat—but I assure you, I am far too experienced a man-manager to ever allow Stanley to know that I feel that way about him." Cyril smiled approvingly; at himself, as far as Don could tell. "For all he knows, I am his greatest admirer."

"That's a great people skill you have there, Cyril," said Don. "Not everyone can do it, you know. On the LOFE committee, for instance, is there anyone who is unable to hide his or her irritation with the secretary?"

"Don't know about that," said Cyril, though his thoughtful expression suggested that Don's flattery had made him inclined to help if he could. "However, the branch librarian—Dot—doesn't seem too fond of that peculiar councillor."

"James Pomeroy?"

"Can't say I'm too fond of him, myself." He sniffed.

"Calls himself a Conservative; not sure he owns a dictionary."

"What is it between James and Dot, do you know?"

"No idea. Personality clash, probably." He tapped his nose. "Just something I've picked up on."

"Those man-management skills, again, Cyril. The army's loss is . . ." Don was going to say *window cleaning's gain,* but even to someone as thick-skinned as Cyril that might come across as a piss-take. ". . . evidently considerable. Did anyone have a problem with Bert Rosen?"

Cyril gave a firm shake of the head. "No, he was easy to get on with."

"You liked him, did you?"

The question didn't seem to make any sense to Cyril. "Not especially, he was just easy to get on with."

"I understand. Did he seem worried by anything, lately?"

"Think he might have found the hero-worship of that child who claims to be the union steward a little embarrassing. Kimberley, they call her. Sort of thing you meant?"

"I was thinking more of whether he was preoccupied, not himself?"

"No, can't say I noticed." No, you wouldn't, thought Don. Cyril clapped his hands together, producing a report like a gun going off. "Right, if that's all, I'd better get back to it. Now, if one of you chaps could just put a foot on the bottom of my ladder while I do that bathroom window there . . ."

"We'd love to," said Don.

"Excellent! Give me a moment to—"

"But unfortunately we can't. We have places to be, I'm afraid."

As they walked back to the car, Don said: "Where's his van?"

Frank pointed towards an elderly bicycle, chained to some railings, to which was lashed a couple of ladder extensions and a spare bucket. "That's his company car there, I reckon."

"Good God. Quick, Frank, get on the phone to the UN—that thing needs reporting as a weapon of mass destruction."

Chapter Eight

"I bloody *love* these places," said Don, as they strode through the propped-open double doors of Bath Street Community Centre. He inhaled a rich lungful of that unique, jumble sale air; dusty but fresh, lively but musty, a nostalgic perfume made up of books and cakes, woollen jumpers and vinyl records. "There was a time, when I was a kid, me and my mum used to go to a jumble sale or a Women's Institute or a garden fete just about every weekend. You could get cakes at the WI that you never saw anywhere else. I suppose you're more of the car boot generation?"

"I suppose so," said Frank. "My gran was quite keen on jumble sales, though. She had a particular umbrella she kept for the purpose."

"Umbrella? No, Frank, if it's held outside it's a fete, not a jumble—"

"It had special spokes," Frank explained, "sticking out through the fabric. And a long, sharp handle."

"Oh, I see—she was a paramilitary Geordie jumble-granny. Now I'm with you." Don looked around, enjoying the sensation of quietly happy memories washing over him. Yes, they were all here: a bloke with a yard-long beard selling LPs; lots of middle-aged women with piles of second-hand clothes, carefully washed and sorted, soon to be reduced to a rubble of rags by heavy-handed browsers; a woman who looked so much like a vicar's wife that no casting director would dare put her in the role sat behind a table full of plants—small succulents, mostly, and potted-on cuttings of spider plant and geranium.

The main change since his childhood was the central heating, which had replaced the portable, smelly paraffin things which had so terrified him when he was a child; they'd always looked as if they might topple over at the slightest provocation—in which eventuality, he had often been warned by adults, they would explode and burn the street down. "Yes," he continued, "they could be pretty competitive events, the old jumble sales. For the buyers even more than the sellers. Of course, in those days possessions were not so easily come by, and getting hold of a bargain might be a matter of some importance. Nowadays, it just gives you a sense of satisfaction, and points on your scoreboard in our national sport. Shopping."

"Some of those car boots get pretty serious," Frank pointed out. "Great big sites, these days, thousands of visitors every week. Turnover to match."

"I don't like them." Don shook his head. "They're businesses, not community events. You don't get bent traders at jumble sales, pretending to be private individuals so as to get round the consumer protection laws."

"Fair point," Frank agreed. He nodded towards a stall at the back of the hall, near the fire escape. "There she is. Busman's holiday, by the look of it."

Don saw what he meant: Dolores "Dot" Estevez—her given name suiting her colouring, but the diminutive more appropriate to her thoroughly English manner—was doing brisk trade at a book stall. A banner nailed to the front of the table invited customers to *Buy A Book—Save A Library.*

"Do we know much about her?" Don asked.

Frank got his notebook out, and flicked to the relevant page. "Age forty-nine, married, two grown children and one grandchild. Popular, by all accounts, with staff and readers alike. Been branch librarian at Bath Street since it opened. She was a deputy elsewhere in the borough before that; seems she's been with Cowden ever since she left library school."

Don indicated a table on which stood three large urns and a stack of paper cups. "We'll take her a cuppa and a bit of cake," he said. "She strikes me as the sort who only remembers to eat when she starts fainting."

She was, as Don had expected and intended, extravagantly grateful for the snack. She squeezed Frank's arm so hard his cuff buttons nearly popped, while Don was treated to a long, moist-eyed look of gratitude.

"Frank was just saying, Dot—this is a bit of a busman's for you, isn't it? Dealing out books on your day off."

"I suppose it is, yes! At least there's no computer to crash here, though. Anyway, I meet several of our Bath Street readers here, which is always lovely."

Don began picking through the books, mostly paperbacks, on Dot's stall. "You're fundraising for LOFE, I presume?"

Dot indicated a clipboard on which was she was collecting signatures for an anti-closure petition. "It's as much a publicity exercise as a moneymaking one, really. Various community groups get together to hire this hall once a month—you can see, there's the Friends of the Hospital over there, and the Animal Rescue, and so on. We don't raise a fortune, but it all helps with the public profile."

"Can you still make finds at an event like this?" Don wondered. "We've become such a nation of collectors, I should think everybody knows what everything's worth these days."

"They do, but that doesn't mean they can actually be bothered to get it. A lot of people just want to recycle their clutter—and replace it with more, of course—and they don't really care about making the full price."

"I suppose the other side of that," Frank put in, "is the folk who've watched too many episodes of *Antiques Roadshow* and think everything old is worth a fortune."

Dot nodded energetically. "Oh yes—when in fact, almost everything is worth nothing."

"Your husband must get fed up with being abandoned," Don said, with a smile. "You're at the library all week, and in here at the weekend."

She re-tidied the books Don had been idly inspecting. "Oh, he's all right. My sister's keeping him company."

She didn't look at Don as she spoke, and he worried that he'd inadvertently offended her. Surely she wouldn't turn on her cake-donating hero so quickly? He hurriedly moved on, just in case. "Talking to LOFE people, Dot, we've picked up a feeling that Cyril and Stanley might not be the closest of pals . . . ?"

She sighed, and pushed a proportion of her hair in the opposite direction to that which it seemed naturally inclined towards. "Oh, dear, yes. They don't get on awfully well, I'm afraid."

"Any idea why?"

"Well, you know, all it is, I think—basically, Cyril believes that his military organisational skills should mean that *he's* our secretary/treasurer, rather than Stanley." She took a bite—more a large nibble, Don thought, if such a thing existed—of her cake, swallowed it, apparently whole, and continued. "To be perfectly honest, Stanley *isn't* as brilliant at money and admin and so on as he thinks he is. Cyril probably *would* be better."

"Is that a general view on the committee?"

"I think everyone's *aware* of the situation, but having said that, there's not much to the job, when you come down to it. There's only a few pounds in LOFE's account, for buying stamps and printer cartridges, and what-have-you. And as for the secretary part, that mainly consists of making sure everyone knows when the meetings are, and keeping the minutes." She smiled, and took a swig of tea. "And it obviously means so much to Stanley, so I really can't see it's doing any harm."

"You're one of those people who gets on with everyone, Dot," said Don, smiling to ensure she knew that his accusatory inflection was a joke.

"Oh, well, I don't know!"

"Isn't there anyone on the committee who irritates you a bit? You can tell us in strictest confidence, you know."

"No, they're all lovely, really. And it's so *good* of them all to give up their time."

Her natural style was so frantic—not flustered, Don cautioned himself, because he suspected she was a perfectly well-organised woman—that he found it difficult to read what, if anything, was hidden behind her words and movements. It was a frustrating and unfamiliar sensation for him. "They're quite a diverse bunch, aren't they—I mean you've even got a Tory councillor on there!"

"Yes, isn't that marvellous? All Bert's doing, needless to say. He was a great believer in what he called the Popular Front. Tactical alliances." She wrinkled her nose. "Or is it strategic? I can never remember the difference."

No, thought Don; if she's got any problems with James Pomeroy, we're not going to hear about it from her. He gave Frank the nod, and the DC asked the question with which by now they were both bored stiff. No, Dot confirmed, she hadn't noticed any change in Bert's manner in the days or weeks before his death.

They were about to leave her to her books, when Don thought to ask her something that had occurred to him the other night, back at the library. "How does the council feel about a branch librarian supporting a campaign against its declared policy?"

She shrugged. "They're not keen, I'm sure, but they can hardly be surprised. What librarian would want her own branch closed down?"

"If the closure does go ahead, would you get another branch?"

Don thought perhaps he could read her face this time: deep sadness. "No, very unlikely."

"I expect they'd stick you in an office somewhere, wouldn't they? Doing paperwork. If your organisation's anything like ours, they wouldn't want someone who'd been a manager working at a lower rank elsewhere in the system."

"It's very similar with us, yes," said Dot.

Don and Frank got themselves some tea and biscuits, and consumed them in the car. "She'd hate that," Don said. "Working behind the scenes. Same pay grade, but lower status—and more importantly, away from the public, which is obviously what she loves."

"You're right," Frank agreed. "She's in her element out front, isn't she?"

"The trouble with this bloody case, Frank, is that most of our suspects seem to have solid gold motives for *not* killing Bert Rosen."

Frank's mobile phone rang.

"She's got news for us," Frank repeated. "The office didn't say what news."

"Well, why not?"

"Because she didn't tell them, I suppose." Frank manoeuvred his car into a space a few yards from Rosa Ledbury's front door. "Perhaps she's one of those strange people who don't entirely trust the police."

"Yes, possibly," Don conceded. "She certainly seemed a very intelligent woman."

The house in which Bert Rosen had written the last chapter of his life was solid, comfortable, and unremarkable. A three-bedroomed end-terrace, with a small back garden and a tiny front garden, it was, Frank, thought, exactly where you would expect to find an elderly widower living with his divorced daughter. He wondered whether he'd be introduced to Mark's famous tortoise.

If Rosa did entertain an antipathy towards the constabulary, it wasn't evident in her attitude towards Don or Frank. She was visibly upset when Frank declined a cup of tea—"I've only just put one out, thanks," he explained—and became quite distressed as he further refused, in turn, each alternative she offered him. It was a relief to all present, Frank felt, when the DI announced that he would happily sell his legs to science in exchange for a very small cup of very strong coffee. Rosa beamed as she served it; Don smiled gratefully as he sniffed it; she didn't notice that he scarcely touched it after that, but Frank did—noticed, and noted.

"I've been sorting out Pops' affairs," she began, and then laughed. Her eyes were red, Frank saw, but her hands were steady. Don had taught him to look at the eyes and the hands, and when Frank had asked why, had replied *You've got to look at something.* "His affairs—that sounds a bit grand, doesn't it? What I mean is, I've been having a look at his bank accounts. He left bequests to good causes, you see, and they're the sort of organisations that could do with the money today rather than tomorrow, so I thought: get on with it."

"On a Sunday?"

"Online banking, Inspector!"

"Oh right," said Don, picking up his coffee cup, turning it round, and putting it down again. "Of course. And you discovered something interesting? *Oof!*"

"Get down, Hammer—leave the inspector alone." A tabby cat the size of a sofa did what cats generally do on receipt of lawful orders from their superiors. It stuck its nose up its bum and went to sleep. "Sorry about that," said Rosa, as Don recovered his breath. "They're bloody anarchists. Just shove him off."

"No, he's all right, I like cats. Where's his mate, Sickle?"

"Are you telepathic, Don?" Rosa looked impressed; so was Frank, after a moment's puzzlement. Of course, the clue had been there, but even so; he was sharp today, the DI, no doubt about it.

"You were telling us about Bert's bank account . . . ?" Frank prompted; he knew how long conversations about cats could continue, if left to grow unchecked.

"Yes, yes I was." She paused to gather her thoughts, reminding Frank strongly of a teacher he'd had in primary school. It was a pleasant memory; he'd enjoyed primary school. "I don't know if it's anything significant, of course, but it is a mystery so, given the circumstances, I thought I'd better report it."

"Absolutely."

"Well, there's three thousand pounds missing from Pops' building society account."

"When you say 'missing' . . ."

"Yes, I should make that clear. It's not *missing*—I'm not suggesting anyone's stolen it. What I mean is that Pops has evidently withdrawn three thousand pounds from his savings, and I have absolutely no idea why."

"And that's unusual? You'd normally know?"

"That amount, yes, simply because it would have to be for a purpose, wouldn't it? It's not pocket money, it's not a simple purchase—some clothes, or a new TV, or even a holiday. If you take out three thousand pounds, you're going to do something particular with it, and I just don't know and can't imagine what that was. I've searched this place, and I'm sure the money's not in the house."

"Was it a single withdrawal?" Don asked.

She shook her head. "Two withdrawals, both in the last week. Here, I've written down the details for you."

As Frank copied them into his notebook, and went over them with Rosa more than once (a piece of standard police procedure which annoyed the ex-teacher rather less than it did most people), Don took his cup through to the kitchen, emptied it silently into the sink and rinsed away the evidence of his lack of thirst.

When he and Frank left the house, he was grinning. "That's more like it—a money motive. Now we're getting somewhere! Some filthy capitalist killed the poor old sod for straightforward gain."

"Why did he take out money secretly?" Frank wondered.

"Was it secret? Maybe he just hadn't got round to telling Rosa yet. But if it was a secret, then so much the better from our point of view."

"More motives to choose from."

"Exactly. Perhaps he was having a secret affair."

"Or he was being blackmailed," Frank offered.

"Or seeing a prostitute, after years of widowhood." Don clearly wasn't going to let go of the sexual angle without a fight. "Or seeing a prostitute and being blackmailed about it."

"Expensive prostitute," Frank objected. "Three grand in a week?"

"Nothing's too good for the workers," said Don. "All right then, maybe he had a coke habit."

"Which the prostitute was blackmailing him about?"

"Cheeky bugger," Don laughed. "He could simply have made a donation to a good cause, but one that his daughter wouldn't have agreed with."

"Or wouldn't agree with the amount," Frank said.

"Good point. And another good point is that assuming someone has had the money off him, for whatever unknown reason—because, after all, he could have put it on a horse or a greyhound, Marshall Zhukov running in the six forty-five at White City—then it looks like they're keeping quiet about it now."

"No proof, no pay-back," Frank agreed. "Whether or not the person who got the money is the same person as the killer."

"But before we follow the money," said Don, "I want to tie up a loose end."

"Which one?"

"Dot and James. If there's something between them, I want to know what it is."

Chapter Nine

"I've never been to a Conservative Party cheese and wine do before," Don told him, and Frank had to bite down hard to avoid giving utterance to sarcasms such as *You don't say!* or *Who'd have believed it!* or even *No!*

Out loud, he settled for "Me neither."

"Well, no," said Don, "but you're a Geordie. Where I come from, Conservatives exist."

Their previous inexperience of the milieu notwithstanding, it was at the Cowden South Conservative Association's Autumn Get-Together that the two detectives now found themselves; summoned there by the magic of the mobile phone. "Can't get out of it," Councillor James Pomeroy had told them. "It is one of the highlights of the social calendar for that shrinking band of diehards, misanthropes, and dodderers in this forgotten borough who still admit to the vice which dare not speak its name, to wit: Conservatism."

"Very Oscar-bleeding-Wilde," Don had said, when Frank, straight-faced even by his standards, had relayed the councillor's words to him, verbatim.

Frank had wondered at the look of revulsion on Don's face and had risked a quick probe. "I expect you agree with him about the Tory Party, but?"

"Not the point, is it? They're the poor sods who turn out for him at election time. If he finds them so laughable, he shouldn't burden himself with their company."

So that was it, Frank had realised; Don had detected the stench of hypocrisy, that crime which always had him reaching for his truncheon and strapping on his biggest boots.

Pomeroy had further warned them that "This afternoon is our equivalent of Halloween—if you dare to come, you will find the dead walking abroad," and they saw what he meant as soon as they entered the large, and far from full, private home in which the event was taking place. On first glance, there didn't appear to be one person in the room who was under the age of seventy. In fact, Frank thought, if you were under seventy in this company, you'd better not give anyone any lip or you'd be in danger of being sent to your room without supper.

"Hello!" Their hostess, the second rasping syllable of her greeting stretching out from her mouth like a teenager's chewing gum, wore just about the most startling makeup Frank had ever seen. It was at least thirty years too young for her face, he reckoned, but then, to be fair, so was her hair. The vibrancy, and sheer number, of the colours involved, and the industrial manner in which they had been applied—apparently from a distance of several feet—left even Detective Inspector Don Packham temporarily unable to speak. Or, in fact, close his mouth.

"Are you new members?" she asked, her eagerness putting Frank in mind of a horror film he'd recently seen, in which the Queen of the Night had exhibited similar lust in her search for new blood. The film had bored him—the only reason he didn't switch it off was because Debbie had gone to sleep on his shoulder, with the remote control clutched in her hand—but here in the flesh, on a suburban Sunday afternoon, he felt less inclined to mock the dark power of the unknown.

"We're here to see Councillor Pomeroy," Don eventually stammered.

The woman leant towards them, enveloping them in the airlock of her Duty Free scent. "Of course—isn't he marvellous? He's just what the Party needs. Young people will really warm to him, I'm quite sure." She dropped her voice. "Are you . . . *friends* of his?"

The sight of an elderly Tory stalwart attempting to pass herself off as an each-to-his-own, liberal modernist was apparently enough to snap Don out of his trance. "We have no friends, I'm afraid. Not that we're Conservatives, as such, it's just that we're police officers. We need to ask the councillor some questions."

"Police officers." She stepped back, and the welcome died in her eyes. This was something Frank had often heard Don talk about: the way in which hatred of coppers, for a century or more the exclusive province of the working classes and the Left, had become, in the last decade or so, almost universal amongst the rich and the Right. The DI had several theories to explain it, only some of which contradicted each other, but to Frank it was simply a nuisance—one more irritating barrier between him and getting the job done and going home.

And then, of course, there was the lecture. Don and Frank exchanged resigned looks; they knew only too well what the antipathy in the Queen of the Night's expression promised. They were right.

"Do you know how many times I've been burgled in the last five years? No, you don't know, because none of you people have ever bothered to actually investigate any of them! You just send me a crime number through the post, for my insurance, you don't actually come round to look for clues, do you? No, you're too busy being politically correct. Learning to speak Hindu and how to shake hands in Japanese and giving guided tours of the police station to one-parent families and—"

"And hobnobbing with homos," Don prompted her.

She ignored him. "If you people spent a little less time giving lollipops to thugs, and a little more time—"

"Very interesting subject, street crime," said Don, taking a glass of white wine from an adjacent coffee table, along with a selection of cheese cubes threaded on a cocktail stick with squares of tinned pineapple. "Now, my own theory is this. Why is the so-called yob culture on the increase, if indeed it is?"

"It *is!*" she cried, clearly affronted that such a central tenet of her faith could be openly questioned in her own home—and by a man who was simultaneously scoffing her pineapple chunks, too.

"Read up on market towns in the pre-1914 era, and you might change your mind," said Don, draining his glass. "But put that to one side. If it is, I think I can tell you why. Lager."

Their hostess nodded. At last, they were in agreement on something. "Lager louts. Drunken yobs with too much money in their pockets."

"Drunken isn't the point." Don shook his head, and held up a hand to silence her. "What are they drunk on, that's the point. Millions of people in this country, during the 1980s—you're not choking on a piece of Gorgonzola, are you, Constable?"

"Not at all, sir." Frank did his best to hide his smile. He didn't consider himself a political man, but even he knew what "during the 1980s" meant: code for "It's Thatcher's fault."

"Millions of people," Don continued, "especially young people, turned from drinking proper, grown-up bitter beer to the more childish, continental, and American-style lager. Now, as any passing brewmaster will tell you, lager is much less heavily hopped than bitter, and therefore less soporific."

He paused to allow the old Tory to speak at this point, but only, Frank was sure, because he knew she was too stunned to do so.

"Therefore," Don went on, "the lager drinker, when drunk, becomes lively—and thus potentially troublesome—whereas the bitter drinker, when drunk, nods off quietly in a corner. Let that be a lesson to you, Constable."

"Sir?"

"Never drink anything that's yellow."

"Sir."

Don returned his attention, with a sad smile, to the silent woman. "It's all a symptom of the infantilisation of modern society, you see. Bitter is a man's drink, lager a teen's. But these days, everyone wants to be a teenager forever." He nodded, and put his empty glass and cocktail stick neatly back on the table. "And that's why you never see women smoking pipes any more."

The woman with the sprayed-on face blinked, swallowed a few times, and then moistened her lips with her tongue (painting much of her chin vermilion in the process). "I see. Well, that's very interesting. More cheese?"

"No thank you, we're on assignment. So you see, madam, the duty befalling a patriotic person such as yourself is clear. You must surrender all your shares in lager companies, and send a sizeable donation to the Campaign for Real Ale on the first of every month. Now, would you please tell Councillor

Pomeroy that we're here to see him?"

"I must confess, I didn't dare hope to see you boys again so soon." In an unused study, on the third floor, James Pomeroy was as charming as ever. Even Frank, who really had very little use for charm, preferring straightforwardness, had to admit to himself that it was quite a potent disarmer; much subtler than CS gas.

"Sorry to disrupt your party," Don apologised. "It's just a quick one, for elimination purposes. People say there was some stiffness in the air lately between you and Dot Estevez?"

"Do they? Well, I won't waste time asking who." Seeming entirely relaxed, Pomeroy lit a long cigarette and smoked for a moment, a picture of contemplation. "For my part, I certainly have no problem with Dot. A splendid woman."

"But might she have any reason to feel differently towards you, whether or not you've noticed it?"

"Well . . . I've no way of knowing for sure, but there is one thing. This is in strictest confidence, you understand?"

"And you understand," Don replied, "that police officers cannot give any such guarantee."

Pomeroy made a great show of reluctance, and Frank suspected that, perhaps, that was exactly what it was—a show. "I understand that the council has made an offer to Dot."

"An offer?"

"Yes." Pomeroy smiled. "An offer of voluntary redundancy and early retirement. Once Bath Street has closed, that is. Now, if she knew that I knew . . . you see what I mean? It might possibly lead to a certain coolness on her part, quite understandably."

"But she wouldn't accept such an offer, surely?" Don sounded quite outraged at the suggestion. "That library is her life."

"What do we know of other people's lives, Inspector? Always less than we think, I would imagine."

"What sort of redundancy package would she get?" Frank asked. "I mean generally—as a councillor, you must have a rough idea."

Pomeroy nodded, apparently in approval at this more practical line of questioning. "Pretty good. She's been with the council forever."

"So if she does know that you know about the offer, she'll be worried that you're going to mention it to people. LOFE people."

"It's certainly possible."

"And have you told anyone?" Don asked.

"I have not. Why on earth would I? I oppose the closure, remember. I've no wish to stir things up."

"Do you know whether or not she intends to accept the offer?"

Pomeroy spread his hands. "No, no idea; since I came out in support of LOFE, as you would imagine, my sources of information within the council have somewhat dried up."

Frank and Don sat in Frank's car, and wondered. They wondered, first of all, whether what Pomeroy had told them was even true.

"Must be," Frank said. "It'd be too easily disproved."

"But is it true that he hasn't told Dot he knows about it—and that he hasn't told anyone else? Obviously the council wouldn't be allowed to make public such private matters, but they'd be glad if it did get out, perhaps even to the extent of deliberately leaking it."

"Divide and rule, you mean."

Don nodded. "Bloody right. So: does this give Dot Estevez a motive for killing Bert? It's a bit of a reach, but say

Bert found out she was planning to stab them in the back: could she kill him to prevent him denouncing her?"

Frank had another idea. "Perhaps he could even have prevented her getting the deal, somehow. I don't know how, exactly, but with his decades of contacts and political know-how, maybe he could have the offer withdrawn."

"Christ, Frank, that's a nasty thought—well done. After all, the council don't care whether she gets the dough or not, only that offering it to her screws up LOFE's unity. Because what is unity, Frank?"

"Unity is strength, so they say. But as a murder motive, it depends on rather a lot of things, doesn't it? Not least, would she take the offer?"

"Seems hard to imagine, I'll say that."

"And would she campaign against the library closure, knowing all the time that she was going to benefit from it?"

"Well, maybe. She could tell her conscience that she did everything she could to stop the closure, fought it right to the end, but once the cause is lost—then there's no shame in benefiting." He clicked his fingers. "Have you got a birth date for her?"

Frank found the information in his notebook. "She turns fifty next month, November eleventh."

"Well, there you go." Don looked sad. "Fifty is the minimum age for local government early retirement deals."

"No, I want more ammunition before we tackle the librarian," said Don, firmly, causing the heads of two lorry drivers at an adjacent cafe table to swivel in his direction. He gave them his best hired-killer look, and they went back to their eggs, bacon, and curried beans.

"Approach the council direct?" Frank asked. "I'm not sure how far we'll get on a Sunday."

"Sod that. Even on a weekday, I imagine we'd need paperwork to get anything out of the council. And fair enough, too—it is a confidential matter, after all."

Frank drained his tea. "So who do we talk to?"

"One of the LOFErs," said Don. "But which one is most likely to have heard any rumours?"

Frank thought about it for a moment, and then replied: "Bert, I'd imagine. I can't see any of the others having an intelligence network to rival his."

"Yeah," Don grunted. Then he snapped his fingers. "Ah! I'll tell you who is plugged into a mains system of gossip, regularly meeting people from other departments, legitimately taking an interest in colleagues' working lives . . ."

Frank smiled. "The shop steward."

Kimberley Riggs was, Frank's mobile soon told him, spending that Sunday afternoon at the James Connolly Bar; not a pub, as it turned out, but the social club owned by the Cowden branch of the local government employees' union—a branch which, for both political and ethnic reasons, had a long and sometimes controversial association with the republican movement in Ireland.

"I suppose it makes a change from Nelson Mandela," Don noted, as they passed the bust of Connolly in the entrance hall.

Kimberley was not, they soon discovered, occupied in drowning her sorrows with subsidised beer. She was not in the bar area at all, but in a small committee room next to the lavatories. She excused herself from her comrades and greeted Don and Frank in the corridor.

"Got time for a quick drink, Kimberley?" Don asked her.

"Sure." She led them through to the bar, which was almost deserted.

Don announced that he was in the chair. "A tonic water

for my colleague, please," he told the yawning barman. "A pint of IPA for me, and for Comrade Riggs . . . ?"

"Half of lager, please."

Don used bonhomie to disguise his disappointment at her choice. "You're not going to have a pint?"

"I'll have half, thanks."

Don shook his head, sadly. "Fear of commitment," he told Frank.

She laughed and shook her head. Don looked at the ceiling.

"So what is it you're up to this afternoon," he asked her, once they were settled with their drinks. "Or are you not allowed to tell me?"

"Quite the contrary," she said, smiling. "One of my duties is to inform the police what we're doing—not you lot, though, your uniformed colleagues."

"Some sort of march, is it?" said Frank.

"Almost. We're doing a twenty-four-hour picket of the town hall. There'll be singing and drumming and fancy dress and all sorts."

"When is this?"

"Tomorrow. It'll last from ten-to-ten to ten-to-ten."

Don grinned. He liked this girl. Apart from the obvious, even, he really did like this one. A girl as cheeky as this, it was a privilege to feed her the lines. "Ten-to-ten to ten-to-ten?" he said, frowning. "But that's only twelve hours."

She could hardly get it out for smiling, but somehow she kept her face together long enough to reply: "No, you misunderstand, Inspector: the picket runs from ten-to-ten to ten-to-ten to ten-to-ten. That's twenty-four hours."

Don worked it out on his fingers. "Of course it is, I see that now. Is this a LOFE event? I can just picture Stanley Baird beating an African drum in time to Doug Ticehurst's toi-toi."

She laughed. "No, it's a union thing, not LOFE. Though I'm sure," she added, with self-conscious loyalty, "that some of the LOFE supporters will turn up, too. Anyway, we're just putting the finishing touches to the posters and that this afternoon." Her face turned sombre in an instant, as she said: "Helps keep my mind off Bert, anyway."

"Of course." Don took advantage of the tactful pause which followed to rethink his strategy. If they were simply to ask Kimberley whether she knew about Dot's redundancy offer, he didn't think they'd get very far. It was obvious to him, now, that her priority would always be the interests of her colleagues, as she understood them, rather than the needs of a police investigation. "Will Dot be at the demo?" he asked her.

She nodded, half her face hidden by her lager glass. "Mm, hope so."

"As shop steward, it must make your job a lot easier—having your line manager so pro the campaign."

"Yes, it certainly helps."

Don sipped his pint. "Can't be an easy situation for her, I suppose. I don't imagine management are very pleased with her."

"No, I'm sure you're right."

"No doubt LOFE and the union will be triumphant in the end—but just supposing you're not, and the worst comes to the worst: what do you think will become of Dot? Seems to me she'd be bereft without Bath Street."

Kimberley gave a tight smile. "We'll just have to make sure we win, then."

So much for the subtle approach, thought Don. "And Bert's death must've made things even harder for her. They were quite close, weren't they?"

"We were all close to Bert," said Kimberley, her voice a

little louder than before. "That's the sort of person he was. You just . . . everyone loved Bert."

You certainly did, poor kid, Don thought. Time to change tack; explore another anomaly which was tickling the back of his mind. "Were you expecting James Pomeroy to join in the occupation of the library the other night? It seems an odd thing for a Tory councillor to do."

"To put it mildly! No, I was very surprised. I assume Bert must've talked him into it."

Of course, Don thought, if Pomeroy was planning to kill Bert, then his staying behind after the doors were locked at the library made perfect sense. Still—it would be a bloody odd setting for a premeditated murder, wouldn't it?

Chapter Ten

"I'm sorry," said Marjorie McDonald—and she looked it, too, Frank thought; sorry, but firm in her resolution. "I know what you're saying, it's a murder investigation, I understand all that. But you've got to understand what I'm saying, too." She stepped out of her porch, clunking her front door shut behind, and squeezing past the two detectives, so that they no longer stood between her and her car. "If I don't work, my kids don't eat. Simple as that."

"We only need a couple of—" Frank began, but Don interrupted him.

"Don't worry, Marjorie—we'll do your deliveries."

"What?" said Marjorie.

What? Frank screamed, silently.

"No problem," Don explained. "You can sit in the jam sandwich seat, I'll sit in the back amidst the parcels, the constable here can drive, and in between deliveries you and I can have a chat. All right?"

"Well, I—"

"Don't worry, he's a very good driver, he won't do any damage." Don let himself into the back of Marjorie's car, giving the others little option but to take their own allocated seats. "He drives like an elderly nun, to be honest with you.

About as much use in a car chase as my great-granny, and the only car she ever got into in her life was the hearse that buried her."

And so the interview got under way, punctuated frequently by brief stops in the gathering gloom, as either Marjorie or the DI, depending on which side of the road Frank was able to park on, jumped out to convey mail order goods to happy householders in exchange for their electronically recorded signatures.

Don particularly enjoyed playing with the digital clipboard. "This is a great gizmo, Frank, we must get these for CID. Hell of a lot easier to fake confessions on one of these, don't you reckon?"

And slowly, as Frank had seen happen so often before when Don was in a cheerful mood, an initially suspicious witness-cum-suspect began to relax.

"I'm going to ask you a straight question," Don told her, as Frank drove from a consignment of cosmetics at Old Park Avenue to a discreetly wrapped sex toy marked Urgent on Uplands Way. "You don't have to answer it, of course. I, for instance, have never answered a straight question from a police officer in my born days, and never intend doing so in the future."

She shook her head and laughed. "Don Packham, what did you do before you joined the police?"

"It was awful," he said. "I had to drink on my own time. However, if you were to answer my question, it might bring us a millimetre closer to finding out who killed Bert."

"Go on, then. Unlike you, I was brought up to respect the police."

Don squeezed the sex toy, and was visibly disappointed when it didn't squeak. "We've been told that there was a coolness in recent LOFE meetings, between Dot and James, or perhaps between Dot and Bert, or possibly both."

"A coolness?"

"That's how it's been described to us, yes. And we were just wondering—"

"You're asking me about Dot's redundancy offer, aren't you?"

"Yes." Don caught Frank's eye in the rear-view mirror, but Frank was already slowing down slightly, making sure they didn't reach their next destination too soon. "Yes, we are. When did you first hear about it?"

She chewed at the corner of her left little finger. "I'm not sure—a couple of weeks ago, I suppose. I can't even remember quite who it was who told me. It was just sort of . . ."

"Just sort of in the air?" Don suggested.

"Yes. Yes, that's exactly how it was. Floating around like a sneeze." She put a hand on Frank's shoulder. "Over here on the left, love, with the big tree."

"So anyone involved in the campaign might have known?"

"Anyone, I suppose. I certainly didn't tell anyone," Marjorie replied, opening the car door. The sex toy delivery was on her side of the road.

"If they come to the door naked, just scream and I'll come running," Don told her as she got out. "Unless you've got your own digital camera, have you?"

The sound of her chuckle was guillotined by the closing of the door. Frank was about to make the obvious remark—that the council might well have leaked news of Dot's deal specifically to Marjorie, hoping to exploit her bitterness towards LOFE—but Don was off down a different burrow.

"Can't be much of a living, this, can it?"

"I was thinking the same myself," said Frank. "You'd have to get through a few deliveries to make it worthwhile, I'd have thought."

"Everything's so bloody cheap these days, that's the trouble. I went to buy a new kettle the other day, you know how much?"

"Cheap, was it?" said Frank, who couldn't quite see what his colleague was complaining about, but assumed he would shortly find out.

"Seven pounds ninety-nine. For a kettle! It would have cost twice that five years ago."

"Shocking," said Frank.

"People think it's a good thing, prices going down every bloody week, but it's not—it's short-termism and it's going to destroy the economy."

"Cheap kettles?"

"What it must lead to, inevitably, is low wages, lack of innovation, lack of investment, all resulting eventually—and before too long, too—in capital flight, declining tax revenues, and a collapse of demand. I'll tell you, Frank, we're heading for the biggest recession since the 1930s. Just be grateful you're a copper, they'll carry on paying us long after the nurses have been laid off. And keep your riot gear polished and pressed."

"Right," said Frank, after a pause to make sure that it was his turn to speak. "So you didn't buy it, then? The kettle."

"Nah," said Don. "I bought two of the bastards."

"Two?"

"Well, at that price it's bound to pack up, isn't it?"

When Marjorie got back in, she had obviously been thinking. "You reckon Bert found out about Dot's offer from the council, and had a go at her about it, and that gives her a reason to kill him. Right?"

"We're not looking at her any harder than we're looking at anyone else, Marjorie—yourself included—but yes, it does seem like a theoretically feasible motive."

"Theoretically, but not really. Not to anyone who knew Bert. Or knows Dot, come to that."

"You know them both pretty well?"

"I'd known Bert since I moved to the area, years ago. And of course I've known Dot ever since the start of Bath Street Library Campaign Group."

"Buzzleycog," said Don. "Or Buslickidge, possibly. And knowing them both as you do, you don't think our motive works?"

"No, no. No chance. First of all, Bert wouldn't have reacted the way you think he would. He wouldn't have hated Dot, or despised her, or denounced her—that wasn't his way."

"It would have been a terrible disappointment to him, surely?"

"*Listen* to me, Inspector. Bert would have tried to help. He'd have given her money himself, if he could."

"Given her money?" said Frank.

"If Dot had to take voluntary redundancy—this is what I mean about knowing *her*—she'd only have done it if she was desperate. Bert would have known it was painful for her and would have supported her. He had his political principles, that's true, but he served in the war, you know? On the convoys."

"In the Atlantic," said Don.

"And I think that had a huge effect on him. The things he saw then, as a young man, the terrible suffering and tragedy. My brother met him a few times, through his work, and he said something that really stuck in my mind—he said Bert suffered from chronic empathy. It was one of his better qualities."

Frank wondered what his worse qualities were; she still seemed to speak of him with respect rather than affection.

"He was like that," Marjorie said again. "I don't mean he was a mug—he was generous to a fault, but he was nobody's fool. But for instance, he took that sad sack Doug Ticehurst under his wing, the one who's so unlucky in love. You know who I mean—the one who looks like he was the result of a phantom pregnancy?"

"I know who you mean," Don laughed. "Well then, Marjorie. Better see to the rest of your round, hadn't we?"

Things changed—fashions, laws, social habits, working patterns—but this remained the same, Don thought: Sunday evening was never a cheerful time in a pub. Never had been in history, never would be through eternity. Even for people who didn't end their working week on Friday and begin it on Monday, there was something about Sundays that called miserably to a race memory of salary slavery in everyone, be they shift worker, self-employed, unemployed, or idle millionaire. And not forgetting bar staff.

It was even worse at this early hour; later on, at least a few pints would have taken the edge off people's awareness of the Monday morning juggernaut hurtling towards them. He and Frank took their drinks to a table as far from the bar as possible, their privacy guaranteed, in any case, by a combination of piped music, played just too quietly to be heard and just too loudly to be ignored, and by the noise of imaginary jackpots clattering out of the unoccupied fruit machine as it cycled through its repertoire of enticement.

"We haven't got much," Don said, "but we've got two things which are well worth having."

"The gun," Frank agreed, "and the money."

"Just so." Don lit a small cigar. "And are the two related?"

"They have to be, don't they? Well, okay—they don't *have*

to be, but the chances are that if we find the money we find the killer, surely?"

"Seems probable," said Don. "Bert was the kind of man—this is what we're hearing—who would help people out quite readily. You didn't have to be especially close to him; if he could help you, he would."

"So someone's borrowed the money from him, to get out of a bit of bother or whatever reason, and is then unable to pay it back."

"Or unwilling. Or never had any intention of paying it back."

"So they've killed the old guy instead."

"I wonder if that approach would work with my Visa card? Definitely worth a try."

"And Bert's carrying the gun because he's somehow realised what is in this person's mind," said Frank, sounding a little less sure of this part of the story.

"Maybe Bert's asked for the money back and the borrower has made feeble excuses—"

"Or no excuses at all, just told him to sod off."

"Right, so Bert feels under threat and gets tooled up. Though *how* is still a puzzle," Don admitted. "He was streetwise, all right, but more in ways of getting the vote out than in matters concerning the procurement of untraceable firearms."

Frank sipped his tonic water. "We'll probably never know that bit, will we? The fact is he did have a gun, so he was planning to defend himself against someone."

"All right, then—who needed a loan from Bert? Could he have given the money to Dot, so that she wouldn't take the redundancy offer?"

Frank shook his head, slowly. "No, it's not enough money, surely? That deal's going to be worth hundreds of thousands to her over the years, with a lump sum and early pension. Three grand isn't going to impress her much."

"Agreed. Who else, then? I was thinking it might be worth talking again to Doug Ticehurst. Sounds like he's been experiencing marital imperfections, and they're always expensive. I wonder what he does on a Sunday night."

Frank drained his glass, which didn't take long, and took out his mobile. "Soon find out," he said.

Nothing much, was the dispiriting, though far from surprising, answer. Mr. Ticehurst was at home, and able to receive guests. He wasn't actually able to seat them, however, there being only two possible perches in his single room abode; or three, to be strictly fair, Frank thought, if one person took the sole chair, and two others sat shoulder to shoulder on the undersized bed. Of course, any number was free to arrange themselves upon the floor. Well, not *any* number—there was room on the brown, balding rug for maybe half a dozen sets of buttocks, provided their owners were all close acquaintances. Provided "They'd all dipped a spoon in the same pot of curry," as Frank's grandad used to put it, when discussing the involuntary intimacy of his own crowded childhood.

The place was as gloomy, in short, as Sunday night itself. Not the Sunday nights of his and Debbie's family life, of course; more the remembered Sundays of childhood, going earlier to bed than on Fridays or Saturdays, with the tedious prospect of school awaiting him on waking, and with end-of-the-weekend adult gloom almost tangible in the air.

Frank himself had never lived in a bedsit—many of his school friends had, at one time or another, but his life had, by chance, worked out according to an older pattern. He knew one thing, however: if he had ever resided in such a place, he'd have been out every night. The pub, friends' flats, evening classes, walking the streets . . . the only thing that could have kept him stuck in here for longer than it took to shower and put on a clean shirt would have been a serious lack of money.

"Not out on the town tonight, Doug?" Don had obviously been thinking along similar lines—even though, in his case, he had inhabited more bedsits and studio flats in his time than a bar full of students put together.

"Fancied a night in. Sunday, you know." Ticehurst was less obviously nervous here than he had been when confronted on his recycling rounds, Frank noted, but not by a lot. Dull as his evening might otherwise have been, he clearly didn't rejoice at their visit.

"Can I ask you something, Doug?" said Don.

"Well, yes—I mean, that's why you've come, isn't it?"

"Good point, of course it is. What I'd like to know is, did Bert Rosen ever lend you any money?"

"Money?" The question set off a short but intense display of spasmodic movements, face-pulling, and limb-twitches. "I don't know what you mean."

Don chuckled. "Know how you feel, mate—I never seem to see any of the stuff, either. But allegedly, it's this papery substance which can be exchanged for beer at registered outlets."

"No." Ticehurst's nervous activity had dwindled to a single tapping foot. "I never had any money from Bert. Why on earth would I?"

Don didn't reply *Because you're recently divorced and living in a dump,* and Frank admired his restraint. "Well, you were a very good friend to him, weren't you? That's what people say."

Ticehurst looked embarrassed; touched, thought Frank, and regretful. Like a grieving friend, in fact, or like a murderer. Or both. "Other way round, really. I don't think I was able to do much for him, but he was very kind to me."

"In what way?" Don asked, sitting quietly on the bed.

"Nothing to do with money!" Ticehurst flushed—with anger this time, Frank was sure, not bashfulness.

"No, no," said Don, "of course not. That was just a routine thing we needed to clear up. Forget I mentioned that. I knew old Bert a bit, you know?"

"I didn't know."

"Oh, yes. For all his fierce politics, he could be quite a fatherly old chap, couldn't he? In his own way."

That brought the first smile of the evening. "Yes. Yes, he was. He was a good listener, wasn't he?"

"Bert? Never been a better," Don confirmed. "He always had time to listen, and as often as not he could offer a little bit of advice, maybe a fresh way of looking at a problem. Don't you reckon?"

"You're absolutely right, Inspector. Yes. That was Bert all over. I could talk to him in a way that I could never talk to any of my . . . he could get on with anyone."

"He got on with everyone in LOFE?"

"Oh, yes, I'm sure he did. Getting on with people, it was almost a religion to him. You know he used to sell insurance? He must've been brilliant at it. He was the oldest person on the committee by far, but differences of age or class or outlook—none of it mattered to him. That young girl from the library, for instance."

"Kimberley?"

Ticehurst nodded. "You'd have thought they were the same generation, the way they chatted together, and laughed. I think she was half in love with him."

Was she indeed, thought Frank. And as he glanced across at Don, he could see the DI was thinking much the same.

Chapter Eleven

You never know what you're going to find in the suburbs: murder, wife-beating, incest, and heroin. But *bugger my cat,* thought Frank—there ought to be limits!

"We're terribly sorry to interrupt your wife-swapping evening," said Don, as they stood in the warm, inviting, knocked-through living room of Kimberley's parents, Alice and Tony Riggs.

Mrs. Riggs, who had been quite flushed when she opened the door to them, giggled like a weathergirl and covered her mouth with both hands. Mr. Riggs laughed more easily, though his laughter came a beat or two behind the band; Frank duly noted the tankard clutched against the bearded man's decent-sized belly. The two naked blokes said nothing.

"Of course," Don added, "Sunday evening—we really should have known. Do you know, I reckon the telly gets worse the more channels there are."

Alice busied herself with some more giggling. The naked blokes looked at each other, and then at Tony Riggs. They were smiling, but their postures were becoming a little stiff. *Forced,* Frank corrected himself: a little forced, not a little stiff. Actually, he saw now, they weren't entirely naked: they wore tiny pouches over their—well, not over their ears, obviously. The sort of thing male strippers wore. Or so Frank assumed; he'd never seen a male stripper. Working, that is; he'd once arrested a pair of male strippers—for armed bank robbery, as it happened—but they'd been fully dressed at the time. They hadn't been on duty. Very fully dressed, really, what with the stockings on their heads and the skin-tight gloves and so on.

And bow ties. Not the bank robbers, the naked blokes. They were wearing bow ties as well as pouches. The bow ties were around their necks, obviously, not . . .

For the most part, Frank kept his eyes on the ceiling. He didn't want to embarrass anyone.

"Perhaps I should explain," said Tony.

"Oh, do you have to?" said Don. "It'll ruin everything."

"I can't help it, I'm afraid." He smiled. "I'm a science teacher." Frank spent a deeply perplexed second wondering why being a science teacher meant that Mr. Riggs couldn't help having naked men in his living room. He was pretty sure that Dr. Mac, the science teacher at his own secondary school, encountered no such difficulties. With or without bow ties. There again, what does a child know of the private lives of teachers? "You see, Inspector, it's our wedding anniversary."

"And the florist was closed for stocktaking?" Don guessed.

"And so I answered an advertisement placed in the local rag by these gentlemen here."

The science teacher politely gestured towards the two naked men, who acknowledged the formal invitation by nodding at the two plainclothes policemen.

"Evening," said the larger of the two men; who was also, Frank estimated, in his mid-forties, perhaps ten years older than his colleague, who made up in tattoos what he lacked in age. His lower chest was dominated by the crest of West Ham

Football Club, the crossed hammers ending just below his nipples.

"Good evening, gentlemen," Don replied. Everyone in the room was grinning now, all trying not to laugh out loud. All except one; Frank Mitchell was having no difficulty not laughing, and was only grinning because it hurt when he stopped. "Are you stripagrams?" the DI asked.

"No, good heavens, no. No, pal, nothing like that." The tattooed nudist, his accent unadulterated West Riding, seemed most amused at the idea that he and his associate might be engaged in anything so eccentric as the stripping telegram business. "We don't do stripagrams, do we, Keith?"

The elder bare person shook his head. Evidently, he too found the whole concept highly comical. "No chance, Ollie! No thank you, don't fancy that carry-on."

"No, what it is, see," Ollie explained, "we're Buff in the Buff." He peered eagerly at the two detectives' faces, and was possibly a little disappointed with what he saw there. "Do you see? Buff as in nude, and buff as in polish."

"And buff as in lovely, in my case," Keith added, giving his love handles a sexy wobble to illustrate his point.

"We're cleaners, mate."

"Ah, I *see,*" said Don. "A special treat for the woman in one's life—not only someone else doing the housework for a change, but that someone being a pair of naked fellas."

"Mother's Day is our busiest time, believe it or not," said Ollie.

"You do this for a living?" Frank asked. He couldn't help himself; the incredulous question burst from him like a belch.

"God, no," said Keith. "We're carpet fitters, we are."

"You mean—"

"No, lad, we wear clothes when we're carpet fitting. Well, you're forced to, aren't you?"

Ollie nodded. "All those fibres."

"Precisely." Keith winced. "No thank you very much. We do this, the nude cleaning like, for charity. For the kiddies' hospice."

Both men smiled expectantly at both policemen. Expectantly and nakedly.

"Oh, right," said Don, the first to catch on. He began fiddling in his trouser pocket, giving Frank an extremely nasty moment, which ended only when the DI produced a ten pound note and handed it to Ollie. "An excellent cause. Well done."

"Ta very much, that's lovely. Every penny goes to the sick kiddies," said the illustrated domestic. He turned his attention to Frank, and then frowned as he followed the young cop's gaze upwards. "We've not done the ceilings yet, mate. There'll be no cobwebs when we have, you can count on that."

Mrs. Riggs also frowned and began scrutinising the ceiling. "There aren't any cobwebs *now,*" she said.

Frank found a tenner of his own and handed it over. He'd have gladly paid three times as much if only the naked men would go and be naked somewhere else. Especially the fat one. And especially the tattooed one.

"Smashing, very kind. God bless the constabulary. Tell you what," said Keith to his hosts. "You've obviously got matters to discuss, so why don't Ollie and I get started upstairs? Now, I hope you've not tidied up ahead of us. People do, you know," he told Don. "Some of the toilets, especially, are spotless. Renders the whole bloody exercise completely pointless."

Frank looked for cobwebs while two bottoms oscillated out of the room, a hi-tech cleaning machine lugged between them.

Don smiled at Alice Riggs. "They've got all the equipment, haven't they?"

She collapsed onto a sofa, again covering her burning face with her hands. "Oh, honestly! Of all the times to get a visit from the police."

"We do our best to add to the general jollity," said Don.

The light mood did not last much longer, however. The sober topic of Bert Rosen's murder began the erosion of jollity, and when the conversation moved on to their daughter Kimberley, the Riggs's wedding anniversary spirits were further flattened.

"I'll tell you the truth," said Tony, setting to one side his tankard of (Frank suspected) homebrew, and sinking his hands into his pockets. "We don't talk to Kimmy that much. Not any more."

"It's not that we mind her still living here," her mother was keen to point out.

"No, certainly not," Tony confirmed. "These days, how can a young person hope to leave home? In London, I mean, with house prices like they are. Anyway, she'll probably be off to university next year."

"Library school, she's talking about, isn't she?" said Alice. "Or at least, she was, the last time she chose to tell us anything."

"I think we ought to stress, Inspector, lest you go away with the wrong idea: it's not *us* that don't talk to *her*—"

"We'd love to!"

"It's her not talking to us. And we shouldn't exaggerate—she's not giving us the silent treatment or anything like that."

"She just won't talk to us about anything important. Things that matter. She's . . ." Alice searched for the right term. "She's *polite* to us, nothing more."

"So you see, if you have any questions about our daughter,

about what's going on in her head or in her life, we're not really the ones to ask."

"I'm sure it's just a phase," Don Packham, the well-known child behaviourist, assured them. "Do you have any idea what started it off?"

An unhappy look passed between Kimberley's parents; not just unhappy, Frank thought—there was more than a hint of exasperation in there, too. A quick exchange of optical semaphore established Tony Riggs as the spokesman on this topic. "What it is—what we think it is—my wife and I, several centuries ago, we were quite active in various good causes."

"Anti-racist, peace, sex equality," said Alice in a blah-blah voice. "You know, all the usual."

"But, as usually happens—I mean, it's not as if we're the only ones—once you get married, you have children, you've got a mortgage . . ."

"You become somewhat less active," Don said.

"Precisely."

"But there's always a new generation coming up, isn't there?" said Alice. "One lot burns out, and the next lot take up the fight. That's how it's always been."

"People like your daughter, you mean."

"Well, you'd think so, wouldn't you?" said her father, exasperation definitely edging sadness out now. "But apparently doing our bit twenty years ago wasn't enough. Apparently we're not allowed to get middle-aged, we're supposed to spend the rest of our lives shouting 'Fascist Pig' at coppers."

"No offence," said Alice. She smiled at Frank, and added: "It's all changed these days, hasn't it?"

"And apparently," Tony continued, "we're a disgrace for retiring from front-line struggle."

"Unlike Bert Rosen," said Alice.

"Unlike Bert Rosen, lifelong cadre, tireless soldier of the revolution, eternal tribune of the people." He reclaimed his homebrew and took a meaningful swig. "Not wishing to speak ill, Inspector, but we're just about fed up with hearing Comrade Rosen's name."

"Bert this," Alice confirmed, "Bert that."

"She hasn't actually got a pinup of the old bugger on her bedroom wall, like she used to have Noel Gallagher—"

"Not 'old bugger,' Tony. The poor chap's dead."

"But she might as well have. That's what Bert was to her, Inspector: a pop star."

"You don't really think it's possible?" said Frank, starting the car up, his mind reeling somewhat from a combination of naked men, and now this. "An affair between Bert and Kimberley?"

"Doesn't have to have been an actual physical affair. But if Bert really was sweet on her . . ."

"He might have given her the money," Frank conceded. "For her college fund, maybe. But even so, does that get us anywhere? It doesn't explain the gun. Surely, nothing except a fear of attack could explain Bert carrying a gun, and he presumably didn't fear Kimberley."

"I've been thinking about that. He was an old man, right? So his fear doesn't have to be a well-founded one. Okay, he wasn't a confused old man, he was all there mentally, but he was still old."

"I suppose so. Except . . . no, wait a minute. He *was* murdered, wasn't he? So his fear *was* well-founded."

Don stared out of the window for a while, but his stare was focussed, not vacant. "I think what I'm trying to get at is, whatever it was he feared and whatever it was that led to his death might not necessarily be the same thing."

"Well . . ."

"No, you're right—an imagined murder plot and a real murder plot surrounding the same man at the same time? The odds are ones a bent bookie would blush at."

"It would be a bit of a coincidence."

"Unless . . ." Don went quiet again. Frank didn't disturb him; he'd learned not to. "Unless, in some way we can't yet get hold of, Bert's imagined threat somehow led to a real threat. After all, you've got to *imagine* a steam engine before you can invent one, haven't you? Ideas create reality, as well as the other way around."

Frank said nothing to that. He wasn't in the habit of inventing steam engines. He waited a few moments, just in case the DI had any more imagining out loud to do, and then said: "So—what next?"

Don checked his watch, and did a double-take. "Oh shit, is that the time? Drop me back at my place, Frank, and I'll see you in the morning."

"Oh," said Frank. "Right."

At the second set of red lights, Don said: "You realise there's one obvious possibility which we've been overlooking? That Bert used the missing money to buy the mystery gun."

"It did cross my mind, but it's far too much money, isn't it? Though he might not know that, I suppose. Maybe he was ripped off."

"No," said Don. "Bert may not have known much about gangsta culture—or gangster culture, depending on who he bought the gun from—but I get the impression that you'd have to be up pretty bloody early if you wanted to con him."

"That seems to be the consensus," Frank agreed. "Which means that even if he did pay well over the odds for the gun, that still leaves a good couple of grand unaccounted for."

On Monday morning, in her reopened library, Dot Estevez was in the middle of a lively discussion with a woman in her late thirties, who wore faded jeans and a matching waistcoat, big boots, and bleached blond hair.

With Frank busy elsewhere, Don waited politely until they'd finished (provided you considered blatant eavesdropping to be the height of good manners), before announcing himself to the branch librarian—who looked, he thought, no more or less frazzled than usual.

"Staff problems, Dot? Doesn't like working evenings?"

"Oh, it's not that—it's another hugely helpful memo from our new political masters. Arrived in the internal post this morning."

"The new council throwing its weight around?"

"With the usual *wonderful* grasp of priorities. And of course, I have to put the notices on the board and make sure everyone's read them, which means they're all my fault!"

"This morning's was a good'un, I take it?"

"The new council has banned smoking on all council property—not just in council buildings, which is the present situation. Which means that half my staff can no longer nip outside for a quick fag on their tea break, because the whole plaza surrounding the library is technically municipal property. If they want to smoke now, they'll have to walk over the bridge, past the old shopping centre, and onto the main road."

Don wagged his head in sympathy. He knew what it was to have idiot bosses. "If smoking's banned on the whole plot, what happens if an OAP is taking a short cut from the main road through to the minicab place, and forgets he's got his pipe in his mouth?"

"Then it's up to you to arrest him, Don."

"Right." Don saluted. "I shall post men at every entrance. The briar-puffing fiends shall not evade us."

She laughed—though not too convincingly, it seemed to Don—and asked him if he fancied a cup of coffee. The staff-room would be empty, she said. It normally was since they banned smoking.

"We're very grateful to the police," she told him, while the kettle was boiling, "for letting us have the library back so quickly."

"Not my department," said Don, modestly, sitting on an ancient municipal sofa, "but I'll tell them. To be honest, I'm surprised the council agreed to re-open. Couldn't they have used all this as an excuse to stay closed?"

"Ah, yes, they *could.*" Dot looked uncommonly pleased with herself. "But I helpfully pointed out to them that if the branch was closed, the entire staff would feel fully entitled to spend the day alongside our shop steward at the picket of the town hall."

"Cunning. It'll be another black mark against your name with management, I fear."

"I imagine it will."

"You're not worried they might be angry enough to withdraw your early retirement offer?"

She'd been just about to hand him his coffee. Now, her face froze and she drew the hand which carried the coffee mug back towards her. Don wasn't sure whether or not the movement was deliberate, but just in case he shifted his weight slightly forwards, from his buttocks to his thighs, and from his heels to the balls of his feet. Most police officers know what it is to have liquids of various kinds thrown over them, and very few actively seek to repeat the experience.

"You know about that, do you? I think I can guess how.

Well, what you apparently don't know is that I've already turned down the offer. In writing. I can show you my copy of the letter if you like."

Don waved away her suggestion, as if it were an irrelevance, and reached out for his coffee. Dot handed it to him; again, he wasn't sure whether she knew she was doing it. There was no doubt she was angry—and, more dangerously than that, feeling foolish. She'd treated this man as if he were a friend, a fellow conspirator against moronic managements, and now he'd revealed himself as nothing better than a cop.

Time to change the subject.

"Tell me, Dot: I keep hearing that spending on public libraries has increased massively over the last few years. But I also hear the opposite—that book funds are lower than ever. So what's the truth?"

It did the trick. She wasn't stupid—she knew what he was doing—but these things mattered to her, and if you wanted to talk about them, she'd talk. "It depends who you ask," she said, sitting down opposite him. "Spending is increasing, but the critics say it's mostly on DVDs, videos, and computers, not on books. Which upsets the traditionalists, to put it mildly."

"Diversification," said Don. "Sounds sensible."

She nodded. "Public libraries have always diversified, ever since they started, and people have always objected to it—especially those who believe that a library should exist purely for education, not for leisure."

"You mean people who were born in about 1827?"

"Oh yes! And there's plenty of them still around. However, even the most reactionary people can be right by accident, and there've been some studies lately which suggest that the more hip and glamorous and modern libraries become, the fewer users they get."

"Ah."

"That what people want from libraries is essentially old fashioned: big piles of paper, easy on the megabytes."

Don sipped his coffee; she did the same, unconsciously mimicking him, he suspected. "And presumably for every study showing that conclusion . . . ?"

"There's one showing the opposite, quite so. Some people say library spending isn't rising at all, and some say even if it is rising, numbers of users—we're not supposed to call them readers any more, which may or may not be significant—are falling. And that the government's response to falling numbers isn't more resources, but . . . can you guess?"

"To set new targets."

She laughed, and he decided he was forgiven. She'd be the sort, he reckoned, who was too mentally busy to be able to hold onto annoyances or grudges, even when she intended to. "Yes, they do love their targets, don't they? The really big argument at the moment is between the government, which tells us the tide has turned for libraries, after years of decline and under-investment; and some in the profession who insist that book spending and borrowing are haemorrhaging, and that the increasing through-the-door numbers are just kids using the free Internet access to visit chatrooms."

"No more 'university of the street,' in other words."

"But others say, so what? Only a lunatic would expect libraries to do the same job in 2004 that they did in 1904. As long as people are using them, that must mean that they are providing a service people need and want—anything else is just nostalgia. A lot of library workers, however, point out that when you *do* increase book spending, big surprise, book borrowing increases."

"So books are what people want? And what do you say,

Branch Librarian Estevez?"

She smiled and shrugged. "When I joined the library service, the big debate was for and against outreach—was a library a passive place, which people came to, or was it an active service, which went out to people? Thirty years from now, there'll be another insoluble argument going on, and thirty years after that, too."

By the time they'd finished their coffee, Don hoped it was safe to return to the main topic. "I'm sure I already know the answer, Dot, but I have to ask. Did Bert Rosen ever give you any money?"

"Money? No, of course not. What do you mean?"

"I can't tell you exactly why I'm asking, you understand, but we have reason to believe that Bert might recently have given a sum of money to someone."

"Well, it wasn't me." She put her empty mug down. "You mean, because of the redundancy offer from the council? Oh, good heavens! I never even mentioned that to Bert. If he'd thought I was short of money, he'd have offered me his life savings."

"Who might he have given it to, do you think?"

"To a passing tramp! To anyone, Don." She leaned forward. "Bert was the real thing, you have to understand that about him. If he thought he could help you, he would. It wouldn't matter whether you were a friend of his or not."

"Doug Ticehurst was a friend of his, I think?"

"Bert was very kind to him, that's true. Poor Doug's not had the easiest of times."

"He's had marital troubles, I believe?"

She nodded. "There's so much of it about isn't there? Poor Cyril, too, he's terribly upset, whatever he says. And I gather that Stanley has been 'seeing a lady' for years, and I'm sure he'd like that relationship to be more than it is." She sighed. "Though their stories aren't quite as dramatic as poor Doug's, of course."

"Dramatic? Was it an unpleasant divorce, then?"

"Well—which one?" She laughed at the look on Don's face, and then put her hand to her mouth, realising she'd said too much. "Oh dear, you didn't know, did you?"

"You'll have to finish the story now, Dot, or I'll be imagining all sorts."

"Me and my big mouth . . . the thing is, I understand that Doug has been divorced, well, *several* times."

"Several?"

"Four or five, I think."

"Four or five?"

"More, perhaps. I'm sorry, Inspector, I'm really not comfortable discussing—"

"No, of course not, I quite understand." Don could afford to be understanding, now that she'd said what she hadn't wanted to say.

At the reading tables in the library, he found a boy of about eleven, watching football highlights on his mobile phone.

"Excuse me, sir." Don showed him his warrant card.

"It's not nicked, it's mine."

"Of course it is, don't worry." Don took out his own, somewhat humbler phone. "Do you know how to send text messages on one of these? I could do it myself, but to be honest with you, my fingers are too big, my eyes are too small, and my patience is too short."

The lad took Don's phone, and treated it to a good, solid sneering session. "You know you can't send movies on this," he said, evidently amazed that such a primitive instrument had survived into the modern era.

"I know. It's a piece of crap. Don't worry, I'm going to

chuck it in the bin as soon as I get home."

"You want to, mate, you really do. Cavemen had better mobiles than this."

"But you can text people on it?" The expert reluctantly admitted that such an operation was technically feasible, albeit distasteful. Don showed him Frank Mitchell's number, and dictated a brief message, asking him to call back at his earliest convenience.

The boy's thumbs moved like electrified maggots. He pressed "send" with an air of satisfaction, and handed the phone back. "There you go, mate."

"Many thanks," said Don. "Much appreciated. And don't worry, I promise not to tell anyone you've been helping the police."

Don smiled to himself. *Frank'll be impressed,* he thought.

Chapter Twelve

"Excuse me a second."

Frank wasn't particularly enjoying his latest conversation with Kimberley Riggs, so he was glad of the interruption when his mobile phone bleeped to let him know that he'd received a message.

He wasn't enjoying it, because it was an inherently embarrassing subject; asking a nineteen-year-old whether she'd mind very much just clearing up a small matter, purely routine Miss, only were you having it away with the late, lamented eighty-four-year-old at all—that was, to Frank's mind, a good definition of embarrassing. And he wasn't enjoying it, too, because young Kimberley's sense of humour got a little wearing after a very little while. The first time she'd greeted a newcomer to the town hall steps with the words "Look, comrade—even the police have decided to join the picket!" it hadn't been as amusing as its reception deserved, as far as Frank was concerned, and by the fifth time of telling, it had been transferred in Frank's mental filing system from the room marked "Embarrassing" to the drawer labelled "Irritating."

Besides which, and not unexpectedly, his embarrassment and irritation had been suffered in vain. On the way over, he'd come up with what he still thought was a pretty neat approach. He hadn't asked Kimberley directly whether she was romantically involved with Bert, but instead wondered if she was aware of any such involvement in Bert's life.

"Bert? No, I don't think there was anyone. Not since his wife." She gave Frank what he fancied was a patronising smile. "It's a sweet thought, though."

"Not that there's any reason why he shouldn't," said Frank. "Far from it. Life goes on. It's just that if such a person did exist, it's very important that she—or he, of course," he added; he thought that was an especially inspired touch. "That he or she come forward, so that we can ask her one or two simple, routine questions."

"Yeah, cool." Kimberley waved at a friend who'd just joined the far end of the picket line. Then she pointed at Frank, and bent her knees, and hooked her thumbs into the imaginary braces holding up her imaginary trousers. Just to be sure, in case her mime was too subtle, she brought her right hand up to her head in a crisp salute, and then pointed at Frank again. The friend laughed. Kimberley laughed. Frank ploughed on.

"Or him. Obviously, it would be none of our business who Bert was or wasn't involved with. Nothing to do with us, or indeed anyone else, and all entirely confidential as far as we're concerned. We just need to know, that's all; just something that needs crossing off our list. You see?"

"Sure," said Kimberley, not quite looking at him.

She was obviously in her element here, Frank thought; buzzing and merry with the excitement and good fellowship of the event. There were fifty or sixty people on the picket line—it was a twenty-four-hour affair, he remembered, so presumably folk were coming and going in shifts—though strictly speaking it wasn't a picket. There was no attempt to prevent access to the building; the aim seemed to be to make a great deal of noise, to give out leaflets protesting against spending cuts in general, and library closures in particular, and . . . well, to have fun. Everyone seemed to be smiling, above their football scarves and below their woolly hats. It was a bright, chilly day, and the protestors kept their hands in their pockets, doing what an old sergeant of Frank's used to call "The Revolution Shuffle," a non-stop, probably unconscious, stepping movement, used against cramp and cold. Unlike industrial pickets, these had no braziers to huddle around: the council would presumably have considered flaming oil drums on their steps to be a liberty too far. However, there were colourful, and in some cases historic union banners—representing firefighters and nurses, Frank spotted, as well as council employees—and simpler, home-made placards, and one or two papier-mâché caricatures of the new council leader and his chief whip.

For all the cold, the protestors looked unfailingly cheerful. They were of all ages, from toddlers to pensioners; readers, Frank supposed, as well as members of the local government union, and a fair turnout of multi-purpose activists, too. And several, no doubt, who belonged to all three categories. The sergeant who'd named the Shuffle had, years previously, served a tour in Special Branch, the Met's political police. He'd made a study of protest movements, the way many coppers studied birds, butterflies, or battlefields, and one of his catchphrases had been "It's a small world, the revolution—you keep bumping into the same old faces."

Not so true now, Frank reflected, as it had been in Sergeant Holden's heyday. Half the country seemed to be involved in protests these days, and there was no shortage of fresh faces, whether it was millions marching against America's wars, or against global warming, or for cancelling Third

World debt; or dozens demonstrating their opposition to the erection of a mobile phone mast next to their children's school playground. Or their love of their local library, indeed. TV talking heads went on about the death of mass participation in democracy, but then they weren't privy to what Sergeant Holden had called "the only indispensable, infallible, involvement index"—coppers' overtime sheets.

If fifty thousand people wanted to shout their way through the streets of London, then a proportionate number of police officers was needed to escort them. When a few score of friendly locals wanted to yell some good-natured abuse at their local politicians, on the other hand, it was felt that PC Standfield could probably keep the peace on his own.

"All right, Frank?" he called, from his post directly in front of the main entrance. "Come to join the picket, have you? 'We shall not, we shall not be moo-oooved . . .' "

"Very funny, Les," Frank mouthed back. "Side-splittingly funny."

"Oh, sorry," said Kimberley, returning from a chat with a friend from the nurses' union. "Are you still here?"

"Yes. So: you can't help us on this? As far as you know, Bert was not seeing anyone?"

She smiled, and tapped his elbow. "How's your little boy?"

"Very well, thank you. So—"

"Have you got a photo?"

"Not at this moment in time, no. Was there—"

"You *must* have a photo, don't be silly!" She extended her hands, as if to frisk him.

Enough, thought Frank: this was a waste of time and embarrassment. Time to try a bit of Don-like crap-cutting. "Kimberley, did Bert Rosen ever give you any money?"

Her hands froze in midair, and all the confidence and self-possession and flirtatiousness which the shivery joy of the picket line had given her dropped from her face in a second. "*Money?* What the fuck are you talking about?"

"Nobody's accusing you of any—"

"The answer's no, Constable." Her hands were back in her pockets now. "Bert never gave me any money. Why would he? What do you think I am, some sort of scam-artist, conning money out of old people?"

Which was when Frank's phone bleeped. *Thank God for technology.*

"Excuse me a second."

"Txt msg frm Don P," said the screen. Frank pressed the appropriate buttons, and the message duly appeared. It was quite short. "U R a Arse," it said. "U R an Hairy arse."

"I'm sorry, Kimberley," he told the young steward. "I'd better deal with this, it's from my boss. Thank you for your help."

She said nothing, and didn't catch his eye. He wasn't sorry.

He dialled Don's mobile number. Evidently, the DI had finally figured out how to text on that expensive phone he'd bought last summer. Which was a good thing, aye, but Frank wasn't sure that infantile insults were the ideal form of test transmission.

"Frank—you got my message?"

"Yes, sir."

"So, what do you think? Pretty good, eh? For an ageing inspector with split thumbs."

Frank wasn't going to get into that. This wasn't the time or the place. Not that any time or any place ever would be the time or the place, but that notwithstanding—this wasn't it. "Did you want to talk to me, sir?"

"Well yes, obviously." Don sounded baffled. "I should have thought my message made that perfectly clear, Frank. None of the terms employed were unfamiliar to you, were they?"

"Not as such, sir, no."

"You do know how to read *txt,* I trust?"

"What was it you wanted to speak to me about, sir?"

"Oh well, I'll send you a fax next time, Frank. Perhaps you're more up to speed with that technology. Or maybe a telegram, delivered by a Cockney urchin wearing a little round hat and a three-button jacket. 'Gawd bless yer, guv'nor, and I ham hinstructed to wait for hay reply, lor' luvaduck.' "

He calmed down eventually—it'd be the excitement of mastering a new skill, Frank thought, and he just hoped it didn't tip him into one of his startlingly manic spells—and finally told Frank the news about Doug Ticehurst's many marriages.

"That is interesting," Frank admitted.

"Interesting? It's gobsmacking. Anyway, I want his marital history dug up, and exhibited for our delight. Can you get someone to see to that, please?"

"Will do. But do we know what we're looking for?"

Don sighed. "No, not really. Just anything odd, I suppose. If something as strange as that pops up in a murder inquiry, you can't help feeling it means something."

"Right you are. I'll get straight on it."

But Frank hadn't had time to bring his notebook up to date, let alone call the incident room, when his phone rang again.

"Frank? The more I think about this, the more I don't like it. Just to be sure, have someone trace the current whereabouts of each of Ticehurst's ex-wives. Have the local force contact each one. You with me?"

"I'll do it immediately."

"And Frank," Don added. "When I say contact, I mean actual, guaranteed eyeball contact. Yeah? Urgently."

They met up again for lunch, their separate tasks seen to. While they were awaiting news of the ex-Mrs. Ticehursts, Don suggested, they should check up on various other marital entanglements.

"I wouldn't mind a chat with Cyril the squeegee-man's wife. Chelmsford, wasn't it?"

"That's right."

"Get an address for his mother-in-law through police resources, not from Cyril. And don't phone the wife in advance; we'll take a chance on cold-calling. With any luck, we'll catch her unawares and uncomfortable."

Right, thought Frank. Plus you fancy a trip out of London, and you don't want the inconvenient unavailability of a witness messing it up.

But when they introduced themselves to Mrs. Mowbray's mother, commiserated with her on her illness and asked to speak to her daughter, her puzzlement was plain. She was perfectly well, she told them, thank you very much, and her daughter's flat was five minutes' drive away.

Not a bad place, thought Don; not luxurious, exactly, but clearly Jill Mowbray's third-floor, two-bedroomed flat, with its spacious living room and gadget-packed kitchen, was a bit more than merely a hole for sulking in. To his inexpert eye, several pieces of furniture, ornaments and so on looked to be pretty good quality. Ugly, in other words, and heavy, and expensive. He wondered whether the flat was let as furnished; he'd have to ask Frank, that was the sort of thing the DC always seemed to know. Very interested in property, was young Frank—almost as interested in property, in fact, as Don had been, at a similar age, interested in . . . well, in lots of things, only some of which were explicitly illegal, and none of which had involved either bricks or mortar.

Different generations; each to his own.

Jill did not ask them to sit down. She was the sort of woman who is sometimes described, not altogether kindly, as handsome. Stiff of hair, dress, expression, and posture, she was certainly not the sort of woman who invites policemen, plumbers, or sewer pipe repairmen to sit on her expensively ugly sofas. Don sat down, and eye-signalled Frank to do likewise. Pain showed on Jill's face. Don felt happy. He always enjoyed getting out of town for a few hours.

Mrs. Mowbray remained standing.

"I must apologise, Mrs. Mowbray, on behalf of myself, my colleague, and the Metropolitan Police Service."

She wasn't at all surprised, her eyebrows told him; she imagined he spent most of his wretched life apologising.

"We seem to be in possession of slightly incorrect information. You see, we went first this morning to your mother's—"

"Where did you get my mother's address?"

"From a computer."

She didn't do anything as demonstrative as shudder, but she did close her eyes and swallow hard. To learn that one's mother was to be found on a *computer,* along with who knew what sort of people; it was only because she was so strong that she could keep going at all.

"The reason we felt it necessary to disturb your mother, was that we understood you were staying with her. While she was unwell."

"As you can see, Inspector, your understandings were . . .

not so." She was, Don noted with some relish, the sort of person who keeps you waiting while she searches for just *precisely* the wrong word.

"It was your husband who—"

"My ex-husband."

"You're not together any more?"

"As I'm sure Cyril explained to you—"

It was Don's turn to interrupt, he decided. "Actually, no; Cyril gave us a bit of a euphemism, I'm afraid. You're divorced, are you?"

"We are . . . cleaved." Her face didn't so much as twitch while she conducted her word searches; it made it a little hard to know for certain whether she was looking for a word or entering a coma.

"Separated? But not divorced?"

"I have no intention of returning to him."

Don caught the implication, but wondered whether it was true, or untrue, or just a matter of opinion. It was a matter of fact, in his professional experience, that almost everyone was almost always the leaver, according to their own accounts, not the left.

"I'm afraid I must ask you, Mrs. Mowbray: why did you leave your husband?" He'd been going to begin the sentence with the more conventional "May I ask . . . ?" but changed his mind when he realised that this particular witness might not treat his question as rhetorical.

"Cyril became . . ."

They waited. Frank fidgeted impatiently, but Don was enjoying himself. What did Cyril become: unreasonable? Malodorous? A werewolf, on the fifteenth of every month?

". . . underemployable," Jill Mowbray concluded.

Ah; so, poor Cyril became poor. One might learn to live with a werewolf—there are all sorts of creams on the market these days—but a drop in career status was a textbook example of what the divorce courts called mental cruelty.

"Still," said Don, "it's sad to see a marriage break down. Cyril seems like a man of depths."

She snorted. "People who say travel broadens the mind have obviously never met a member of the armed forces."

"Do you have any children?"

"No children," she replied, "and no . . ."

Dogs? Cats? Imagination?

"No correspondence."

Don looked at Frank, but there was no help there. "Correspondence?"

"No one else," she explained. "On either side."

"Yes, I see. Of course. Well, that's a mercy, anyway. So, you'll be getting divorced?"

She almost shrugged; Don could have sworn he saw a small movement in one of her shoulders, if not both. "When I get around to it, I suppose. I'm very busy."

And enjoying letting Cyril dangle, no doubt, thought Don; or should that be *dandle?* "And how does Cyril feel about that?"

Her look of satisfaction was the first complete expression she'd yet shown them. Don wondered if her frozen face was the result of competitive strain injury. "He still thinks I'm coming back, the idiot. Phones me every day. I don't pick up. My family are right—best not to encourage him."

Frank was quietly puzzled, Don could tell without looking at him. There was something about the lad when he was working hard to follow what was going on; a bit like the way a fridge will buzz slightly off key, just before its icemaker dies. Frank was puzzled about why this cold, stuck-up woman was telling her most intimate secrets to a pair of strangers, and puzzled about why, exactly, she wanted rid of her husband.

To Don it seemed obvious. It would be tautologous to say that Cyril and Jill had married in folly, but this particular folly was more doomed than most. She was obviously considerably posher than he was, and probably had more money, but as long as Cyril was in the army there was always a faint chance of advancement. Once she saw him in civilian dress, however, she knew finally and certainly that he was an incurable nothing, and so she dumped him.

And he reacted to this in the time-honoured manner of loud-shirted, boom-voiced men everywhere: he refused to believe it had happened.

Don wondered whether he could explain all this to Frank without actually addressing a word to him. To Jill Mowbray, he said: "Are you aware of what Cyril does for a living now?"

She succeeded in suppressing a shudder, but not in naming the trade at which her estranged husband now worked. "He's . . . he's . . . he's started his own . . . small affair."

Frank looked more confused than ever now. Don helped him out: "His own small business, that's right. As a window cleaner." He turned to Frank. "It was window cleaner, wasn't it, Constable?"

Frank—the light was dawning, no doubt about it—made a show of consulting his notes. "Window cleaner, sir, that's correct."

"Window cleaner." Don nodded. "Thought it was window cleaner. I imagine he began this venture after you'd left?"

"It certainly wasn't while I was there! I don't know why he bothers, it brings in no money whatsoever," she added, looking around her at the presumably unsatisfactory quarters in which vile fate had billeted her.

"You've suffered dreadfully," said Don. "But strength and good breeding will see you through, I'm sure of that."

Jill looked at him quite hard for quite a long time, and then said: "Inspector, would you care for a cup of tea?"

Chapter Thirteen

"Ambition," Don announced on the drive back to London, "is an almost wholly female vice, you'll find."

Frank wasn't entirely convinced it *was* a vice, per se, but he concentrated on the road. Don took a call telling him that two of Doug Ticehurst's exes had been located, alive and well. The call completed, he returned to his theme.

"Men, as a general rule, are much happier just toddling along. Or todgering along, as our dear chum Jill would no doubt put it."

"Unusual woman," said Frank.

"God, let's hope so. But her existence means that Cyril is a man who could really do with getting his hands on a few grand, fastish."

"It does." Frank had been working it out. He knew he didn't make the instant, intuitive leaps that seemed to come so easily to Don, but he reckoned his more methodical route was at least as likely to arrive at the correct destination. "Either to keep her in the manner to which, or else to win her back."

"Hard to know why he'd want her back, though. Not only is she horrible, but she's clearly finished with him."

"Pride, I suppose. An important man like him, he can't be

left by his wife. Self-important, at any rate. It's a blow to his dignity."

"My thoughts exactly, Frank. Plus, let's never forget, Cyril is the only trained killer in the picture."

As far as Don was concerned, Frank knew, "ex-Forces" was just another way of saying "psychopath." That was an interesting question, in fact; would Don be happier, at the end of this case, to arrest the ex-soldier with the loud voice, or the great white hope of the Cowden Tories?

"We don't know that for sure," Frank pointed out. "He might not be a trained killer—might have spent his whole career in the catering corps."

"Don't be daft, Frank," Don said. "The catering corps? They're the first ones they teach unarmed combat to. They have to, to protect them from angry soldiers."

"I used to go out with a girl who worked in a library," said Don, during a tea break on the journey back to London. "Did I tell you?"

"You mentioned it."

"Lovely girl." Don lit a small cigar, stuck it in his mouth, and leaned back with his hands clasped behind his head. "Lovely shoulders, from lugging stuff about all day long. Bringing up dirty great bound volumes of *The Times* from the basement, you know, and reams of spare paper for the photocopier. Cakes on people's birthdays. Take this tip from me, Frank, you ever want help moving house, you round up a load of library workers. Juniors, that is, not the professionals—none of *them* ever did a day's turn in their lives." He took in a happy drag of smoke, and studied the ashy tip of his cigar. "Oh yes, I do like a woman with a bit of muscle tone."

Frank would have been more interested in hearing what sort of women Don didn't like; it would have been an intriguing, and indeed much shorter, list. "I don't suppose they do so much carrying nowadays. It'll all be on computer, won't it?"

"Well," said Don, "be fair. Computers are pretty heavy, too."

Stanley Baird, they both agreed, was due another visit. Not that either of them could bring themselves to fancy him as a killer: "Still waters might run deep," said Don, "but you can't go scuba-diving in a bucket of milk." Even so, his name seemed to have come up in conversation more often than they might have expected. Besides, Don pointed out, "As secretary-treasurer of Loose Olives Forge Ecstasy, he might know more about what's been going on than he knows that he knows."

"We've got no hint of a motive for him, have we?" Frank asked. He knew full well that "we" hadn't, but sometimes things went on in the DI's head which he forgot to tell you about—and he was later astonished to find that you weren't fully au fait with them.

"Not particularly, Frank, unless you're keeping something to yourself?"

"Nothing, I'm afraid. The place he lives in seemed okay, didn't it? Not rich, not poor."

Don agreed. "Also, I got the impression he was a bit tight. And you rarely find mean people short of money."

"I suppose it's vaguely possible he could have had a really big fall-out with Cyril—but how that would lead to Bert's death, I don't know. Could he have killed Bert by mistake? But no: there was a light on in the office where Bert died, and he and Cyril didn't look much alike, even from behind."

"Maybe he was plotting something against Cyril, and Bert found out or even tried to stop him?" Don shook his head, and stubbed out his cigar. "No, none of it sounds very likely, I know. But we've got to give Stanley Baird his fair chance to be nicked for murder—otherwise he'll sue us for discrimination against prats."

"Just a hobby, Inspector, you understand."

Stanley didn't look especially embarrassed, Frank thought, though the smile on his female companion's face was, perhaps, a little fixed. She was about Stanley's age, maybe just a bit older, with an amiable, if careworn face. Oddly enough, even though Stanley didn't look embarrassed, or even sound embarrassed, his words sounded as though they *ought* to sound embarrassed. If you saw them written down, Frank reckoned, they'd look like the words of an embarrassed man. The tone in which they were spoken, however, was almost bouncy.

"No law against skip-diving," Don assured him. Frank had to suppress a snigger as a cloud passed across the DI's face; transparently, he was wondering whether in fact there might be any laws against skip-diving. Not that he would let such a technicality bother him for long, Frank was sure.

"Clare and I are not destitute, you see," Stanley Baird continued. "Nor are we running a rag-and-bone business. It's merely a bit of fun."

It didn't look much fun to Frank, and he was a little surprised to discover Stanley enjoying such a pastime. It seemed out of character—but then, of course, it might all be the girlfriend's idea.

Frank and Don had happened on the skip-divers more or less by chance. Getting no response from Baird's mobile or landline phones, they'd been driving towards his home when they'd seen Stanley himself, accompanied by a woman, dragging a leather armchair along the pavement. Don had remembered what Dot had said about a "lady" with whom she thought Stanley would like to be more than a friend. "There don't seem to be many happy pairings in this case," he'd remarked.

"Except James Pomeroy, perhaps," Frank had pointed out.

"That's a fine bit of furniture you've got there," Don said now. "Amazing what people throw out, isn't it?"

"Isn't it extraordinary?" Clare agreed. "There's absolutely nothing wrong with it. It hardly even needs cleaning, and it'll fit perfectly in Stanley's spare room."

"Doug Ticehurst would be impressed," said Frank. "By your commitment to recycling, I mean."

"I don't know why everybody doesn't do it," Stanley said. "You could easily furnish an entire house from skips, if you're methodical about it."

They were leaning against a wall, all four of them, Stanley and his friend getting their breath back, each keeping a proud hand on their trophy. Don and Frank had decided that there wasn't much more they could usefully discover about the money angle while they waited for the officer in charge of the incident room to sort out checks on the suspects' bank accounts. Meanwhile, they were back to wondering about the mysterious, out-of-place gun.

If Bert was so afraid for his life, then surely *someone* must have noticed it? Okay, so he was ex–Battle of the Atlantic, a veteran of Cable Street and everything else, but he wasn't superhuman—and he was an old man. Surely being so scared that you take a handgun into a public library was going to show in your demeanour? And even if, unlikely as they both agreed such a possibility was, Bert had been carrying the weapon for the only other logical reason—to kill someone, not to prevent someone killing him—then that would affect his behaviour even more so, wouldn't it?

"We just need a quick chat, Stanley, and then we'll let you get back to your labours," Don said. "We'd offer you a hand, but I don't think that thing would fit in DC Mitchell's car, I'm afraid."

"Not to worry, Inspector," Stanley assured him. "The exercise won't do us any harm. It's all part of the fun."

"I can't tell you why I'm asking, as you'll understand, but this is very important. You're an observant man, so I ask you to think carefully: during the day, or perhaps weeks before Bert's death, were you aware of any sign of stress or unusual behaviour? Anything at all that seemed out of character?"

Baird dabbed at his moustache and forehead with a threadbare handkerchief while he considered the question. "I really can't recall anything of the sort," he said eventually. "And of course it's not the sort of thing one would minute, I'm afraid."

"No, quite. Just for the record, when exactly did you last see him? Before that last, fateful committee meeting, that is."

"Let me see . . ." He closed his eyes to concentrate, and his tongue flicked at his moustache. Odd that he has to make an effort to remember, Frank thought; it's the sort of detail I'd expect him to have at his fingertips—or at least, in an ever-present diary or notebook. "It must have been the Thursday before he died, I think."

"What about?"

"I'm sorry . . . ?"

"What did you see him about," Don asked, "on that Thursday?"

"Oh, just some committee business, you know, very boring. Just a routine matter. I needed his signature on something or other." He gave them what he presumably thought was a disarming smile, and hurried on. "But I can't say he seemed in a state about anything, no. Given that he was always a man with bees in his bonnet about carrier bags and nuclear disarmament and this, that, and the other. Certainly, as far as I can say, even in retrospect, he was his usual, polite self."

Which was pretty much the answer the detectives had expected—puzzling as it was.

"Well fancy that," said Frank, putting his mobile away, and starting the car.

"Fancy what?"

"They've okayed the Scottish trip."

"You're joking!"

"For both of us," said Frank.

"Bloody hell," said Don. "Frank, you haven't been taking secret photos of the Commissioner wearing a tutu again, have you? Because if that's it, now's the time to tell me."

"I am wholly innocent of the charge, guv'nor," Frank insisted.

"Well, fancy that." Don sat back and crossed his arms, luxuriating in the warm bath of anticipation. "Ages since I've been to Edinburgh. Brilliant city. Tell you what, if you can get permission from Debbie—and young Joe, of course—we'll fly up tonight, before the accountants change their minds."

"Better phone Bert's son, first, tell him we're on the way." Frank pulled the car over to the kerb, and retrieved his phone from his jacket.

"No, hold on," said Don, holding up a hand to stay his colleague's dialling finger. "Shouldn't we book the flight first, so we can tell him when we're arriving? Or would it be wiser to . . ." Don screwed his eyes shut, the better to work the problem out.

"Well, either way, I'd best start by phoning Bert's

daughter—and get the son's number from her."

"Good point, Frank—well done. Yes, quite right, that's step number one. Step number two is to buy comics and sweets for the journey."

Frank phoned Rosa Ledbury. They spoke, though not for long. Frank put his phone away again.

"Well fancy that," said Frank.

"Fancy what?" Don asked, not sure he altogether liked the ironic look on the DC's face.

"Bert's daughter informs me that Bert's son is with her, just now, at her home."

"Ah," said Don. "Down to help with the funeral arrangements, no doubt?"

"So it would appear."

"Well fancy that."

"I thought they were estranged," said Frank. "The father and son."

"Not sufficiently estranged, it would seem, for our purposes." Don opened his window fully, and lit a small cigar. "Lovely city, Edinburgh. It has no equal."

"Well fancy that," said Frank.

"My sodding thoughts, precisely," said Don.

The generation gap between brother and sister was immediately obvious, not only through the physical differences between a pensionable woman and a man in early middle-age, or even late youth—but also in attitude, as expressed through bodily posture, through speech patterns, and even through accent. Rosa spoke with an authentic cockney accent of a sort which scarcely existed any more, albeit one with the edges ground off during decades as a teacher. Don had heard it often in his earliest years in the capital, but it had now been almost entirely replaced by the general-purpose, southeast

England sound, with its Australian inflection, Californian lack of breath control, and stubbornly London nasality.

Tom, Bert's son from his second marriage, born and raised in suburban Cowden, exhibited a textbook example of the contemporary articulation—with, if this wasn't just Don's wishful fancy, a hint of Auld Reekie.

He was well-dressed for a Trotskyist, thought Don, whose subconscious had, he acknowledged, been expecting strange hair, ill-fitting jeans, builder's boots, and a wounded leather jacket. Instead, Tom was largely bald, neatly shaven where he wasn't, and wearing inexpensive, inoffensive, dull and generic clothes of the kind which used to be called "smart casual."

But however they were dressed, whenever and wherever they were born, whatever they sounded like—in short, whoever they were—there was one question which all witnesses, suspects, friends, or relatives in this frustrating case were destined to be asked by DI Packham and DC Mitchell.

"Anxious?" said Rosa. "You asked me that before, Don. What are you getting at?"

"I can't say, Rosa, I'm sorry. But you still say that you noticed nothing?"

She shook her head. "No, I'm quite sure there—"

"Yes actually, Inspector, I think Pops might well have had something on his mind."

Rosa's astonishment seemed to add years to her eyes, Don thought, as if the idea that her brother might have some private knowledge of their father had taken her to a new level of bereavement. "When did you talk to Pops? You *never* talk to Pops."

Tom answered her question, but addressed his answer to Don. "He rang me on Thursday. We weren't alienated, despite what Rosa thinks, we just weren't as close as we used to be."

"Your father didn't approve of your particular brand of socialism?"

"Well, yeah." Tom lit a roll-up; Rosa passed him an ashtray with a resentful look. "But all that was . . . it didn't matter lately the way it had twenty years ago. How could it? Things have changed, there's less room for sectarianism now."

"Tell that to your Fourth International friends," said Rosa.

Tom spread his hands, and again spoke to Don, not to his sister. "Well, there you go."

"What did Bert ring for?" Don asked.

"Ostensibly just for a chat, which I will admit wasn't something he did all that often."

"Ostensibly?"

Tom nodded, his face grim. "I thought there was something more. But whatever it was, he didn't quite get round to it. I gave him a couple of openings to say what was on his mind, but he didn't take them."

"But there was something in his voice, or in what he said . . . ?"

"Nothing that he actually said, but yes—his voice, his manner, I just got the impression there was something he wanted to discuss. Not necessarily with me," Tom added, looking at his sister now, "just with someone." Rosa looked disgusted, and busied herself with her teacup.

"And this was the day before the library occupation? The Thursday?"

"That's right. About seven in the evening. I was still in the office." Tom, Don saw, was rhythmically tapping his fingers against the arm of his chair; left hand Morse, same as his father.

"Rosa," said Don, "having heard what your brother's said—"

"I didn't see much of him that day," she replied, her mouth narrow with regret and perhaps, Don thought, shame. "We were both busy with different things. I had a Peace Group meeting in the evening, and he was in bed by the time I got home."

"Do you know what your father was up to on Thursday?"

She thought about it for a moment. "Went shopping in the morning; he generally did on Thursdays. In the afternoon he had a meeting to do with the library—or, possibly not a meeting, maybe he just had to see one of the committee members. And then later on, around tea time, I imagine he went for one of his walks."

"Litter patrol," said Tom. "He was still doing that?"

"Always," she said, and a smile of shared memory passed between the siblings; the first Don had seen them exchange.

He let the moment loiter as long as he could, and then asked again: "Even thinking about it now, Rosa, there's nothing from that day . . . ?"

He tried not to make it sound like an accusation—it wasn't one, as far as he was concerned—but even so a defensive expression occupied Rosa's face. "No, but then when you're with someone all the time, looking after them every day, perhaps you don't notice things which someone who's more distant—"

"Oh, Rosie!" Tom slammed his cup on the table. "Don't start all that at a time like this, for heaven's sake."

"I'm not starting anything," Rosa protested. "I'm just saying—"

"You'll be around for a few days, Tom?" Don interrupted.

Tom looked at Don, and then at his sister. "I hope so," he answered.

Chapter Fourteen

In a dull, deserted pub, Frank put his mobile back in his pocket. "They've identified the murder weapon," he reported. "The leather belt, used as a ligature."

"Didn't belong to one of the suspects, I suppose?"

"No such luck; it came from the lost property box, which is kept in the office where Bert was killed. Couple of members of staff recognised it; it'd been there for a while."

"So it was just to hand," said Don. "Which could mean a lot, or could mean nothing."

"No prints on it, the lab says gloves were used; waterproof nylon gloves, probably."

"And if I remember correctly, the only gloves recovered during the search of the suspects were woollen, yes? Damn."

"How the hell," Frank wanted to know, "does someone lose a belt in a public library?"

Don waved his cigar. "I did *tell* you about libraries, Frank. If you don't want to listen, that's not my fault."

"Sir. Also, the checks on the suspects' bank accounts have come up with nothing."

"Okay, get your notebook out. Let's have a look at the runners and riders. If there are any runners, that is."

"Well, starting with the occupant of the office in which the body was found—"

"Yes, good point, Frank. To be honest, I do feel this is probably a male crime, but given the age of the victim, I accept we can't exclude a woman."

"Both Dot and Kimberley, as library staff, could have known about the handy belt in the lost property box. Even if it wasn't a premeditated crime, they'd have known where the box was kept."

"I don't think that's worth much, to be honest," said Don, after a pause for thought. "Unless the lost property box was kept in a locked safe behind a secret panel activated by a magic word known only to the Elders of Dewey—"

"I'll check." Frank made a note in his notebook.

"Then all it means is that the killer scrabbled around for the nearest ligature, and happened to come up with what he happened to come up with. Besides, I daresay all the LOFErs have been inside Dot's office at one time or another, on committee business."

"On top of which," said Frank, "Dot claims she's already turned down the ER/VR offer, thus scuppering the only possible motive we've got against her name."

"If the council really wants her to take it, though," cautioned Don, "no doubt she could change her mind any time she likes. But in any case, I can't see her killing Bert for the money. Maybe for pride; to stop Bert telling people if she *was* thinking of accepting the offer. Except that everyone agrees that he wouldn't have done that. And I think they're right, and I think Dot knows it."

"What about her apparent falling out with James Pomeroy?"

"Whether or not Pomeroy did tell people about the possibility of Dot jumping ship, she probably believed he did. But that's all that is, I'm sure."

"Okay." Frank made another note. "And Kimberley?"

Don stubbed out his cigar, rather slowly and without undue physical force. "Granted that it's a meaningless expression, but she really doesn't seem the sort, does she?"

"You mean, to kill an old man," asked Frank, who wanted to be sure what they were talking about, "or to string him along as a sugar daddy?"

"She doesn't seem the type for either," Don replied. "But that means nothing, of course. *He* doesn't seem the type either, and that means less. Suppose she was, as you say, stringing Bert along. Where does that take us?"

Frank shrugged. "I don't really see how it provides a murder motive."

Don thought about it, tapping his lighter against his chin. "Maybe Bert finally decided he wanted what he was paying for, and she didn't want things going that far. Or perhaps he came to his senses, realised he was being rooked, and wanted his money back."

"Which she'd already spent."

"We're going to have to put it to her," Don said, his mouth showing distaste at the thought. "But she's not at the front of my mind, I must say. You agree?"

"I do. So, let's move on to someone I suspect you have more of an eye on."

"Ah!" said Don. "Time for Cyril, is it? Right: well, he knows guns, we presume. Knows how to kill."

"Oh yes," Frank interrupted, "I had a text message about that while you were in the bog."

"Mr. Mowbray's service record?"

"Or at least the headlines thereof: nothing dodgy, is the basic story. Served honourably, left honourably. Further details will be released if we can demonstrate a need to know."

"So when we arrest him, they'll be willing to tell us he's been a suspect in nine previous ligature-related discipline incidents? Never mind, forget the army. The important thing is, Cyril has a desperate need for money, to get his wife back."

Frank made further notes, in a methodical hand, something he did partly as a way of creating pauses during these sessions with the DI; pauses during which he could be sure he was keeping up. *Money,* he wrote. It looked as though Don still liked the idea that the murderer had borrowed the missing money from Bert, and decided not to pay it back. "Three grand's not going to go very far in saving that marriage."

"Three grand's better than no grand," said Don. "Maybe he could put it towards a decent car or something, whatever might impress the frozen-faced old bag."

Himself, Frank couldn't see it. "Yeah, but three grand . . ."

"Look, Frank: we could say that about *all* the bloody money suspects! Three grand is not a fortune, and that is a problem for us, I accept that. But if we follow that logic to its conclusion, then you must have dreamt that case you were on last month, where that car park attendant was put in Cowden General on a life-support for the contents of his wallet. Which came to how much?"

"Three pounds thirty-five and a packet of condoms." *But,* Frank thought, the robber in that case was a crack addict. Bit different, surely. No point in pursuing it though. Not just at the moment. "Okay, so Cyril is a hot suspect. What about Stanley Baird?"

Don laughed. "The man's a joke."

"Wouldn't be the first solid gold wally to commit a murder, but."

"No, you're right, Frank. All the same . . . okay, he's as

tight as a microbe's nostril, so maybe he would kill for three grand. But he doesn't seem to need money, does he? And anyway, he's such a nothing. You know just by looking at him that all the decisions that changed his life were taken by other people."

"True enough. He doesn't exactly seem the proactive type, does he?"

"Exactly. Can you see him killing someone?" Don held up a hand, to delay Frank's answer. "No, I don't mean in theory—I mean literally. Can you, in your mind's eye, actually *see* him killing someone?"

"It's hard to imagine," Frank agreed.

"Keep him on the list, though; we live in hope." Don grimaced. "You know he reuses his teabags?"

His expression stern, Frank took his mobile out of his pocket and held it to his ear.

"Who you calling, Frank?"

"The Armed Response Team," said Frank. "I'll have Stanley picked up for a bit of rough justice. You know how the men feel about teabag re-users, sir. They have to put the bastards in isolation in prison."

"Stop arsing about, you idiot!" Don gasped, through his laughter. He was one of the very few men Frank had ever met who really did love to be had by a joke, provided only that the punchline justified the setup.

"One thing about Stanley Baird, though," Frank pointed out, his phone back in its nest. "He met Bert on the apparently significant Thursday, so could theoretically be considered the cause of Bert's upset."

"Theoretically. Who's next?"

"Well, Marjorie McDonald is also broke, so the three-grand motive fits her, too. With the same proviso as everybody else, that it's not much money to kill for."

"Of course," Don mused, "it *is* much money, if it's the exact amount you need—to clear a debt for instance."

"Okay, but then you borrow it. You don't kill for it."

"Unless the reason you need the money is not only urgent, but shameful or damaging. So you need the money, and the certainty that no one alive knows you've had it."

That made sense, Frank thought. "Can't see what there might be of that sort with Marjorie, though. Family woman, hardworking."

"We're agreed she wasn't that fond of Bert. Respected him, but didn't like him. Why, do you suppose?"

"Perhaps just jealousy at LOFE taking over from her gang?" Frank knew better than to suggest to Don that this wasn't a motive, but he felt safe enough saying it wasn't a credible motive for this particular woman.

Don agreed, as far as that went. "But if there is something else in their past . . . ?"

"What about Doug Ticehurst? All the ex-wives are now accounted for, all safe and well. So he's not a mass wife-murderer."

"Again, he shares the money motive. And we know Bert was keeping a particular eye on him, so he's a good candidate for the secret loan."

"All right." Frank wasn't going to say it again: *he wouldn't kill for three grand.*

"But the only thing about him that really sticks out is this business of the many wives. Okay, he hasn't chopped them up, but there must be a reason why they keep leaving him."

"He's gay, and doesn't know it?"

Don tapped his lighter on the table: once, twice, three times. "We need to talk to one of them."

"The ex-wives?"

The DI nodded. "Pick one at random and arrange a meet."

"Will do. So, finally—James Pomeroy. Money motive's no good there, unless he's unbelievably good at keeping up appearances."

"Yeah, he didn't do it for the money, that's for sure. And it's hard to think of anything more personal that would be worth the risk of killing for."

"Do we cross him off?"

"No, Frank, there *is* one thing that still worries me about him. Worries me a lot, in fact. What the holy hell was he doing at the occupation of Bath Street Library?"

Frank flicked back a few pages. "He says—"

"I know what he says, and it's a load of balls. Him at that occupation—it simply does not fit."

"He's really that right wing?"

"Right wing?" Don snorted. "He makes Tony Blair look like the leader of the Labour Party! Back in the early eighties, our James—in common with most of his libertarian tribe—made his political start in the Conservative Party's student federation. It was so extreme, the party had to close it down in the end. I've seen a photo of young James wearing a 'Hang Nelson Mandela' T-shirt."

"Hang Mandela?"

"Oh yes, Frank, in those days Mandela wasn't a saintly grandfather. To Reagan and Thatcher and all their kind, he was a terrorist with too many communist friends. It was only mad old lefties like Bert Rosen who wanted him released from prison."

That was one of the things about working with Don Packham; you got the odd history lesson along the way. Emphasis on odd. "Extraordinary. Still, times change, I suppose."

"We can but hope so, Frank. We can but hope. No, I didn't think much of Pomeroy's explanation for being at the occupation when he gave it to us, and the more I've thought about it since, the less I think of it."

Frank didn't bother trying to make a note of that. "It's true that the others seemed surprised to see him there."

"They did, didn't they? Unless we can establish a good reason for his behaviour, we have to at least wonder if the answer isn't that he stayed behind so as to bump Bert off."

Frank couldn't quite resist. "For reasons unknown," he said.

"Motives." Don was halfway through lighting another of his small cigars, but now he chucked it back into its box. "We go on and on about motives as if they're the be all and end all, and okay, we'd rather not go into court without one, but that's only because juries feel short-changed if they don't get a decent story."

"So we're not looking for a motive?"

"There *are* no motives, Frank. Not for murder. We should be looking at personalities, not motives."

"Right. Very interesting. Moving on—"

"Or rather," Don continued, taking the cigar out again, and this time getting as far as tapping its ends on his thumbnail, "there are three motives."

"Not none." Frank nodded. "Three. Aye, I'm with you."

"There are two motives for unpremeditated murder—anger and fear—and there's one motive for premeditated murder, which is madness. By definition, anyone who would think about killing someone, plan it, and then go through with it, is round the twist. Aren't they? Think about it."

"I am."

"A sane person simply cannot kill in cold blood. That's what sane *means*. And if that's not true, then do you really want to live on this planet any longer?"

Frank thought about it. "Depends. What are my alternatives, exactly?"

"What they should do, is get rid of all the detectives. Sack us all—"

"I haven't got to go back into uniform, have I?" Frank asked. "Only, I find the public don't vomit on you so often when you wear a suit."

"Sack all the detectives, and bring in a load of psychiatrists. They can interview all the suspects, find out which one is bonkers, and bung him away. Simple."

"What if more than one of them's bonkers?"

Don crossed his arms, and smiled. "In that case, you've got yourself a proper result, haven't you?"

It was a mild evening. Before the pub's dreariness could finally overcome them, like fumes from a faulty boiler, they decided to continue their conversation while walking across the common. Frank kept his eyes downwards; suburban dog owners were a thoughtless breed, he'd learned.

"The neatest way," he said, "to tie the gun to the money is still the direct way: he took out the money to buy the gun." He didn't especially believe it, but it needed to be said.

"I reckon that's even less likely now than it was before. Don't you?"

"Before what?" Frank asked.

"The son. Tom says his dad was upset about something on Thursday evening. Nobody noticed him upset before that, but he'd already taken the money out by then. So—if he withdrew the dosh to buy the gun, then he did so because he was already in fear of attack."

"And if he was in fear of attack, why wasn't he in a state? Yeah, fair enough." Frank thought about that. Don smoked; and thought, too, probably. "Which suggests that the money wasn't for the gun, but also, perhaps more significantly, that whatever the money *was* for, it was something that wasn't a cause for concern."

"Good point, Frank." Don exhaled slowly, looking away into nothing. "It does suggest that, doesn't it? He wasn't paying blackmail, for instance, if all our witnesses are right about his mood. The money wasn't connected to something frightening or shameful. So it was, as we've already speculated, something like a loan."

"That still leaves a number of questions—"

"You could say that, Frank, yes!"

"First of all, the son is the only person who reports him agitated, and that's on Thursday night; no one says so before, and no one says so *after,* either."

"Ah, yes . . . I see . . ."

"Which sounds as if the problem was resolved. But it wasn't—Bert was subsequently killed. Which is about as far from resolved as a problem can get."

"Perhaps he mistakenly believed he'd solved it, which is how he came to lower his guard sufficiently to get himself killed."

"No, that's no good," said Frank. "He was still carrying the gun. Why was he toting a gun, if he thought his problems were behind him?"

Don rolled his cigar between his fingers. Frank watched with some interest; it was a small cigar, already half-smoked, and if the DI wasn't quite nimble he was going to get his fingerprints altered. "Maybe that was *why* he was more relaxed—he'd bought a gun to protect himself."

"I can't believe carrying a gun would bring much peace of mind to a man like him. I wonder if he even knew how to fire a gun. I mean, I've never fired one, have you?"

"I have, actually."

That was news to Frank. "What, you've done a firearms course?"

"No, no. This was nothing to do with the police."

Right. There were some conversations with DI Packham which wise men did not pursue. "But I doubt if Bert had ever used a gun in his—oh hold on, mind, he was in the war, wasn't he?"

"Yes, but did they do a lot of shooting in the Battle of the Atlantic?" Don wondered. "Could you do much damage to a submarine with a pistol from the crow's nest of a convoy ship? Anyway, I agree with you. A man like Bert Rosen could only have taken up the gun out of total desperation. So whatever scant comfort it might give him, I can't believe it would work on him like a Valium." Don went back to staring into nothing, and also back to juggling his ever-shrinking cigar. After a few seconds of this, he said "Ow!" then he said "Bugger!" and then he bent down to retrieve his cigar stub from the ground. Frank looked elsewhere.

After a moment's first aid, Don removed his right index finger from his mouth, and said: "Something to beware of here, Frank. We're maybe putting too much weight on second-hand reports of someone's apparent mood. Bert spent a lifetime in politics—a certain amount of it under real threat—so he must have been a decent actor, good at hiding his feelings. Not perhaps from his own son, but from more casual acquaintances."

"All right then," said Frank, who increasingly felt that there was something completely wrong with this whole case. "That's true. So let's look at something more solid: a timetabling problem."

"Go on."

"Thursday night, seven-ish, Bert speaks to his son from his landline at home, he's worried about something. According to Rosa's statement, she saw him briefly about quarter to eight, then she went out to a meeting, got home ten thirty, and Bert was in bed. So *when* did he buy the gun?"

"Yes . . ." Don put his finger back in his mouth and, distracted, left it there. Frank hoped he wouldn't have to mention it; it wasn't a conversation you wanted to have with a senior officer.

"The incident room has had sight of phone records from his mobile and landline, and they offer nothing."

"No calls to Pizzas'n'Guns, delivery within thirty minutes or you get the bullets and garlic bread for free?"

"Nope." Frank remembered a documentary about body language he'd seen on BBC2. Something to do with how involuntary human movements were the same as those of other apes; but of more immediate relevance they'd conducted an experiment in which . . . well, it was worth a try. He put his right hand next to his mouth for a second, and then used it to rub his nose. Sure enough, the programme had been right: the DI mimicked him exactly. The finger-in-mouth embarrassment had been resolved. Amazing what you could pick up on telly. "Now," he continued, "if whatever's worrying Bert has been going on for some time, then no problem; he could have bought the gun the previous day, the previous week, the previous month. But there is some circumstantial evidence—not overlooking your point about not putting too much weight on interpretations of his mood—for his problem arising on the Thursday."

"The fact that he rang his son at all."

"Exactly. Bert suddenly rings Tom, for no ostensible reason. Which, given their recent relationship, is unusual enough for Tom to be quite surprised. Bert tries to ask him about something, but can't quite spit it out. He eventually decides, perhaps, that he doesn't want to spread his burden, doesn't want to drag his son into whatever unpleasantness he's got involved in, and that's the last anyone hears of Bert Rosen having something on his mind. Which, if all the ifs line up, suggests quite strongly that he bought the gun that evening, or at least that day."

"True," Don said.

"But *when?* Surely it takes an eighty-four-year-old retired insurance agent a bit longer than forty-odd minutes to find an illegal gun? Unless, you know—he'd certainly led an interesting life. But was he on good terms with any gangsters?"

"Or gangstas, come to that," said Don. "More likely to be gangstas than gangsters these days, from what our Kiwi mate told us. But I see what you mean. Can old Bert really just pop out for half an hour, in a quiet suburb, and come back with a shooter in his raincoat pocket? Good work, Frank. But what does it all mean?"

Frank sighed, and spread his hands. "I don't know, I don't get it at all. But if the ifs *do* work out, then could it mean that we're simply putting the piece marked 'gun' into the wrong hole?"

"It could. Yes, I'm afraid it could. Which is something to bear in mind, but doesn't actually take us anywhere specific at the moment." Don looked at his watch, and Frank wondered where they were off to next. "I think we'll pack it in now, start afresh in the morning."

"Pack it in now?" Frank looked at his own watch, though he wasn't sure why.

"Yes, I'm going out tonight, I need to shower and change first."

Frank looked at his watch again. He still wasn't sure why. "You're going out tonight?"

"Yes, Frank! It wasn't *me* that was murdered, you know."

"No, right. So—what are we doing first in the morning?"

"You choose, Frank. Better yet, ask Debbie's advice."

Chapter Fifteen

At nine minutes to six on Tuesday morning, a thought flitted across Frank Mitchell's mind as he lay awake in bed, and he reached out to snag its hind leg at the ankle. He made a mental note of its plumage, and then got up.

He was annoyed to find himself thinking about work when he wasn't at work; this broke one of his own most important rules. Even worse, it suggested that he was on his way to becoming a typical CID hack. *Got to watch that.*

At eight thirty, he picked Don up, and asked him if he'd had an enjoyable evening.

"Fine thanks."

That was that conversation done, then. Frank decided to share with the DI that which had forced him from his bed an hour or so earlier. "What if the money Bert took out wasn't handed over to anyone, after all? What if Bert was carrying it on him at the time of his death?"

"You mean, whatever he planned to do with it—"

"He hadn't done yet." Frank nodded. "And it was taken by his killer. Making the motive for the killing a simple robbery."

Don combed his black hair with his fingers. "He had his wallet on him when he was found dead, with money, cards, and so on still in it, so the assumption was that he hadn't been robbed. But you're saying perhaps he was . . ."

"But only of the three thousand pounds, that's right. You see what I'm thinking, Don? It would explain why we can't find a reasonable personal motive for anyone to kill him. It wasn't personal; it was just money."

Don held up a hand. "Hold on a mo. You're the one who keeps saying that three grand isn't enough to kill for."

Frank had been thinking about that, while he was supposed to be enjoying an audience with Master Joseph Mitchell at the Breaking of his Fast. "It just seems more believable, somehow, when it's straightforward robbery. Instead of planning a murder for such a pathetic amount, the killer simply saw the bundle of banknotes, needed them, grabbed them, killed their owner. Impulse. All over in a couple of minutes."

"And the killer wouldn't have known how much was in the bundle; just that it was a lot. Yes, you're right, it does sit easier on the imagination, somehow, this way round. Okay, but how did the killer—the thief—know the money was in Bert's pocket? I doubt he was flashing it around."

"They got a peek of it, when he was getting his appointments diary out, something like that?"

"No, sorry, Frank. I can't go with that. Bert grew up shit-poor. He was a working man all his days. The sale of his house, that was the first time in his life, I'd bet, that he'd ever had a penny sitting in the bank doing nothing. I'd be very surprised if he had ever held as much as three thousand pounds in his hands before. It would have been very safe indeed, carefully buttoned in an inside pocket, and no one would have got so much as a sniff of it."

"No, that's true." Frank wasn't sure he'd ever physically handled such a large sum either; this was a society run on credit, not cash. Damn. Had his lost morning been a waste? "In that case, we're more or less back full circle: if it was stolen, then the thief and the killer must have been the same person he was going to lend it to anyway. They simply decided to have it as a gift instead."

"From what we've heard," Don pointed out, "and from more than one witness, Bert would probably have *given* it as a gift if he'd been asked. There was no need to kill him."

"The person didn't know him that well, maybe? Didn't realise the sort of bloke he was."

"Or knew, but was too proud to ask." Don gave a small smile. "Yes, before you ask, I have known villains who would rather kill someone for a few quid than beg them for it."

"Not in the present case, though, I would think."

"Possibly not, Frank. I hate to say it—this is good stuff you're coming up with here—but there's another problem. How was the thief going to get Bert's money out of the library? He must have realised—surely, even in a panicky situation—that he'd be searched before leaving the library, once the body was discovered."

Frank felt his neck go cold. "But in that case," he said, speaking slowly, as if his mouth couldn't believe that his brain wasn't blundering into a pit of stakes, "then if the money *was* stolen from Bert in the library . . ."

"It could still be there," Don finished. He spoke slowly, too, Frank noticed. Perhaps his mouth feared the same stakes.

Bath Street Library had been searched after the discovery of Bert Rosen's body, but there had been no reason to search it to any great depth. There had been no suggestion of anything having been stolen from the corpse, and both the site of the killing and the weapon employed had been obvious and undisputed.

For that matter, Don and Frank's follow-up examination of the locus could hardly be described as microscopically detailed. It was an eyes-only search, conducted while the business of the library went on around them; closing the branch would have meant further disruption to an important public service—and more importantly, in Don's view, might have played into the hands of the council bosses. Besides, a sudden closure would have announced their thought processes to the murderer.

An amount of money, hidden in a hurry; that was what they were looking for.

"Not necessarily in a hurry," Frank pointed out. "The hiding place might have been recce'd beforehand."

"Either way, it's got to be something the thief can get to quickly, having killed Bert in the librarian's office, and without attracting attention. What I'm saying is, I don't think we need to tear the plaster off the walls or prise up the floorboards."

The office itself, as the specific location of the murder, had been thoroughly inspected on the night of the crime, so Don and Frank gave it only a cursory tossing. The lavatories, both staff and public, merited greater attention, as did the rest of the upper floor. Having found nothing, they moved on to the ground floor: lending, children's, disabled lavatories and all.

"I think I mentioned I used to go out with a library assistant," said Don, an hour and a half into the exploration.

"I think you did," Frank agreed.

"In her time, and I imagine it's the same now, the juniors began the day doing shelf-tidying—before the library opens to the public, they each take a section of shelving, and check that the books are in order, class number and alphabetical, and also straighten them, so that the spines are all aligned properly with the edge of the shelf."

Frank saw what he was getting at. "So if the thief simply stuffed the money behind the Agatha Christies, it'd probably have been found by now."

"I would think so. In which case, what we're looking for is—"

"Excuse me, could you tell me where you keep the consumer reports? I'm looking for kettles."

Don had got so used to not looking like a detective inspector that he was astonished to discover that he did, apparently, look like a library assistant. There could be worse things to be mistaken for, he reflected. "Kettles? Now then, are you looking for cheap or are you looking for good?"

"Good," replied the reader, firmly. "I've tried cheap, and it's a false economy."

"You do right," said Don. "You're not wrong. I think you'll find the consumer reports upstairs, in reference."

"Thanks a lot."

"Not at all. Good luck." The happy reader headed off towards the stairs, and Don turned back to Frank. "What we're looking for is a hidey-hole. Somewhere easy to reach, but out of sight. And the problem is—"

"We're finding too many, right." Frank looked around him. "This place is full of good, temporary hiding places. Behind the books, under the computer trolleys, in the draws of the issue desks . . ."

"I think you've put your—"

"Excuse me?"

Don smiled as he resumed his librarianship duties. "Yes, madam?"

"Have you seen *The Guardian*?"

Don nodded. "I saw it once, in 1982. I don't suppose it's changed much."

"Ah—no, what I actually meant was—"

"If you ask at the issue desk, madam," said Frank, "they'll be able to help you there. Thank you."

"Oh. Right."

"I think you've put your finger on it, Frank. The word *temporary* is the crucial one. We've found nothing, but we have established that the library is stuffed with hundreds of hiding places—especially for something that nobody's looking for."

Frank had, in between bibliographical interruptions, come to a similar conclusion. "The money could indeed have been hidden here, and then retrieved before we thought to look for it. Is it worth asking the incident room to compile a list of which of the suspects has visited the library since it reopened, by interviewing staff and studying CCTV footage of the entrance?"

Don thought about it, then shook his head, regretfully. "Hell of a lot of manpower for very little result, don't you think? Even if we knew for sure that the money had ever been hidden here, what's the betting the answer to which suspects have been here since would be all of them, or most of them? Given that they've all got good reasons to be here. With the possible exception of James Pomeroy."

"True enough. So we'll just report 'Nothing Found,' and leave it at that?"

"I think we'll have to. This was a neat idea, and very definitely worth doing, but I'm afraid we have to accept that it's eventually led nowhere. Don't be downhearted, Frank!"

"No, no."

"You were working well, coming up with all this. The old Geordie grey matter was bubbling away like nobody's business. That's how it goes in the detecting lark, you know that.

When you have eliminated the unlikely, whatever remains, no matter how blindingly obvious, is almost bound to be the truth. But first you have to do the eliminating. Speaking of which, it's time to start eliminating some of these bloody suspects."

Frank smiled. "Interesting choice of word."

"Don't tempt me, Frank. Don't tempt me."

Of all the former Mrs. Ticehursts which Frank might have chosen, he'd picked the one whose workplace was nearest to Cowden. He suspected that the DI might have made his selection using less prosaic criteria, but that was tough: he'd asked Frank to choose, and Frank had chosen Ms. Sheila Ticehurst, a City analyst, who had kindly made herself available for interview during her lunch hour. That she was the most recent Mrs. Ticehurst struck him as a handy bonus. That she still used her married name was intriguing, he thought.

"Didn't think they had lunch hours," said Don, "City analysts. I thought they were too important to eat lunch."

"I'm not entirely sure what a City analyst is," Frank admitted, "let alone what their dining habits are."

"Oh yes, City analyst," Don explained. "That's someone who analyses stuff in the City. Very high-powered."

Frank managed to find a parking space not more than ten minutes' walk from the wine bar in which Sheila had promised to meet them. "Can't entirely see Doug Ticehurst with a high-powered wife."

"Neither could she, obviously. That's why she divorced him."

In this assumption, it turned out, Don was significantly mistaken. "He dumped me," said Sheila, a not obviously attractive woman, who was drinking a not noticeably small glass of red wine, mopped up with some French bread and pâté. She gave an apologetic shrug, as if she still couldn't quite grasp what had happened. To a City analyst, no less.

"I must say, I find that hard to believe," said Don, his tones at their most gallant.

"Well, this is it," she said. "People do. They see poor old Dougie, not really making a great success of anything, and they hear about the women he's been married to: a barrister, a software development executive—"

"A City analyst," Don added, "brilliantly analysing things for the City."

"Quite; people see, as I think you have, a pattern. Successful women, good-looking but unambitious man, and they assume that sometime after the honeymoon, the women come to their senses, remember their careers, and quietly dispose of the handsome failure."

"But they're wrong?"

Sheila took a while to swallow some pâté and wash it down with some wine. She blinked several times, and continued swallowing, Frank fancied, even after all the food and wine had gone down. "I've actually met one of his other wives; Fiona. She's the barrister, in fact—company law, not criminal."

"Naturally," said Don.

"And she says the same as me. She'd still be with Dougie, if he'd still have her." Sheila gave a pale smile. "If that goes for all of them, then I suppose I'd be at the end of a long queue. Anyway, he'll have married another one soon."

"And divorced her, too?" asked Frank.

She nodded at him in sad approval. "Precisely."

Don coughed. "Is Doug—"

"No, Inspector. That's everyone's *second* idea. I can assure you Dougie is not gay, either knowingly or otherwise. Fiona confirms my views on that."

"I appreciate your candour, Sheila. I realise this is a painful business for you."

An expression of real concern creased her face. "He's not a serious suspect, is he? For murder, I mean?"

"Let me say," Don replied, "that he is not at the top of our list. We simply need to try and . . . well, understand him a bit better."

"There I can help you, I think. Even though it's too late to help me." She mopped her mouth with a thoroughly crumpled paper napkin. "It's taken me and Fiona a good few bottles of red to sort it out." She smiled. "But I think we've got it, now. This murder of yours, it's the old man killed in a library, is that right? I saw it on the local news."

"That's the case we're working on, yes."

"Do you know why Dougie goes to the library so much?"

"Well," said Don, "we assumed that he was a bit lonely, what with the divorce and so on, and that perhaps he was hoping to meet—"

She held up two hands; an economical and highly effective gesture, Frank noted, which he guessed served her well in the high-powered world of City analysing. It sounded like the sort of profession which would involve shutting people up quite a lot, especially if you were a woman. "No, I don't mean why did he get involved with this protest group. I'm sure you're right about his motives in that regard. I meant—why is he such a regular patron of the public library?"

"Goes there to borrow books, I suppose," Frank suggested.

"But do you know what sort of books?"

"Ah," said Don, some light dawning. "Self-improvement

manuals. Would that be right?"

"You've got it, Inspector. If someone repeatedly marries, and never stays married, and is always the one who brings the marriage to an end, what would you assume about him? Now that you know he's not gay, that is."

"How would I analyse the situation, you mean? Well . . ." Don made a show of thinking about it, though Frank was pretty sure he didn't need to. "He must be getting married for a reason which never, in reality, works out."

"Correct." She lit a menthol cigarette, as if to reward herself for her student's progress.

"And given the social status of his various brides, and the nature of his favoured reading matter, I would have to conclude that his aim is, as the books proclaim, self-improvement."

"Not quite." She held up just one finger this time. It was still pretty impressive, Frank thought. "Almost, but not quite. He doesn't want to improve *himself*—"

"He marries women who he hopes will improve him," said Frank, suddenly seeing it.

"Exactly! Dougie is looking for an ambitious, successful wife who will transform him into an ambitious, successful husband. Not understanding, I'm afraid, that if we'd wanted such a man, we wouldn't have been attracted to poor Dougie in the first place. Fiona and I—and the others, I'm sure—meet men like that all day every day. Dougie was different: attractive, nice, generous."

"He marries women who he hopes will bully him into being more than he is, and then he dumps them when they won't?" Frank couldn't help himself; this just seemed awful to him. "I think you could add 'ruthless' to the list of his qualities, couldn't you?"

Sheila Ticehurst's mouth snapped shut, and her eyes went

quiet. She'd been quite happy to talk to them all day, provided the topic was her ex-husband's niceness. But Frank's impetuous honesty, once uttered, could not be recalled, and the interview was, effectively, at an end.

Chapter Sixteen

"Not to worry, Frank. I think we'd got what we needed." One thing about Don Packham as a boss: he never had a go at you if you cocked something up through excessive engagement. If you cocked it up because you couldn't be bothered, by contrast, then you would feel the imprint of his boot right up your bum and into your colon for months afterwards.

"We found out that there's nothing sinister about the many wives of Dougie Ticehurst, you mean? Nothing that Bert might have found out, for instance, which Doug might have killed him for." Frank started the car.

"That," Don agreed, "but also that Doug Ticehurst is, as you rightly said, ruthless to the point of—"

Frank's mobile rang. He turned the car off. "DC Mitchell speaking."

"Hi, Frank, it's Nicole here—from Scenes?"

"Oh right, hi, Nicole." He mouthed *SOCO* at Don.

"I've just heard that you and your DI have been doing a research of Bath Street Library?"

Oh, shit, thought Frank: injured professional pride. "Yeah, listen Nicole, this was to do with something new that came up, it's absolutely no reflection on—"

"No, don't panic, Frank, I'm not ringing up to give you a

bollocking. Just tell me, you were looking for some victim's property, hidden, yeah? How big an item?"

"Just a pile of bank notes—about three thousand quid, presumably in large denominations."

"Right . . . well, I should think this would do. I noticed it at the time, but it wasn't relevant to anything—we weren't told we were looking for hidey-holes!"

"No absolutely, quite right, our fault not yours." *Knew it,* Frank thought. "So what's this hiding place?" Don raised his eyebrows; Frank replied with a shrug.

"Do you want to have a butcher's at it? I can meet you there in ten minutes," Nicole offered.

"Make it half an hour, can you?"

Twenty-seven minutes later, Nicole from Scenes of Crime gave Frank a huge smile with her teeth and eyelashes, gave Don a curt "Sir," and led the two detectives past Horror & Fantasy, towards 920 (Biography & Autobiography) which occupied a large bay against the back wall of the ground floor. She knelt down next to the life stories of Mao, Mountbatten, and Muggeridge, and indicated the false skirting board between the carpet-tiled floor and the front of the lowest bookshelf.

"I noticed it on the night of the murder," she explained, "because it was a bit clean, whereas the surround was quite dusty."

"Contracting out," said Don. "The cleaning firm is private sector these days, not council labour."

"Whatever, it had a polished look about it. So . . ." She pushed at a length of the skirting, using just two fingers, and it gave almost immediately. She pulled the piece away, and shone a pen torch into the small cavity thus revealed.

"I notice you're wearing gloves," said Don.

"No, don't get excited, just habit. I tested it the other

night, and I did it again just now while I was waiting for you two, and there's no prints."

"None at all?"

"That's the good news, I would think—no prints at all, no scuff marks from shoes, no dust, nothing."

"So it *has* been used as a hidey-hole," said Frank. "It's been wiped clean."

"Not my department, guys," Nicole replied, "but it sounds pretty likely, doesn't it?"

"But it was empty when you checked it on the night?" Don asked.

"Yup," said Nicole. "Empty then, empty now." She left them with their empty mouse hole, taking her kit and their thanks with her.

"So it *wasn't* used," said Don, when he and Frank were alone. He had his warrant card ready in his hand this time, to put off any information-hungry members of the public. "Not in this case, anyway. There's no point in the thief hiding it after the murder and then retrieving it the same night."

"He'd be caught with it on him," said Frank. "You're right. Okay, how about this: Bert was supposed to have the money on him that night, so the killer planned to take it, kill Bert, hide the cash in this pre-prepared place, come back for it after the police had given up the building. He wiped it clean after he'd done his recce; would have wiped it again, after he'd put the money in there."

"But Bert didn't bring the money," Don carried on. "For whatever reason. And the killer killed him anyway—in anger."

"Or else he didn't know until *after* he'd killed him that Bert didn't have the money. So the hidey-hole was prepared, but never used."

"Two possibilities, then: Bert never brought the money in

here, in which case he'd already done whatever he was going to do with it; or the killer did get it, and somehow managed to evade the scrupulous search techniques of our painstaking, eagle-eyed super-uniforms. On which possibility I'm not going to comment."

"Neither am I," said Frank.

"Oh, I was rather hoping you would."

"You'll be disappointed, I'm afraid," said Frank, who still had friends in the uniform branch—an accusation which could never be made against Don Packham.

Still, both men thought about the possibility. Could the money have been smuggled out of the library that night?

"No. Three thousand quid in notes?" said Don, eventually. "No, even a bunch of uniforms in the early hours of the morning couldn't miss that. They might nick it, but they wouldn't miss it, surely."

"And they were searching in pairs," Frank reminded him, "in accordance with guidelines. No, it would have been noticed, and logged, and once the missing money angle came up, the collator would have spotted it. Or someone would have remembered it, anyway."

"All right then, where *is* the money? Rosa says she's searched her and her Dad's place and can't find it."

"Theoretically she could be lying, to avoid paying tax on it or something, but that does seem pretty far-fetched."

"It does. We may have to get her place done again, even so. For the money, or for something Bert might have spent it on."

The house Rosa had shared with her father had already been searched, for something obvious to provide a motive: threatening letter, evidence of blackmail, that sort of thing. With this in mind, Frank said: "Same thing applies, though, doesn't it? If the money was there, the search team couldn't have missed it. Unless it was seriously well hidden. And they'd have noted it."

"Somebody's got the money, Frank. It's got to be somewhere."

"Oh, it's you two. I was just about to phone council security."

"Hello, Kimberley," said Don. Frank busied himself with his notebook. "Are we causing a disturbance?"

"One of our regulars reported that she couldn't get at the 920s, because there were some strange people loitering there."

"She was right," said Don. "Sorry about that."

Kimberley Riggs reached past him, and plucked a biography of Muhammad Ali off the shelf. "Is this the one, Mrs. O'Rourke?" she called.

A nervous-looking woman in her seventies scuttled over and took the book from the girl's hand, without making eye contact with the strange men. "Thanks, darling. Everything all right over here?"

"Don't worry, Mrs. O'Rourke. They're only coppers."

Mrs. O'Rourke risked a glance at Don. "What, both of them?"

Kimberley giggled. "I think one of them's doing community service."

Once the fight fan had retreated to the safety of the issues desk, Don asked: "Have you got a moment, Kimberley?"

"Not really. I am on duty."

"Well, so are we, love. That's the thing."

"You haven't arrested anyone yet, then."

"We're getting closer, I think we can say that. Isn't that right, Frank?"

It was news to Frank. "Definitely, sir. Getting closer all the time."

"I hope so," said Kimberley, looking for the moment much more like a teenage girl than either a library assistant or a shop steward. "It's just terrible, I just can't . . . the only comfort is that right up to the moment he died, he was active. On the very day he died . . ." Her voice faded.

"You're absolutely right," Don told her. "Not everyone has the strength of character to keep up the struggle year after year, right till the end of their lives."

She shook her head—in disgust, evidently. "Some people give up after a couple of years. And then they spend the rest of their lives talking about how cool they were."

Think I can guess who that was aimed at, Frank thought.

"Of course," said Don, "to be fair, life has its distractions, doesn't it? You fall in love, you have kids, you get a career . . ."

"Yeah, yeah." Her face showed how little she thought of that argument—and how often she'd heard it before. "Bert was married, Bert had kids, Bert had a full-time job. And how about Dot? She never misses a departmental union meeting, and her husband's bedridden."

"Married twice, in fact," Don said. "Bert was. I only knew him when he was old, as you did, but you could see from his face that he must've been a good-looking lad. Bet he had the girls in the Young Communist League queuing up, eh? In his day."

And Frank could see from Kimberley's face that the idea—of an eighty-four-year-old man having been, decades before she was born, a "good-looking lad" simply had no real meaning for her. "Yeah, no," she said. "Yeah, I'll bet."

Don smiled, and let her go. "No need to ask the final question, Frank. Was there, really?"

Frank was impressed, but he wasn't sure how to express it. It was easy for a senior officer to compliment a junior—even if most of them, in practice, found it impossible—but how did it work the other way around? It was impressive, though; Don liked to watch faces, and he'd taught Frank to do the same, and both of them had seen in Kimberley's expression complete innocence of the only possible motive they'd been able to think up for her. She hadn't had a crush on Bert Rosen, that was clear. But equally clear, without having been directly addressed at all, was that even if Bert had felt that way about her—she hadn't known about it. If she had, she'd have blushed, at the least, or exhibited distaste, or annoyance, or even shame. But she hadn't; all they saw on her face was a generation gap of imagination which no amount of comradeship could ever hope to bridge. And if she hadn't known that he fancied her, then it didn't matter whether he did or not: she had no motive.

But how did you tell your boss that you thought he'd done brilliantly, without sounding like you were taking the piss?

"I reckon you're right, Don," was what Frank settled for. "Reckon we can cross her off the list."

"Yeah . . ." Don was tapping his lighter against his chin. Surely even *he* wasn't about to light up in a library? "Unfortunately, the same can't be said of Dot Estevez. If she's got a bedridden husband, then she might have a very compelling reason for taking the redundancy offer."

Bugger, thought Frank: I missed that.

"Pull over a minute, will you?" Don asked Frank, as they drove from Bath Street to Dot's house.

Frank, who'd been on the CID driving course—the "Skids and Prangs Diploma," as one of his haughtier colleagues called it—made a fairly impressive emergency stop, subsequent to an even more impressive emergency skid from the centre of the road over to the kerb. "What is it, Don?"

"No, sorry mate, it's nothing. It was just an idea struck—did you see *that?*"

Frank had indeed seen the angry woman in the 4x4 raising the middle finger of her right hand in their direction. "Very rude," he said.

"Rude?" Don raised his own middle finger, and the one next to it, forming the time-honoured British signal for "Go away," the immortal V-sign. "*That's* rude," he said. "Giving the finger is just some stupid American thing she's picked up from some girlie TV show. It's like saying heck instead of hell. Or drinking decaffeinated coffee. Good god, you'd think people could at least be patriotic with their obscenities, wouldn't you?"

"They should make it a federal offence," said Frank, but his wit went unobserved on this occasion.

"Bloody right. She should be thrown in jail for that." Don peered along the road, in the direction the 4x4 had taken. "In fact, do you think we could catch her?"

"Possibly not," Frank advised. "What was your idea?"

"Hmm? Oh, that. Yes. Call up your pet SOCO, will you? We need to see her again."

Frank pressed the phone against his face, glad that it wasn't one of the more fashionable, thumb-sized models; the bigger it was, the more blush it covered. She *wasn't* his pet. "Hello, Nicole? It's Frank Mitchell—yeah, fine. Have you got time for another meet, just briefly? DI Packham would like a word. Back at the library?" Don nodded. "Yeah, that'd be great. Thanks."

Nicole was parked outside the library, and on the whole Frank thought it might be less complicated if they met in her car. There was something about Don in a library which seemed to attract . . . well, *silliness,* basically. And they were supposed to be investigating a murder, which was supposed to be a serious business.

"Thanks for seeing us again, Nicole," said Don, sliding onto the back seat. "What I wondered was: when you searched Bert Rosen's house, the house he shared with his daughter, did you find where he kept his gun?"

She shook her head. "No sign at all; no cleaning equipment, no residue of oil or anything else. Absolutely nothing to say a gun had ever been in the place."

"That's what I thought, from the report." Don was staring off into space, so he missed the SOCO's eye-rolling. Frank gave her an apologetic smile. "To you, does that suggest he hadn't owned the gun for long?"

"Assuming there's nowhere else he might have kept it, then yes, could be. But there was something else, too—no ammunition. None in the house, none on the body, and none in the gun."

"Well," Frank explained, "we thought he didn't want any ammo because he wasn't really planning to shoot anyone. Just to threaten someone who he thought might be planning to attack him. And being a responsible citizen he wouldn't want to run the risk of having a loaded gun around, or even a gun and ammunition kept separately."

She gave him a sceptical look. "So you're saying he's a responsible citizen—and he defends himself from threats by buying an illegal firearm, albeit unloaded, instead of talking to the cops?"

"He didn't really trust cops," said Don. "He was an old Communist, you know."

She wasn't convinced. "I don't care if he was Fidel Castro, if someone's going to attack you, you call the police, surely?"

It cost Don visible effort to bring his attention back from

wherever it had floated in the last few minutes. "Bert was an old East End Jew," he told her, once he was ninety percent back in the car. "When he was growing up, the cops were probably the ones most *likely* to attack you. Then he was a red in the 1950s, a trade union militant in the seventies, a campaigner against police racism in the eighties . . ."

"Yeah, I take your point, but—"

"I guarantee that man never received a single phone call in his life that wasn't listened to by Special Branch. But having said all that—a gun? I'm with you, Nicole. It doesn't work for me either."

Back in his own car, their journey to Dot's resumed, Frank asked: "So what do we make of all that, then?"

"I don't know . . . I suppose it's a negative, so it doesn't really prove anything, but perhaps it reinforces the idea that Bert bought the gun in the last few days before he died. If true, and added to other equally iffy bits of quasi-evidence, that would mean that the whole business occupies a pretty brief timescale. A threat to Bert arises, Bert gets a gun, Bert gets killed. And Bert takes a pile of money out of his savings, though we don't know where that fits in the running order."

"But all of it within a few days."

"It's looking that way, isn't it?"

Dot didn't look as if she was enjoying her day off. If anything, she looked more flustered at home than she did at work. She answered the door holding a sweatshirt in one hand and a bag of potatoes in the other. The lack of enthusiasm in her greeting, Don thought, was caused less by fear of arrest for murder, than fear that they would steal some time from her which she was unable to spare.

Don immediately came to a decision: there was no point in asking her blunt questions about early retirement. If there was anything to tell, she wasn't going to tell it, and if she lied about it, they wouldn't be able to spot it; Dot's face was the perfect place for a lie to hide, amidst all that worry.

He spoke quickly, to pre-empt Frank. "Sorry to bother you, Dot. I can see you're up to your eyes. We really just wanted to ask you a quick question about two of your LOFE colleagues. Is, ah . . ." He pointed towards the staircase. "Is this a bad time?"

At least they got her to sit down long enough to drink half a cup of tea with them, and eat a biscuit—or, if not actually eat it, then certainly give it a damn good looking at. That would count as their good deed for the day, Don thought; except, of course, that the chores which kept Dot on her feet were not imaginary ones. If they weren't done now, they'd have to be done later.

"He's not well, I understand? John, isn't it?"

In a plain voice which suggested that she'd told the tale many times before—and that no matter how boring it became to her as a story, she was no nearer to comprehending it as a series of actual events—Dot said: "Two years ago, he went to see the GP about a pain in his back. Right after breakfast, just popped in on his way to work; they started his cancer treatment the following afternoon. He never went into work again."

"I'm so sorry," said Don. "That's terrible. Is he dying?"

"Not really. Well, *no.* The treatment has been quite successful. But he's not—you know, he can't be left on his own."

It's all in code, thought Don; it generally is. What was she saying, exactly; was it some sort of brain cancer, or had a complication of the treatment itself disabled him? He'd ask Frank later to ask Debbie; handy to have a nurse in the family.

The details didn't matter anyway. That her husband was

permanently ill was enough to give her an excellent reason to make a deal with the council, no matter how it went against her heart and her history. Would she, having made such a deal, kill to protect it? He couldn't picture it. But imagination and common sense were often, as he knew well, a feeble match for real life. Most victims of homicide loved, liked, or were related to their killers; sometimes all three. Murderers kill friends, more often than they kill strangers.

"We won't take up much more of your time, Dot. I just wanted to ask you whether you knew what kind of history there is between Bert and Marjorie McDonald?"

"History?"

"We've got the impression that Marjorie wasn't especially fond of him. Was that just because—"

"Oh, you mean that business about the halfway-house?"

Don fixed a noncommittal smile to his face. "That caused a bit of bad feeling, did it?"

"Well, people worry, don't they? About property prices and so on. But of course, Bert was all for it."

"As you'd expect. I don't suppose the value of his house was ever uppermost in his mind."

"But as it turned out, you see, Bert sold up anyway—he moved in with his daughter. I think, perhaps, Marjorie thought—well, it's all right for him, what about the rest of us?"

They left her to her labours. Outside, Frank asked: "Does that take Marjorie off the list, because now we know why she wasn't all that fond of Bert, and it's nothing to do with anything; or does it put her back on the list, because she does at least have a reason to dislike him, however petty?"

"A good, if convoluted, question, Frank. On the whole, I think it means that she's worth another little chat. But first, do you have, in your magic notebook, a complete list of the items found on Bert's deceased person? Pocket contents, and that?"

"Yeah, hold on." They got into the car, and Frank found the appropriate page. "Few pounds in notes and change. One handkerchief, red."

"Naturally. The workers' blood had dyed its every fold, no doubt."

"Not specified," said Frank. "One crumpled supermarket carrier bag, plastic. Various keys on key ring with union logo fob. Pair of glasses, reading. Wallet, leather. One handgun, obviously. Packet of mints."

"No rubber bands, are there?"

"Rubber bands? Oh. See what you mean." Frank scanned the rest of the list. "No, nothing like that. As far as I can see, nothing that might be used to hold a bundle of banknotes. None of those paper bands the bank put round them. But then, if the money was stolen from him, the thief would have taken it with the bands still on, wouldn't he? More convenient."

"I expect so. It was just a thought. No bank receipts, anything at all that might suggest he had the money on him when he went into the library?"

"Nothing to suggest he did," said Frank, having read the whole list through again, twice. "Nothing to prove he didn't."

"Oh well, forget it." Don sighed, and stretched his shoulders. "If it wasn't for dead ends, we wouldn't get no ends at all."

Chapter Seventeen

They drove in the general direction of nowhere in particular, but not by the direct route.

Frank was used to aimless driving on days when Don was too down to make decisions, but that wasn't it today; the DI's unusually extended run of equanimity seemed to be continuing. This was something rarer, and potentially more productive—this was Detective Inspector Packham having a ponder. It was pretty intensive pondering, too, judging by the degree of lip-chewing, chin-tapping, and assorted grunting which accompanied it. Don was, according to all available clues, on the edge of a major thought.

Can't be lunch, thought Frank; we've had that.

"Pomeroy," said Don, after ten minutes or so of contemplation. "James Pomeroy. Our trendy Tory."

"Oh, aye," said Frank.

"We're agreed that if his participation in the campaign to save Bath Street Library is surprising, then his participation in the occupation of the library is downright astonishing. Yes?"

"I'll go along with that."

"And that it makes sense only if he stayed behind in order

to kill Bert. Which would, presumably, mean that Bert knew something about him."

"But what?"

"Haven't we been past that kebab place already, Frank?"

"No, sir, only three times."

Don began to give him a look, but gave up halfway through. "Do we know what Pomeroy actually did at the library that night? Is there any indication of how he spent his time?"

"I think I have got something in my notes. Shall I pull over?"

"I think you'd better, don't you? Unless you're confident of your ability to read with one eye and drive with the other."

"No, that wasn't what I—"

"I used to know a bus driver who did that. He was studying for an Open University degree. Classics, I think."

Frank swung the car onto a deserted garage forecourt. "This'll do."

"Mad bastard, he was," said Don. "His widow was a good sort, though."

"Here we are," said Frank, notebook open on the dashboard. "According to statements, he just spent his time as you'd expect, chatting to some fellow politicos."

"Anyone in particular?"

"Mostly, it seems, James spent his time with a LibDem ward chairman called Patrick Underwood. Well, I don't suppose there were many other Conservatives there to keep him company."

"This Underwood, he's a dissident in his party, presumably."

"According to Dot, yes. And according to the local rag, a maverick candidate for leader of the group, should the current administration totter."

"Well, well. Let's give him a bell."

"I am a gentleman, I hope," said the gentleman who lived in what the developers called a contemporary townhouse—meaning that it was even slimmer and had an even smaller front yard than traditional townhouses—on the outskirts of south Cowden.

He didn't *look* gay, Don decided. A fat man in his early sixties, he seemed to live alone, and had about him the air of one who was moderately prosperous, in a small-business sort of way. But Don didn't think he was gay. Not that he pretended to be infallible in such matters. He had wondered about it: could James Pomeroy have been discreetly meeting a lover, or potential lover at the library occupation? He lived with a partner in a posh flat, but when all was said and done he was a Tory politician; if that tribe had known how to keep their trousers on, they'd still be in power.

Thus: the conversation between Patrick Underwood and James must have been about politics. Or football. Or wine. Or the weather. Or . . .

"I'm sure you are a gentleman, Mr. Underwood, but—"

"There can be no buts, Inspector, I'm afraid; you are asking me to divulge the contents of a private conversation, which has nothing to do with the matter you're investigating. I have already stretched a point, given the importance of the matter at hand, and confirmed that Councillor Pomeroy and I enjoyed a conversation—"

"A lengthy conversation?" Frank asked, notebook in hand. Good lad, thought Don; interrupt the rhythm of the pompous bugger's lectures—that'll rattle him.

"A conversation of some duration, yes," Underwood allowed. "I can confirm that such a conversation took place, but I cannot—I will not—say what it was about."

"I must remind you, Mr. Underwood, this is a murder invest—"

"Oh please, Inspector!" Underwood winced, and held his hands protectively in front of him. "Such a dreadful cliché—and one which, as you well know, has no legal force whatsoever."

It was pretty obvious from the start that he wasn't going to budge. Still, Don was happy to keep trying. He kept trying for half an hour, in fact, because the way he looked at it, it was better to waste as much of this pompous ass's time as possible than . . . well, than not to waste it.

Eventually, Mr. Underwood became bored with the game—or with his audience, perhaps—and, when his phone rang, he made it clear that this would be a convenient moment for the detectives to leave. They did so, not with much grace, and were just about to get into Frank's car when Frank's mobile rang.

"It's Mr. Underwood," Frank reported. "We have been recalled."

They both looked at up at a living room window on the second floor of the contemporary townhouse. Underwood stood framed within it, mobile to his ear, impatiently gesturing at them to come back in.

"Why couldn't the old tosspot just bang on the window?" Don wondered. "Do you suppose he gets free local calls on his network?"

"I have changed my mind," Underwood told them, as soon as they entered the room. His cool pomposity had been replaced, Don sensed, with sweaty anger. "Councillor Pomeroy and I were discussing the possibility of his joining the Liberal Democrats."

"A defection? Ah yes," Don smiled. "Now, that does make sense."

"Why did you change your mind about telling us?" Frank asked.

Mr. Underwood composed himself to give them an answer they would like, but unfortunately Don spotted him doing it, and interrupted his preparations with a rude guffaw. "That phone call you took just as we were leaving—Pomeroy's not joining your lot after all, is he? Oh dear oh dear! What, then: is he to head up a public services reform think tank for New Labour?"

"One of my party colleagues has heard certain rumours," Underwood confirmed. His face clouded. "Sod James Pomeroy, and sod the gentleman's agreement he rode in on!"

No one was home, at Councillor Pomeroy's residence. Instead, upon pressing the doorbell, Frank was invited by an electronic voice to leave a message via the entry phone.

"An answering machine for doors, what will they think of next," said Don. "Drip-dry shirts and portable record players, most likely."

"Shall I leave a message?" Frank asked.

"Sod that. Get him on the mobile."

That proved harder done than said, James Pomeroy being such an important and busy man, but eventually Don was able to speak to the councillor, who informed him that he could not meet them immediately, as he was officiating at a reception for a visiting gay rugby team from the USA.

"I didn't know they played rugby," Don told him. "Bit of a rough game for them, isn't it?"

"You disappoint me, Inspector. I wouldn't have expected such stereotyping from you. Why shouldn't gays—"

"Gays? No, I meant Yanks."

They made an arrangement to meet later on that evening. As Frank turned towards the car, Don chuckled. "Tell you what, we will leave him a message." He pressed the doorbell, and when instructed to speak clearly following the tone, he said, in a high, piercing voice: "This is Lady Thatcher. We know what you've been up to, young man, and you've let us down badly. You deserve a jolly good spanking."

"Ah, Don," said Frank. "Was that a good idea?"

"Relax, Frank. He won't know it was us."

Frank said nothing; silently, he pointed above the door, at the blinking light of the security camera.

"Oh bloody hell, Frank—you might have warned me!"

Marjorie McDonald was clearly exhausted, having finished her latest round of deliveries only five minutes before the detectives knocked on her door, and was almost pathetically grateful when Don told her to sit down while he made her a cup of tea.

"It's not easy," she said, once the three of them were seated in her living room. "It's not easy, on your own."

"It can't be," Don sympathised. "And I suppose the vicious circle is that you're less likely to meet anyone, because you're too busy coping."

She sipped her tea. "That's nice. Thanks. You know, I actually tried computer dating once, a couple of years back."

"Really? Any good?"

"Well, to be fair, the computer did pair me up with several guys who matched my age, my weight, my personality, and my lifestyle." She smiled. "Pity really, I'd have preferred someone normal."

That brought a good laugh from Don which, Frank noticed, she seemed to find as comforting as the tea.

Don obviously noted it too, as he chose this moment to ask the question they had come here to resolve. "You felt Bert let you all down, didn't you, Marjorie? When he supported the halfway-house for alcoholics. And then sold his house before it was opened."

Her sigh spoke of regret far more than it did of fatigue, and Frank could almost see Don crossing her off his mental list of suspects. "I called him all sorts, I'm afraid. I wish I hadn't, now. We were never close friends, but he was a decent neighbour. He only did what he thought was right. And, you know, who was the hypocrite, really? Everyone agrees there should be places like that, but no one wants them on their own doorstep. Except Bert Rosen."

"Of course, it wasn't his doorstep for long, as it turned out."

"I had a go at him over that, and we never really got back on good terms afterwards." She put her mug down, and blew her nose on a tissue. "I know what it was, now."

"How do you mean?"

"He was alone, like me. He was widowed too, you know? And then he *wasn't* alone—it was all so simple. He just sold up, moved in with his daughter. Moved on."

"You envied him?"

She laughed, which didn't go too well; she had to grab for the tissues again. "I know how that sounds. I mean, I didn't honestly want to swap my life for that of a widowed man in his eighties! But you don't always think clearly when you're . . . when you're not thinking clearly."

"It sounds as if you'd got over it all by the time he died."

She nodded. "Oh yes, it was just nonsense. It's not as if I'm alone, either, am I? I've got the kids. But it's just so *hard* all the time. Everything, every day. I suppose I should be grateful, really."

"Grateful?"

"I suppose it'd be even worse if I'd been divorced—no pension."

In the car, Frank said: "Presumably that's why Doug Ticehurst is so broke—he's not only divorced, he's divorced over and again."

"It is an expensive business, from what I've heard," said Don, with all the smugness of a lifelong bachelor. "Even if there aren't any children, and your ex earns more than you do, there's always the lawyers to feed." He looked at his watch. "Right—just time for some fish and chips before we go and arrest James Pomeroy for murder."

"Hmm," said Frank.

"Hmm?"

"Just thinking—let's hope he hasn't had a chance to look at his security tape yet."

"Shut up, Frank. You'll put me off my pickled egg."

"I was intrigued by your message, Inspector," said James Pomeroy, showing them through to the aquatically enhanced living room.

Don chose not to wonder—let alone to ask—which message he was referring to. "We're going to need some straight answers from you now, Councillor," he said. "And it's only fair to warn you that if we don't get them, you will undoubtedly end this interview as our prime suspect for the killing of Bert Rosen."

Pomeroy cocked his head. "You've been talking to someone, I think."

"We have spoken to many people," Don replied. "Now it's your turn. You're about to defect from the Conservative Party. Yes?"

"*Defect* is perhaps a little melodramatic. It conjures images of a deserted Berlin bridge by moonlight. Politics in Cowden is less theatrical—if only marginally."

Don said nothing. Pomeroy had to understand that this

was a time for confession, not badinage.

The message seemed to get through. "You're quite right. I have come to the painful conclusion that there is no future in British political life for the Conservative Party, as it is at present constituted. I am scarcely alone in having such thoughts, I'm sure you'd agree."

Don was far from confident that Pomeroy's pessimism was justified. The world's oldest and most successful political party had cheated death before, in its long history. But, again, this was not the time for intellectual debate. "You don't believe you'll ever hold office again as a Conservative," he said, "so you're moving on. As you say, you're hardly the first—so why the secrecy?"

"Negotiations have been ongoing," said Pomeroy, bluntly, "concerning my price. I haven't—or, I should say, *hadn't,* until very recently—quite made up my mind as to which rival camp might best provide a home for my talents."

That rang true, Don thought. Pomeroy was a colourful character in an age of blandness; his change of allegiance would be worth some printer's ink, and not only in the local press. "I can see that the timing of your announcement had to be perfect—your value on the political commodities market could tumble alarmingly, if you didn't control the moment."

"What a charmingly cynical turn of phrase you have, Inspector. You've never considered standing for office yourself?"

"They've yet to build the party that could hold me," said Don. "Besides, my evenings are fully booked. I suppose if Bert had found out about your intentions—"

"And Comrade Rosen tended to learn of everything that occurred in Cowden politics, sooner or later,"

Pomeroy interrupted, nodding.

"He could have used that knowledge to bugger things up nicely for various of his opponents at once: the Tories, your new party, and the party you ultimately rejected."

"Not only could he have, but he would have taken great pleasure in doing so." Pomeroy's easy smile vanished for a moment. "I really am very sorry he's dead, you know. The way a soccer fan would feel, on hearing that Pele was no more." He frowned. "Or am I thinking of Nobby Stiles?"

"You were at the library that night to continue your negotiations with the LibDems?"

"Precisely. I should have known better, but matters were approaching a critical juncture."

"Tautology," Don said. "And Bert twigged what was going on?"

"Of course he did." Pomeroy laughed. "The old bastard, I was guilty of hubris if I thought I could evade his scandal-detector. That's why I stayed when the occupation began, you see."

"To kill him?" Frank asked.

"Not at all, Constable, not at all. Far from bumping him off, I hoped to sound him out."

"To find out how much he knew, or suspected," Don said. "And what he was planning to do about it. And *then* bump him off."

"To find all that out, yes—and having established it, to see if he, too, might not be open to a little late-night negotiation. He was the most dangerous kind of idealist, you know: a pragmatic one."

"What did you think you could offer him in exchange for his silence? Apart from a ligature, that is."

"Well, as my opening bid, I thought I might offer to take a much more public and vigorous role in supporting LOFE—a strategy which, in the best tradition of such deals, could have served us both."

"Could have?"

"Yes, Inspector. Try as I might, I never did get a chance to speak to Bert on his own. And now, of course, I never shall."

"And now, of course," Don echoed, "you don't need to."

Chapter Eighteen

"All makes sense," Frank commented, as they walked back to the car, "but we've only his word for it. It makes just as good sense that Bert found out, threatened to ruin Pomeroy's precious timing, and Pomeroy killed him."

"Hmm," Don replied—or rather, didn't reply; Frank turned to find the DI standing several feet behind him, tapping a small cigar rhythmically against his chin.

"Don?"

"I'm just thinking . . ."

Frank waited a moment, to see if any more clues might be forthcoming. Once it was clear that there wouldn't be, he said: "Thinking what?"

"About what Marjorie McDonald said. How getting divorced makes you poor."

"Right . . ."

"But why is Cyril Mowbray so poor?"

"Well . . ." Was he missing something here? "We've just said, haven't we? Because his marriage has broken up."

"No, but why specifically is *he* so very poor? He was an army officer for years, he must be on a pension. And he must earn something, even if it's not much, from the window cleaning. Okay, so he's split with his wife, but he's not actually divorced, don't forget—there's no lawyers' bills yet."

"That's true."

"I suppose there's two rents to pay, assuming he has to pay hers as well as his."

"Would he being paying both, do you think?"

"She might insist on it. Seeing that the separation is his fault."

"Is it his fault?"

Don smiled. "I think that's how she sees it; he should have made a better go of the army, but he didn't. And having retired from the army, without having achieved the rank of field marshal, he should have made a better go at civilian life. Which in her book doesn't mean wiping other people's double glazing with a bit of grimy chamois. Why, Frank—that's almost like being in service."

Okay, thought Frank, but in that case . . . "So, you've answered your own question, haven't you? Cyril's broke because he's paying his ex-wife's rent."

"Yeah, could be."

"Don? Shall we get in the car?"

"What? Oh right, sorry." Don lit his cigar, and slid into the passenger seat. "I wonder if he's paying her debts, too."

"What debts?"

"Woman like that's bound to have debts. Credit cards, store cards, whatever. I wouldn't be surprised if she landed him with those, as well. It's a man's job to provide, you know; women don't pay bills—women arrange dinner parties."

"Division of labour, like?"

"You can count on it, a woman like Jill Mowbray."

This obviously wasn't idle chatter; the DI fancied he was onto something. Frank thought about it. "I can see that, aye."

"For a man like Cyril—you see what I'm getting at,

Frank?—a man in that position, three grand could be a life-saver."

"It would fill a hole, right enough."

"We wondered why Cyril seemed so determined that his marriage wasn't over, when according to her it was history, no question. Yeah? And we thought it was just his pride. But I don't think it was: it was money."

"Money?"

"Look at his life, Frank, and what's happened to it. He's got used to having a rich wife, and without her his living standards and status drop through the floor. However, if he can somehow manage to keep her, during their separation, in the manner to which she reckons she was born to be accustomed, then maybe he can prove to her that he's still a real man."

"What, and she has him back? Just because he pays off her MasterCard? He can't really believe that. He's not that much of an idiot."

Don inhaled from his cigar and lovingly, almost grudgingly, exhaled. "Desperate men can believe *anything;* how many domestics did you attend when you were in uniform, where you found some drunken geezer chucking pebbles at his ex's bedroom window? And when you nick him, at her request, he fights you because he knows for sure that if only he could talk to her alone for five minutes she'd forgive him?"

"Drunken," Frank pointed out. "That's the key word there."

"Besides," Don continued without deviation, "Cyril knows her a lot better than we do. Perhaps he's right. Perhaps she is just teaching him a lesson, setting him a task."

Well . . . "It's true she hasn't actually started divorce proceedings against him."

"Exactly! Bloody good point, Frank." Don ground out his cigar and buckled his seat belt. "You know what? I think we've finally found someone for whom three grand is worth committing a murder."

By starting time the next morning, Frank had decided that if they were going after Cyril Mowbray—and they were, he accepted that, because once Don Packham had settled on a suspect, nothing short of a sledgehammer could convince him he'd picked the wrong horse—then at least he was going to force the DI to answer a few questions of his own first. If he was really lucky, he might even get Don to *ask* some questions.

"If Cyril did kill Bert for his money, then how do we prove it? Has he still got the money at his place?"

Don didn't need to search long for an answer to that one. "No chance; he'll have hidden it."

"No point in searching his gaff, then?"

"None whatsoever. Forget it, Frank. Waste of manpower. We'd have to search all of them, anyway, we haven't got enough to justify singling him out."

That's because we haven't got anything, Frank didn't say.

"And I don't want to go on a fishing trip, not unless we really have to. That kind of thing alienates people, shuts them up. And you usually come up empty-handed, anyway. By the same token, though—he won't have spent it yet."

That was true, Frank admitted to himself. The killer couldn't know whether or not the police were looking for the money, so he daren't have any unexplained activity in his bank account.

"We could put him under surveillance until we find out where he's hidden the dosh," Don continued, "but unless he's an idiot he won't go there until we've all moved on. We could be watching him for bloody months."

On nothing but half a hunch, Frank didn't say.

"You're not saying much, Frank?"

"Thinking, sir."

"Course you are. Sorry, didn't mean to interrupt. Tell you what—we'll ask Stanley Baird. He's supposed to know about money, isn't he? He used to work in finance, sort of."

"Ask him what?"

"Ask him, if you had three grand where would you hide it?"

"He won't know, will he?"

"No," said Don, with a grin, "but if he hates Cyril as much as vice versa, which I suspect he surely must, then he might spread the word. Careful though, we can't actually *tell* him it's Cyril we're looking at. But we can insinuate. We can also tell him that we've no idea where the money is, but we're going to be searching everyone's houses very soon, and as soon as we find it, we'll be making an arrest."

"What good will that do?"

"With luck, word will get back to Cyril and he'll panic—do something daft."

"Like what?"

"Scarper. Move the money. Meanwhile, we'll phone his wife, ask her if her old man has sent her three grand lately."

"But are those two even talking?"

"They will be, Frank! She'll phone him, demand to know how come he's got three grand which she hasn't seen a penny of. Assuming she hasn't, of course. And the same result—one panicking murderer."

"We hope."

"And you and I watch Cyril."

"Just the two of us?"

"No need to involve anyone else," Don said.

Aye, thought Frank, with their nitpicking objections to

wild goose chases, and their modish obsessions with intelligence-led policing.

Stanley Baird didn't offer them a cup of tea—and in fact, didn't even invite them to sit down, possibly because he was worried about depreciation of the furniture.

Don told him, in strictest confidence, that three thousand pounds had been stolen from Bert Rosen around the time of his murder, and asked him how, in his professional opinion, one might go about hiding such a sum from the police?

Somewhat to the two detectives' surprise, Baird made no pretence of being interested in this bogus question. Instead, he went straight to the meat: "Do you suspect one of *us* of having taken this money? Someone in particular?"

"Oh dear," Don said, as if he'd been brilliantly tricked into revealing more than he'd intended, by Stanley's unrivalled dialectical wiles. "I can't answer that question, can I, DC Mitchell?"

"Certainly not, sir."

"But I suppose it would be reasonably harmless for me to say, Stanley—again, in confidence—that it's someone you know."

Baird licked his lips. "Someone I know?"

"Yes," said Don, "okay. Look, I can't deny it's someone you know. Though not necessarily a friend of yours, if you see what I mean."

"Not necessarily . . . ?"

"Nope. Stanley." Don held up a hand. "I can't say any more, I really can't. Obviously, we'll be getting warrants to search everyone's homes, garages, lock-ups, and so on, but the bureaucracy takes its own sweet time, as you can imagine. We just thought your professional expertise as a former money-man might be able to give us a short cut."

"I'm—no, I'm sorry." Baird wiped his face with a handkerchief. "I'm sorry, I really can't help."

"No? Well, just a thought, not to worry. Sorry to have disturbed you."

Outside, Don rubbed his hands. "Who do you think he'll phone? Dot Estevez?"

The Chief Super, probably, Frank didn't say, *to lodge a complaint.*

"He's a military man, remember. He'll move under cover of darkness. Dusk, at the earliest."

Don's mind was made up on that point, so Frank spent the remainder of Wednesday engaged in desk work, while Don . . . well, Frank didn't ask. He just did his paperwork and minded his own business.

As afternoon gave way to evening, and daylight to streetlights, they met up again, to sit outside Mowbray's flat, a block or so from Bath Street, in an unmarked pool car with dirty windows.

"If the money's in a vulnerable place," Don was sure, "he'll move it tonight. He won't delay."

That was assuming Cyril had yet heard of their interest in the three grand, which Frank considered a rather large assumption. No point in saying so, though. "But it won't be in a vulnerable place, will it? He'll have it somewhere safe."

"Like where? It's got to *be* somewhere safe, that's the point. Not buried in the public park, or down by the canal."

"That's what I said: somewhere safe."

"Not somewhere safe from *us,* Frank—somewhere safe from someone finding it accidentally. Or it being scooped up by a litter warden. Or eaten by foxes. Now, by definition that's got to be somewhere connected with him: an allotment shed, a garage, a lock-up where he keeps his window cleaning stuff. Therefore it's somewhere we *could* have found out about, and he can't risk that we won't have a search warrant for that place."

Which did, to be fair, make a certain amount of sense. "Then why don't we just search everywhere connected to him?"

"Because I'm assuming the actual hiding place will be somewhere less obvious than his lock-up, which we might never find, or not find for ages, or not find without huge supplies of manpower. But he can't take that chance, don't you see?"

"He has to assume we're about to knock on his door with a search warrant for the hiding place. Okay. So where will he move it *to?*"

"I don't know, Frank! Somewhere even more obscure. Maybe he'll post it to himself by same-day courier—that should make it vanish for at least a week."

Frank settled himself for a long watch. Don's scheme—of spreading a rumour in order to flush out a suspect—was standard CID practice, sure. But for dealing with teenage shoplifting gangs, not ruthless murderers. He tried not to display his scepticism, though. And by the same token, he tried not to exhibit astonishment when, after a mere forty-minute vigil, they saw Cyril Mowbray come bustling out of his front door, wheeling his bicycle.

"From the body language," said Don, "I don't reckon he's off to the pub for a quiet pint, do you?"

"Doesn't look that way," Frank admitted, as Cyril hurled himself astride his bike and wobbled off down the street, standing up on the pedals, his bright yellow knee-length socks pumping up and down. Frank allowed him a small lead before starting up the car.

It was not the easiest follow-job Frank had ever been involved with. If the car had to go any slower, he feared, it might give up altogether and start going backwards. Unfortunately, their quarry's speed was severely limited by the fact that he'd been in too much of a hurry to remove the ladders strapped to the sides of his bike, and the stiff autumn winds kept blowing him off course. Cyril's journey involved several remounts, but eventually he arrived at his destination.

"Oh God," said Frank, when he realised where they were. "He's not going to move the money—he's going to thump the bloke that's spreading lies about him. This is Stanley's place."

"Oh shit," said Don, but he brightened almost immediately. "Maybe he's here to bump off a witness."

But they had no such luck. When the two detectives entered Stanley Baird's flat through the open front door, they found Stanley attempting to disappear into the stuffing of an armchair, while a red-necked, purple-faced Cyril stood over him, shouting loud enough to deafen, let alone waken, the dead.

"Okay, Mr. Mowbray, let's calm down a bit," Frank told him, trying to get between the enraged ex-soldier and the object of his wrath.

"I want this twat arrested," were Mowbray's first words to the police. "He has been spreading slander. I just got a hysterical phone call from that shop steward kid, weeping and wailing that I'd killed Bert Rosen to steal his lifesavings! And she knows it's true, if you please, because *this* bastard told her the police were just about to arrest me."

Don said nothing, possibly because he had complete confidence in his DC to bring the situation under control, or possibly because he was busy contorting himself in order to sniff a sticky substance adhering to the bottom of his left shoe. There was some on the carpet, too, but it was only mud, Frank concluded, from the calm look on the DI's face.

"Now Mr. Mowbray, I'm sure we can sort this—"

"I am *not* a thief, and I'll fight any man who says otherwise. Is that understood?"

"That is fully understood, Mr. Mowbray. Now why don't we just—"

"I have never stolen so much as a chocolate bar in my entire life. I am going to sue this little numpty for every penny he owns."

Frank had a horrible, growing feeling that Cyril's protestations were sincere. His anger certainly seemed so. One glance at Don, however, told Frank that the DI believed Mowbray was just a good actor.

"Did he hit you?" Don asked Stanley, as Frank finally persuaded Cyril to sit down in a chair on the other side of the room. "We can nick him for that."

"No, he didn't." Stanley stood, unsteadily. "You got here before—before anything untoward occurred."

"Are you sure he didn't hit you? Just once, perhaps?"

Stanley was clearly eager to be rid of them all. "Let's just forget about it, please."

Don tried once more: "Maybe he hit you so hard you've forgotten?"

"No, no, it's all just a misunderstanding. Now please, I have chores to attend to."

In the absence of a witness statement, they had to let Mowbray go with an informal warning. Frank escorted him to the pavement, and noticed his clean shoes as the still-fuming man swung his leg over his crossbar.

It was while Don was on his mobile, trying to persuade a patrol car to pick up Cyril for riding an unsafe bicycle, that Frank said to Baird: "Been doing some gardening, Stanley?" He indicated the mud on the carpet. "May I have a look at your shoes?"

Don, his peripheral hearing never having failed him yet, abruptly concluded his phone call. "Sod off, then, but don't come to me next time you want your mother-in-law arrested for procuring. What is it, Frank?"

"That's yellowish," said Frank, getting down on his knees to examine the mud. "London clay; if it was topsoil, it'd be brown."

"He's right, Stanley. That stuff's been dug up. And since it's still on your left shoe, I'm assuming it got there so recently that you haven't had a chance to change yet."

Stanley Baird reached up to a shelf over the fireplace, and handed Frank a torch. "You'll need this," he said, before sinking back into his chair, surrender written all over him. "But please don't turn it on until you get outside—the batteries, you understand."

Don snorted. "Tell you what, Stanley, we'll have a cup of tea back at our place. It's foul, but at least it's not secondhand."

Chapter Nineteen

Bert Rosen's missing money was found half-buried in Stanley's garden. "Not so much a shallow grave," Don noted, "as a shallow safe."

"I'd been keeping it in the house," commented Mr. Baird, under caution, "because I wasn't quite sure who it rightly belonged to, following Mr. Rosen's death."

"That's why you buried it, is it?" said Don. "Bollocks. Try again. You nicked it."

"No, no. He leant it to me."

"And you thought, no need to pay it back now he's dead. Yeah, I get you. What do you need the money for, anyway?"

Using highly advanced interrogation techniques—such as sighing impatiently, snorting derisively, tutting irritatingly, and staring implacably—Don dragged Stanley's story out of him. Dot Estevez had been right; Stanley was not much of a treasurer. Various of the small accounts he managed on behalf of diverse organisations had, he admitted, "developed irregularities." A shared look between Don and Frank was all that was needed to translate that into cop-talk: Stanley had been dipping, perhaps to cover up incompetence. A little borrowed here, a little there . . . but it all added up. In the end, it added up to an amount which was as easy to hide as a hippo in a hat shop.

Bert Rosen, never one to see a man dragged down by cruel fate or personal shortcomings, had leant Baird the three thousand to put right his debts once and for all. If it had become public knowledge that LOFE's treasurer was on the fiddle, it could have been a serious blow to the campaign.

Stanley had taken possession of the money on Thursday evening; though he would not admit it—yet, at any rate—he had obviously seen Bert's death on Friday night as an opportunity to avoid repayment of the loan.

But he denied any knowledge whatsoever of Bert Rosen's murder, and the detectives, reluctantly, believed him. They bailed him (though Don was determined to find something nice to charge him with, as soon as he had time to work out what), and were just about to turf him out, when a thought struck Don.

"Hold on, Stanley—you believed we were after Cyril for the money, yes? And you rang young Kimberley to tell her that, which was what set Mad Mowbray off. So why were you burying the money?"

Baird explained, in pedantic detail. At first he thought Don had been referring to him: someone he knew but not a friend. Their visit, he supposed, had been intended to startle a confession out of him. So he'd hidden the money in the garden. Then he'd suddenly thought that perhaps, instead, they'd been talking about Cyril; it didn't take much of a leap of the imagination for him to see Mowbray as a villain. So he dug the money up, went back inside and phoned Kimberley—out of sheer spite, he didn't add, but Don and Frank intuited. But then he'd had third thoughts; why would the police think Mowbray had the money when, after all, Stanley knew he hadn't.

"I panicked, frankly," he concluded, "and took the money

back to the garden, to bury it again. Which was when Mowbray turned up."

"Blimey, you have had a busy night, haven't you?" said Don. "Quite the crowded agenda."

Baird's face took on what could only be described as a look of very small triumph. "I was right, though, wasn't I? You *were* watching me. You must have been to get there so quickly."

"You haven't thanked us for that yet," Don pointed out.

Cyril's motive had gone, Don and Frank agreed over a quick half in the nearest cop-free pub. Don was understandably downhearted, and Frank thought this would be a good moment.

"Don? What *was* the Battle of Cable Street?"

It worked like a charm. Don's mood recovered as he regaled his colleague with the glorious story of October 4, 1936, when the swaggering British fascist fuehrer, Sir Oswald Moseley, attempted to lead a march of provocation and intimidation through a largely Jewish area of the East End. Ten thousand baton-wielding police escorted Moseley's thugs, but even they could not beat a path through the half million workers—Jewish and Gentile, and largely organised by the Communist Party, but mobilised from the grassroots themselves—who barricaded the streets of London. The result was a humiliation for the disarrayed Blackshirts, from which British fascism never recovered.

If Mosley had won that day, some historians later wondered, would Britain still have held out alone against the Nazis, in the first years of World War II? In other words—if Bert Rosen and his comrades hadn't stopped Moseley, might Hitler have won the war?

Frank nodded periodically, and said *Fancy that,* and *Fasci-*

nating, and *Makes you think,* though in fact none of what Don said was new to him; he'd looked it all up on the Internet a couple of days earlier, just in case it proved relevant.

"Okay," said Don to Frank, after a reviving smoke. "Forget the money."

"Back to the gun?" said Frank to Don.

"Bloody right. Forget theft. Who was Bert afraid of? That is, and always has been, despite all distractions, the central question."

"Has to be, now."

"Always was. We took our eyes off it, and more fool us, Frank: an octogenarian turns up dead in a library with a gun in his pocket? Nothing else matters, and we should have seen that. Forget the money."

"I've forgotten it."

"Good man. Now, look at that lot, our suspects. Who was Bert afraid of? It can only be Cyril. Who else? A teenage girl, a middle-aged woman with funny specs, a bloke who keeps getting divorced because he can't find a woman to henpeck him enough, a politician with a fucking pond in his lounge? It's *got* to be Cyril."

Frank waited to see if Don would add the obvious codicil, and when he didn't, did it himself. "Okay. I can believe Cyril killed him. But why?"

Frank's phone rang at ten to one on Thursday morning. He was asleep. He often was, at ten to one on a Thursday morning.

"Frank? Why *one* carrier bag?"

"Don?" Frank signalled Debbie that she should go back to sleep, and tried to signal himself that he should wake up.

"Bert Rosen's pocket contents. That list you read me. Why did he have one carrier bag on him—an empty carrier bag? We assumed he'd picked it up on his way to the library. But if so, why only one? Did he only find one pair of witches' knickers all the way from his place to the library? In this town—no chance!"

Frank's eyes opened. He hadn't realised they were closed; no wonder it was so dark. "It wasn't one he'd picked up; he was carrying something in it. But nothing *was* in it. So . . ."

"Exactly."

"So, okay, he used the bag to carry the gun to the library, so what?"

"So I think I know where he got the gun from—he *found* the sodding thing, probably in that very carrier bag, while he was on witches' knickers patrol. You see, Frank? He didn't buy it at all, he found it. That Scotland Yard gun bloke, the Kiwi, he told us, didn't he? He said guns are so cheap, they're often dumped after use. Disposable guns."

Why couldn't Don have phoned on the mobile? At least Frank would have been able to go for a pee. "All right, so now we know how he got it, but that still doesn't explain why he kept it. To protect himself, presumably, but if he had a reason to be afraid of someone, we've still no idea what it was."

Don was silent for a while. Then he said: "Suppose Bert found the gun last Thursday, the one day we know he was unhappy. Rosa says he went out on bag patrol that afternoon, that's most likely when he found it. He called his son, upset, looking for advice. But during the conversation, suddenly, he seemed not to be so worried any more. Why?"

"Just from hearing his son's voice, perhaps?"

"Perhaps. But first thing after breakfast, let's talk to Tom Rosen again. Frank?"

"Don?"

"Can you do frozen waffles in a toaster, do you know?"

"The postmen's union," said Rosa, bending down to slip a LOFE leaflet through a door, "has been campaigning since the 1950s to get ground-level letterboxes banned. They're a serious health and safety hazard. They're illegal in Ireland."

"I can see they'd not do your back much good," said Frank, "if you were having to stoop to them dozens of times a day."

It was only just after breakfast time, but Bert's son and daughter were already out on their rounds, distributing pro-library propaganda on a former council estate.

The familiarity and ease with which they accomplished the duty, low-level letterboxes notwithstanding, suggested they were old hands at the game.

"Activists tend not to have fat children," said Tom, taking a fresh batch of leaflets from his sister's knapsack. "All that marching and leaflet delivering and door-to-door canvassing."

"How much of the estate do you plan to cover?" Don asked.

"We'll have most of it done in a couple of hours," said Rosa. "I've been delivering on this route for decades; the miners' strike, CND, you name it. I know every letterbox on the estate. You know, when your mail is late, it's probably because the Post Office is using causal labour."

"True," Tom agreed. "It takes a novice, or someone unfamiliar with the round, a lot longer to deliver mail. The regular roundsman will get through in half the time—and put the letters through the right box, too."

While Rosa continued her late father's work, Don and Frank borrowed her assistant. Sitting in the car—it was sunny, but none too warm—they asked Tom to give them, as near as he could, a verbatim account of his last conversation with Bert. With a degree of recall which was impressive but hardly surprising, considering his profession, he took them through the opening pleasantries.

"Like I said before, I could tell something was up. After a while it was obvious he wasn't going to spit it out, so I tried to prod him a bit."

"What did you say?"

"Something like, 'Everything okay down there, Pops? Luxy's hale, is she?' "

"Luxy?" Frank looked up from his notebook.

"It's what I call Rosa."

Don smiled. "She was named after Rosa Luxemburg?"

"Actually, she was named after her auntie, but it winds her up, and that's what brothers are for. She gets her own back; I *was* named after Tom Paine, so you can imagine that gives her certain opportunities. Anyway, Pops said something like, 'Not to worry, just got a lot on my mind.' Something like that; dismissive, you know. Or trying to be."

"But you were still worried?"

He shrugged. "Only a bit. I can't pretend I had any great premonition. I said, 'Is it to do with your library campaign? How goes the struggle, Commandante?' And he said, 'Oh, not bad, we're getting there. We're occupying the place tonight.' Well, I thought that was dead cool, naturally. Direct action? I'm all for that, and . . ."

"And what?"

Tom had been assembling a cigarette, but he'd stopped halfway through, somewhere between the roll and the lick. "In fact, now I come to replay it, he seemed to cheer up after that. We talked about the library for a bit, and then a bit of football, and then . . . that was it."

"He didn't say anything else about this problem, whatever

it was, or give a hint as to why his mood suddenly changed?"

"No. Not a word more was said about it, on either side. So much so, that I forgot all about it until you two came round to Rosa's the other day. Perhaps I just imagined the whole thing."

"They talked about the library occupation," said Don, relishing his third cup of tea and second currant bun in a cafe not far from Bath Street, "and after that, Bert wasn't worried any more."

"But who *was* Bert planning to use the gun against?"

"He wasn't!" Don put down his bun for emphasis. "Remember Cable Street, Frank; remember the miners' strike, and Grunwick, and News International, and Southall and . . . remember who Bert was. A cuddly old man with eccentric politics, yes, but also a lifelong revolutionary fighter, for whom even the most honest, sympathetic cop is merely a lackey of the imperialist establishment."

"I thought we were sadistic, thieving perverts?"

"No, that's us, Frank—I'm talking about uniform."

"Oh. They're the lackeys?"

"Keep up." Don finished his tea and his bun, in one mouthful. "Bert wasn't keeping the gun, when he put it in his pocket and took it to the library. He was getting rid of it!"

"How?"

"You can't just chuck a gun in the bin, can you? Anyone might find it, a kid or a madman. He wanted it disposed of safely—and he couldn't or wouldn't take it to the police."

"Because they're lackeys. All right, but why the library?"

Don just looked at him, smiled, and waited. It didn't take long.

"Oh my God . . ." said Frank. "He took it to the LOFE meeting to hand it over to the one person who would surely know how to safely dispose of a firearm."

"Right," said Don. "Got to be. The ex-military man. LOFE as in Local Officious Firearms Expert."

"All the same: I hate to keep saying it," said Frank, who didn't, particularly, "but that's not actually a motive for murder, is it?"

"Not as such," Don had to admit. He went to the counter for another round of tea and buns; seemed a long time since breakfast. When he returned to the table, he said: "Wonder what sort of books Cyril borrows from the library?"

"No idea. War stories?"

"Maybe."

"Could we find out from the library's computer?"

"Frank!" Don's bun-hand froze halfway to his mouth. "What a dreadful suggestion. In a democratic country, you are not allowed to spy on people's library records. We're a civilian police service, not the FBI or the KGB."

"Right. Sorry."

"On the other hand," Don continued, "there's no constitutional impediment that I know of to gossiping with library workers."

"We won't have to kill them afterwards, will we?"

"I don't think we'll talk to Dot, too close to home. And too savvy, anyway."

"We could see if Kimberley's on duty today."

She was on duty, and glad enough to break off for a few minutes from shelving a trolley-load of art books. "The Major?" Kimberley straightened her shoulders, and contorted her face into a passable caricature of a blimpish military gent. "He likes his crime, and of course, he's another one for the self-improvement racket. Why do people fall for that crap? *You Could Be All You Can Be But Only If You Will Be.* There's one born every minute, I suppose."

"So Cyril's into self-improvement, too. Can't say I'm surprised. And by crime, you mean whodunits—bodies in libraries, all that nonsense?"

"Oh, no: true crime, not fiction. Famous murders, unsolved crimes. We've got a whole bay of the stuff. Very popular, especially with old people, for some reason. The more gruesome the better."

Frank really was becoming embarrassed about saying it, but ten minutes later, sitting in his car, he had to say it yet again: all that they had heard and speculated about Mowbray this morning was very interesting. "But none of it provides a motive for killing Bert Rosen."

"You're absolutely right," said Don.

"Am I?" Frank wasn't sure he liked the sound of that.

"Start the car, Frank."

"Where are we going?"

"We've been looking for a motive for the wrong victim."

"Suspect, you mean?"

"No." Don shook his head. "I mean *victim*. Cyril hasn't got a motive for killing Bert, you're absolutely right. And neither has anyone else. Get driving will you, Frank? What are we waiting for?"

"Where are we *going?*"

"No motive for Bert," said Don. "But Cyril's got a motive all right."

Chapter Twenty

They didn't immediately arrest him, when they found him at his home a few minutes later, but that didn't mean the DI was playing games.

"When you killed Bert," Don said, as soon as Cyril opened the door, "you were disturbed. Not as in mad; as in interrupted. Before you got what you'd come for."

"Don't know what you're talking about," boomed Cyril, his voice louder than either detective had ever heard it before.

"We found the hidey-hole, Cyril. We know the whole plan. You were going to stash the gun under the 920s, and come back for it when it was safe."

"Oh yes? And you found my fingerprints all over it, I suppose—this 'hidey-hole' of yours? Must have, Inspector, otherwise you wouldn't have bothered mentioning it, since you wouldn't be able to use it in court." Mowbray was wearing an enormous but joyless grin, like a flatulent meerkat.

Don's smile, by contrast, was small, and twitched with frustration. The one thing they didn't have in this case, Frank knew, was physical evidence. But then, it seemed, the sun came out; Don's face cleared and his smile broadened. "Prints? I'll give you prints, Cyril. You handled the gun. Didn't he, Constable?"

It took Frank a moment to interpret Don's mime: putting something in his back pocket? *Of course* . . . when Don took the gun from the dead man's back pocket, it was upside-down. And it was in his right rear pocket, although Bert was left-handed: that's what Don was miming—the unlikely awkwardness of using your left hand to put an upside-down gun into your right bum pocket.

"That's right, sir," he said. "The person who stuffed the gun back into Bert's trousers must've handled it to do so."

"You were disturbed by someone, a noise or something," Don continued, "and so you just shoved the gun back into Bert's pocket, as best you could. Is that prints enough for you, Mr. Mowbray?"

But Mowbray's unfeigned sneer told Frank that he wasn't falling for that. "I forgot to say 'What gun?' didn't I? Never mind. Supposing there was a gun, and supposing I had handled it, you can be bloody sure I didn't leave traces on it. I'm not one of your ganja-smoking car thieves, you know!" He grabbed a hank of his thinning hair and brandished it at them. "You don't see any dreadlocks, do you? And another thing: I would be grateful if you would address me as *Major,* not *Mister!* I am entitled to my rank."

His neck was colouring, as it had when he'd attacked Stanley Baird. He was losing control, and he wasn't even trying very hard to keep it. *He was guilty*. At that moment, Frank truly believed it for the first time. He knew it. And thinking about the printless gun, he suddenly knew something else, too.

"I'm sure you're right," he said, flicking back through his notebook. "You wouldn't have left any traces on the gun, because you were wearing gloves, weren't you? But you didn't have any gloves on you when you were searched that night."

"Can't have been me, then, can it? The killer was gloved, I

was not. You may leave, gentlemen, as soon as you wish." He clapped his hands together.

"Cold night to be without gloves," said Frank, dialling a number on his mobile phone.

"Forgot them. Left them at home. Always doing it. Bloody idiot; bloody cold on that bloody bike."

"Yes," said Frank into the phone, "it's DC Mitchell, I'm interested in the contents of the lost property box from Bath Street Library." He put his hand over the mouthpiece, and addressed Don in a stage whisper. "It's the properties manager back at the nick, sir. He's just checking. Yes, hello? Great: and are there any gloves in there, at all?"

Don smiled at Cyril, and nodded towards Frank. "Bright lad," he said. Cyril, Frank couldn't help noticing, looked less happy, but still resolute.

"Ski mittens? Yes, that'll do. Have them transferred to the lab immediately, will you, Sarge? On Mr. Packham's authority. Check to see if they've been in contact with a non-discharged firearm and also for identifiable human traces, please. Cheers." He put the phone away.

"I could have lost a pair of gloves in that library any old time," said Cyril. "Any number of pairs. Told you, always losing them. Leave them strewn across London like sweet wrappers."

"Adding up though, isn't it?" Frank said.

Cyril shrugged. "Adding up to very little. I'm no murderer, I'm no thief."

"Ski mittens," mused Don. "Do you ski, Cyril?"

"Have done."

"Big clumsy things, aren't they, those ski mittens? No fingers. Okay for handling large objects, but useless for fiddly work." Both detectives felt that electric, flushing thrill—which can only ever be fully appreciated by people in the people-hunting professions—as they saw a horrible realisation take Cyril Mowbray in its iron jaws. "Constable Mitchell," said Don. "Would you be kind enough to redial that number on your mobile? Thanks . . . hello, yes, DI Packham speaking. I'm inquiring about a pair of witches' knickers found in the pockets of a deceased Bolshevik . . . plastic bag, that's right. Yes, I'll hold." It was his turn now for the pantomime; the covered mouthpiece and the piercing whisper. "I do hope the bag's still there; you can get perfectly nice prints off carrier bags. And of course, you can wipe a gun clean—but I'm not sure how you'd wipe a plastic bag. Any suggestions, Cyril?"

Cyril had nothing to offer.

Chapter Twenty-one

"NATO standard," said Don, putting Cyril Mowbray's plastic cup of coffee on the plastic table in the interview room at the police station. "Milk, two sugars. Is that right?"

"Thank you." Mowbray lit a cigarette.

Frank primed the tapes, and repeated the formal caution.

"To start us off, Cyril," said Don, "perhaps you could tell us when you decided to kill your wife."

"My client," Mowbray's lawyer interjected, "is here to answer questions concerning the death of Mr. Rosen; not to discuss any hypothetical offences which have not, in fact, occurred."

"No harm in me indulging in a touch of the hypotheticals, though?" Don stretched out his legs, folded his arms, made himself comfortable. "I don't believe Cyril wanted to lose his wife, let alone kill her. He was horrified, I'm sure, and mystified, when she left him. At first, he was convinced she'd come back—women are moody chaps, aren't they, Cyril? At the best of times."

Mowbray sipped his coffee. His eyes never left Don's.

"But recently, I think Cyril has come to the reluctant conclusion that Jill really does mean to divorce him."

"Her family have always loathed me," said Cyril.

"Dreadful snobs." His lawyer put a cautionary hand on his arm.

"Which realisation has somewhat simplified Cyril's dilemma. To put it bluntly, he has to kill her before she begins divorce proceedings, to ensure that he inherits. Straightforward matter, really, of analysing a situation, identifying objectives, and executing a plan. Right, Cyril? Not difficult for a fellow of your qualities."

Mowbray shook off his lawyer's restraining grip. He straightened his back, and pointed his chin at the detective inspector. He was a man, his posture said, who knew his worth. And knew that when a game was up, all that was left was dignity. "Harder than you'd think, Packham. Made a study of accidents, first. Best method from the point of view of not being detected, but made trickier by the fact that we weren't living together. She'd only meet me on neutral ground."

Don grimaced, sympathetically. "Cunning woman."

"Typical of the sex. Next, I researched poisons, using commonly found items such as over the counter medicines; fine, but problems as above, plus too slow. Suicide's out; did you know the suicide rate in this country is at an all-time low? One of the lowest in the Western world." He shook his head, perhaps in disgust at his nation's spineless contentment.

"But a gun," said Don, his voice heavy with admiration. "Very bold, if I may say so."

"Mr. Mowbray," the lawyer began, but it was clear he no longer existed in Cyril's universe.

"Gun's perfect. A woman not used to living on her own, shot by an intruder. By an asylum-seeking druggie, as it might be; no one would think twice. Only trouble: how to get a gun which couldn't be traced back to me."

"Good old Bert," said Frank.

"The old chap was obsessed with carrier bags, don't know if you knew. On the Thursday, he was out collecting them up for recycling, and he found one, shoved right under that little hedge they've got round the car park by that German supermarket. Opened it up: handgun inside. Well, well."

"Why didn't he call the police?" Don asked, for the benefit of the tape, knowing that such a question would surely arise in court.

"Fair point," said Mowbray. "Way he told it to me, he had an idea who might have dumped the weapon. Some local toerag, with aspirations to become a Yardie. Bert planned to talk to him." He laughed. "Fat lot of good that would have done! The situation's way beyond talking, it's time for action, that's what the Bert Rosens of this world can't grasp."

"So he, too, faced a dilemma," said Don.

"That's it. Hand the gun in, and it gives the police—of whom he was not wholly enamoured, begging your presence—an excuse to roust the local youths. On the other hand, if the gun had in fact been used in a serious crime, and was evidence, he must hand it over. Decided to wait twenty-four hours, keep an eye on the local news, and assuming he heard no reports of a killing, a robbery, what-have-you, he'd bring it with him to the LOFE meeting."

"He assumed that, as an ex-soldier, you'd know how to dispose of the thing safely."

"Assumed correctly," Mowbray confirmed. "Chuck it in a bloody deep river, that's how you dispose of a gun safely!"

"But when he managed to get you on your own for a moment—in the librarian's office, where it was relatively private—you saw an opportunity."

"Like a sign from on high," said Mowbray, his eyes wide as if he still couldn't believe his luck—indeed, as if he'd forgotten that his luck hadn't, in the event, been so good after all. "I quickly established that no one else knew Bert had the gun. You see, I'd looked into all this. A street-bought gun is always potentially traceable—if they find who sold it, eventually they'll find who bought it." He leaned towards Don, making sure that the DI fully appreciated his moment of inspiration. "But this gun not only could not possibly be connected to me—it couldn't even be connected to the person I obtained it from. The chain was broken twice!"

Obtained, thought Frank; nice word.

"Brilliant," said Don. "So even if the cops somehow managed to identify the gun used to kill your wife, it had nothing to do with you."

"Even better than that," said Mowbray, displaying, Frank thought, the first genuine smile he'd ever shown them. "I'd have deliberately left the gun at the scene. You see, it might have come up on your computer in connection with past crimes, sending the police off in all manner of wrong directions."

"You killed Bert there and then?"

"Certainly not. Preparation is nine-tenths of victory, Inspector."

"Of course. I apologise."

"Mr. Mowbray," said the lawyer again, though his voice lacked conviction. Just doing enough to make sure he wouldn't be struck off by the Law Society, Frank suspected.

"Not now," his client replied, without looking at him. "Later. I told Bert to stay where he was, tell no one what he'd told me, I'd fix it. Wouldn't be long. And I wasn't. Took me about three minutes to find the loose skirting. Surprised? You shouldn't be: I've done a lot of contraband searches in my time. This was the same process in reverse."

"Masterly," said Don. "So, having sorted out where you were going to stash the gun . . ."

Frank held his breath.

"Went back upstairs," said Mowbray. "Killed the old man."

There it was.

"What with?"

"Strangled him. Used a belt, found it in the lost property box on the librarian's desk."

Nailed down: unless he turned out to be mad, they'd got him.

"Ha! Ironical—killed both *by* and *for* lost property. See?" Cyril looked directly at his solicitor for the first time in the interview; Frank had the distinct impression that he was expecting the lawyer to record his bon mot for future generations. In fairness to that man's professional standards, he did in fact write down the remark. Next to it, Frank could see, he wrote the word "Pillock."

"And then—" Don began, but Cyril hadn't finished.

"What was so marvellous, you see: no one would know there'd ever been a gun, so, number one, no one would search for it; and number two, I had no motive to kill the old chap."

"But something disturbed you, before you could take the gun."

Mowbray shook his head. "Bloody shame. The gun was back in Bert's pocket, of course, in its plastic bag. I got it out, still wearing the gloves. Took the gun from the bag, put the gun in my pocket. Then I heard a noise, outside, in the corridor—someone going into the toilets, probably. Well, I couldn't risk it, could I? They might come into the office, next. Had to abort. I shoved the gun back in Bert's pocket—the back pocket, it was the only one I could get at with the stupid mittens on. Took them off, bunged them into the lost property box, where I'd got the belt from. Then I saw the bloody carrier bag, still sitting on the desk!"

"So you hurriedly shoved that into Bert's pocket, too. And made good your escape."

"Exfiltration was achieved without incident," Mowbray confirmed. "But I never got a chance to go back for the gun, before that neurotic library woman found the corpse." He shrugged. "So all that effort wasted, I suppose."

"More than you know," said Don. "The gun wasn't loaded, you pathetic little dipstick."

A flicker of confusion crossed Mowbray's face, registering the change in Don's attitude towards him, but he quickly brushed it away. "Told you—I've never stolen anything in my life."

"Do you mind me asking," said Frank, "why you got involved in the campaign to save the library?"

"Perfectly simple. I was using it for my researches. If it had closed, and I'd had to go to another branch, it would have been bloody inconvenient. I've only got a pushbike, you know, thanks to that bitch."

Researches, thought Frank; almost as good as "obtained."

"Just a matter of interest, Cyril," Don asked, as Frank dealt with the tapes, an hour or so later, when everything had been gone over and gone over again. "What exactly did you do in the army?"

Cyril Mowbray gave him a look of such weariness and contempt, that Frank felt compelled to stop what he was doing and pay attention to the reply. "I was an infantry major. I served on the front line in Belfast, Bosnia—all the major theatres."

"Right."

"You're disappointed, aren't you? You wanted me to say that I counted paperclips in Aldershot. People always do. What does that say about you, Inspector Packham? What does it say about me?"

Don stood, and took his jacket from the back of his chair. "It says you won't be attending many regimental dinners in the next twenty years."

"So the motive for murder," said Frank, "was murder."

"Or money," Don replied. "Or love, or pride. There is only one motive, Frank, I told you."

The air was more fresh than cold as they leant against Frank's car, Don slowly smoking a small cigar.

"If you told me that one was bonkers, I'd believe you," said Frank. "Whatever the court says."

"I just don't know how they can do it. I don't understand how you can physically *do* that, to someone who's no threat to you."

"Well," said Frank. "I suppose you're in the right job, then."

Don laughed. "That'd be a first."

Frank didn't agree, but it wasn't his place to say so. Time to get home; it'd be a busy day tomorrow. "Do you think they'll save it? Bath Street Library."

Don shrugged. "If Bert was here, I'm sure he'd tell you: if we don't win this one, we'll win the next one. That's how you keep going."

"We won this one." Don nodded, but not much. "So, are you going out tonight?"

"Me? No, I don't think so. Why, you fancy a pint?"

"No," said Frank, who fancied few things less, at that precise moment. "No, I just—I thought maybe you were . . . seeing someone."

"Oh, that," said Don. "Well, there's a bit of a story behind that."

From anyone else, that would have been an invitation to further inquiry; but from Don it was simply a statement of fact. If the DI wanted to tell you a story, he just told you—he didn't do teasers. "Actually," said Frank, "come to think of it, I wouldn't mind a quick half."

Don studied his watch for a moment, and jiggled his car keys. "Go on, then," he said. "I could probably manage a swift one."

They walked ten minutes to an old-fashioned, backstreet pub, with lino on the floor and no mirror in the Gents, a local favourite of Don's. They ate peanuts, talked about murder, and drank a pint each, slowly.

When Don went off to the loo, Frank thought he'd give his boss a laugh. Not that Don seemed to be in need of cheering up, particularly, but all the same—he was a man who was always able to extract full nutritive value from a laugh. He'd send Don a text message, right now, similar in style and intent to the one he'd received from the DI the other day. It wasn't Frank's sense of humour, to be honest, but each to his own.

He took out his mobile phone, put down his beer, and set his thumbs to work.

About the Author

As well as being author of the Packham and Mitchell mysteries, Mat Coward is a Dagger- and Edgar-nominated short story writer, whose collection, *Do the World a Favour and Other Stories*, was published by Five Star Publishing. Coward lives in Somerset, in the UK, and writes children's fiction, science fiction, and humour. His latest book is a guide to the writing life called *Success and How to Avoid It.*